DAYS

LOUIS PAUL DeGRADO

13 DAYS

iUniverse books may be ordered through booksellers or by contacting:

iUniverse
1663 Liberty Drive
Bloomington, IN 47403
www.iuniverse.com
1-800-Authors (1-800-288-4677)

Because of the dynamic nature of the Internet, any web addresses or links contained in this book may have changed since publication and may no longer be valid. The views expressed in this work are solely those of the author and do not necessarily reflect the views of the publisher, and the publisher hereby disclaims any responsibility for them.

Any people depicted in stock imagery provided by Getty Images are models, and such images are being used for illustrative purposes only.
Certain stock imagery © Getty Images.

ISBN: 978-1-6632-0133-1 (sc)
ISBN: 978-1-6632-0135-5 (hc)
ISBN: 978-1-6632-0134-8 (e)

Library of Congress Control Number: 2020911344

Print information available on the last page.

iUniverse rev. date: 06/18/2020

Also available from author Louis Paul DeGrado

The 13th Month

Editor's Choice, iUniverse

Finalist, Foreword Reviews Book of the Year, 2015

Have you ever wondered why bad days linger, why moments of regret stick with you, or why bad situations seem surreal? What would you do if you found out that evil existed in these moments and that forces of evil were working to control and extend them by warping reality? Would you have the faith to stand and fight?

Evil once controlled the thirteenth month and is looking to do so again.

When a revered priest, Father Frank Keller, investigates a tragic murder in his parish, he is thrust into a covert battle between forces of good and evil.

While seeking answers, Father Frank is contacted by a group consisting of a holy man from India, a Native American shaman, a college professor, and an attractive middle-aged psychiatrist. The group's mission is to fight shadows: parasitic creatures that lurk in moments of time and warp reality to take control of their host.

The leader of the group, Adnan, is convinced that the shadows, once banished from the world, are gaining a foothold. The only way to stop them is to go to the place where the shadows come from and turn the tide.

Father Frank must face his own insecurities and desires in order to find the faith to help the group and combat the evil that threatens those closest to him. He must prepare himself to cross through a portal where the shadows come from, a portal that may lead him directly to the gates of hell.

The Calling of the Protectors: Book One, The Legend of Chief

Gold Award, Literary Classics, 2017

Editor's Choice, iUniverse

A small amount of courage has a giant impact in this book that is fun for the whole family. When a small, fluffy cat has to find her courage and overcome impossible odds, she teams up with an advice-giving canary, a cockatoo, some jazz-loving alley cats, and a fancy mouse. Come join this inspiring story of fellowship and witness the birth of a hero.

This series comes with seventeen original songs in the story and is sure to inspire!

The Calling of the Protectors: Book Two, The Mighty Adventures of Mouse the Cat

Editor's Choice, iUniverse

Our fluffy heroine returns in an adventure to save her friends and other animals from a perilous fate. Mouse risks her life to take the animals on a journey to a safe place while her father battles to keep their home safe. Join the adventure as a team of alley cats, mafia-style rats, pigeons, a cockatoo, a canary, and a fancy mouse overcome great obstacles and teach a lesson of courage and belief. With seventeen original songs, this story is sure to inspire.

Savior

Finalist, Foreword Review Book of the Year, 2001

Glimpse the future in this exciting science fiction thriller!

How far will we go to save ourselves? Faced with its own demise, humankind turns to science for answers, and governments approve drastic measures in genetic testing and experimentation.

Battle lines are drawn when a religious crusader and the medical director of the largest research firm in the world, clash over thousands of people frozen in cryogenic stasis who are being used as human test subjects. Caught in the middle is Kyle Reed, the director of the company, who has been brought back after two hundred years to face his greatest dilemma: support the company he founded, or expose the truth behind its plans.

The Questors' Adventures

The Round House and *The Moaning Walls*

This combo pack includes the first two stories in *The Questors' Adventures.*

What do you call a group of boys who set out to explore the unknown? They call themselves the Questors, and they're ready for excitement, adventure, and mayhem. Join the adventure as the boys, ages ten to thirteen, must overcome jittery nerves and active imaginations to investigate a haunted house in their neighborhood. An engaging series for young readers!

The People across the Sea

Editor's Choice, iUniverse

Within the towering walls of the city by the sea, a dark secret is kept. The city's history was wiped out by foreign invasion, and even now, the city stands poised to repel another attack from the dreaded people across the sea.

A culture based on fear and the threat of invasion has spawned a leader, a council, and the Law of Survivors. Aldran Alfer is now the keeper of the law and the council leader. He knows the hidden terror that threatens to rip the city apart.

Aldran's sons, Brit and Caln, find themselves caught in a web of danger and mystery. Brit finds himself on the run from the Black Guard, veiled men who prowl the streets and crush any who oppose the council's will.

While Caln remains in the city, struggling to hold his family's position on the council, Brit heads to the forbidden desert to seek out the Wizard, a man with strange powers who was banished from the city. In the company of the Wizard and a mythical desert wanderer, Brit will find his destiny. He must cross the land of the sand demons, fierce predators who stalk the desert, where he searches for a way to carry out his father's plan to lead their people to safety and end the threat from the people across the sea.

CONTENTS

PROLOGUE

"**K**eep me free from harm and safe from those who would have my soul. Lord, bless your servant and protect him." Father Frank Keller shivered in the darkness and cold as he said the prayer. The farther he stepped away from the garden that he'd made his home, the colder and darker his surroundings turned, but this was the only way for him to complete his task. He followed the shard of light from its origin, a place where he knew he was safe. Whenever he moved away from the light into the darker areas, the shadows attacked him and ripped at his flesh. His left hand moved over the scar on his arm from one of the nastier attacks.

At five feet ten and with a muscular build, Frank was no ordinary priest but one who had prided himself in his fitness. A carryover from his high school sport days and his military service, this characteristic had given him the ability to keep up with the youth in his parish. In his current predicament, his fitness had helped his state of mind but did not keep the shadows from attacking. He knew he needed to stay in the light as much as possible. The shard of light he followed grew thinner as he approached his destination, and he knew it was only a matter of time before he would have to venture into the dark area.

Behind him lay a garden with trees and lush grass; water flowed, and there was heat from the light. Out here, the land grew barren and rocky until it became consumed by darkness that made travel any farther impossible.

"There," he whispered to himself, more to hear himself talk and keep his sanity than because he believed anyone at all was listening.

Upon his arrival to this place, he'd searched but found the place void of any human forms; with the exception of the shadows, he was alone.

The sound he followed was a weeping, this time a female voice—young, troubled sobs. He knew it was probably another youth; the shadows picked on them the most, and he suspected it was because of the insecurities they harbored.

"Give me strength, Lord. Help me combat this evil," Frank said aloud. He spotted the abnormal shapes just outside of the light he followed. He'd reached his destination. There were many shadows hovering around the form—a small, vivid light in the shape of a ball that wasn't solid but wasn't liquid. It had form but pulsed in and out of the shape and changed in luminosity, going brighter and then fading. The more shadows that surrounded the ball of light, he had learned, the more it was dimmed. It was as though they fed off the energy in order to travel to its source, a place they wanted to be.

Frank prepared himself for the task and went to the edge of the light, or what remained of it. The shadows hadn't noticed him yet. He stepped forward and reached for the shape. *There!* He'd made contact before the shadows could stop him. His mind swirled. He was no longer on his feet but felt elevated and then found himself in a bedroom. Pictures of horses lined the walls, and a queen bed with a giant, fluffy lavender comforter and matching pillows was centered in the sizable bedroom. Soft music played from a notebook computer that lay open on a white desk, a depressing song of love lost. The window shade was drawn, and a candle flickered to its demise, leaving the only light in the room a dancing screen of colored swirls that moved along with the music. Through the streaming strands of light, Frank spotted a blonde-haired girl in a dark-colored nightgown lying on the floor between the desk and the bed; her knuckles turned white as she clenched the pillow beneath her, sobbing, half-asleep. In her left hand was a bottle of pills with the top closed.

"I still have time," he said. He reached out and touched his hand to her head. He had used this technique many times before and knew that the person he was helping could hear him. He whispered, "You are not alone in this world. Have faith. Your pain will not last; you have strength and courage to overcome this. You are a beautiful child, a child of God. Don't listen to the shadows; they are here to harm you. Reach out to those around you, find your place in this world, and move forward past this time of trial. You are strong beyond imagination."

"I'm tired. It hurts too much," the girl sobbed.

"Pain subsides," Frank said. "There is so much more for you to look forward to in life—love, laughter, and wonderful experiences."

"I can't," the girl said. "I don't have faith. I don't believe in God."

"You only have to believe in the good that's inside of you." Frank paused. The name came to him, a gift that he had acquired and didn't understand. "Heather, cast the darkness away from you. Awake from this nightmare with renewed spirit."

"But they said they can show me a way to get rid of the pain."

"No, they are going to hurt those who are trying to love you. They are faceless liars who will only make the pain worse for you. Reach out and you will feel they are cold."

"Why are you here?"

Frank put both his hands on her head and concentrated. He sent all the hope and love he could to her and felt power he couldn't understand but knew came from the light. The girl stirred, her legs moved, and she sat up, rubbing her eyes. Frank wasn't always certain that the person he was helping could see him, but Heather focused on him.

"I feel like a burden has been lifted," Heather said.

Frank smiled and held out his hands to help her to her feet. "There, see, you can move forward now." He had broken the grip of the shadows.

A warm sensation overcame him, and he held on to the feeling because he knew that what would come next would test his strength. He waited for a moment until Heather got in bed and pulled her covers tight. He waited until the long breaths of sleep were upon her and he knew his mission was done. He looked to the bedroom door. Beyond it was the world he had once lived in, but he couldn't step to it because he knew he wasn't truly in the room; only a part of him was—a kind of reflection of himself but not truly his whole being. He caught a glimpse of his reflection in the mirror across the room; he reached up and touched his face and noticed that his black hair needed a comb.

He closed his eyes and felt the sensation, a pulling, back to the place where he'd come from, the world of the shadows. He opened his eyes to the fading light of the portal as it shut, leaving him in darkness. "One less soul for you to torment," he said, giving into the sensation and preparing himself for what was to come. He knew he would need total concentration to keep focused on his goal—to get back to the light.

In the darkness, he sensed the black creatures before him, but the circular form that they had reached out to hold was no longer there. He had protected it from harm. The hollow eyes of one of the shadows turned to him. He had been recognized and knew he needed to get back to the path of light. Thin as it might be, it was his only escape.

He ran, but the creatures were on him before he could reach safety. He felt the creatures gnash at his skin, their teeth hot and sharp as they ripped. The dark, formless shapes became solid enough to tear his skin and go deeper at times—causing not just physical pain but mental too. Every doubt he'd ever had about his faith, about his purpose, played before his eyes. Frank was used to the attack; he'd dealt with it hundreds of times since he'd been in this place. The onslaught lessened as he reached the path of light and headed toward the source, the garden he knew was safe. Several of the creatures released their grip, but one remained. He recognized one that seemed more powerful than the others; they'd battled before, and he recognized the hate as it slammed into his brain and thoughts. Frank resisted and pushed back. Then the creature found a thought that caused Frank to stop—people he cared about.

"No!" he shouted. In a moment, Frank felt the need to fight back more than run, and the creature hesitated—it started to release him. He was close to the only source of light in the dark land, a place where he felt safe and where he was stronger than the shadows. This time, instead of letting the form flee, Frank reached out for it and found a place to grasp. He had watched another person he'd followed do this before but had never tried it himself. He tightened his grip and held the form captive, not so much by the power of his grip but by the power of his thoughts, which reached out. His thoughts were met by a foe that was foul, full of hatred, turmoil, and confusion. Frank felt the force trying to pierce his thoughts, threatening to attack those he cared about and was connected to. Instead of struggling, he reached out until he found what he was looking for: a thought, a moment of realization that he was separate and stronger than the thing trying to attack him, making it weaker.

He started moving back, dragging the creature with him along the path. He felt it struggle to get loose as he neared the light, but he reached out with his mind and held on. He dragged it past the line of trees, and it stopped fighting. He was in control and could see images that were not his—the shadow's thoughts and responses. The creature lashed out at him one more time, this time connecting with his body, and Frank felt the pain in his abdomen, as though a claw had torn into it. He grabbed the wooden cane he'd left lying against the rocks and swung it toward the shadow, making contact. It was gone. The cane he held, made from sacred wood, was a gift from the man who had taught him about the shadows. It was a powerful weapon. He considered whether he had somehow killed the shadow but didn't dwell on this because another thought from the creature had escaped before it vanished.

"The group has found a way in," Frank said. "They are trying to cross over to where I am. But it's a trap. The shadows know they are coming." He looked out into the dark world before him to seek out a path to one of the friends he had left behind, but the pain he felt reminded him of the battle he'd just fought. He looked down and saw blood flowing from the cuts in his chest. Knowing that the cuts in his back were even deeper, he walked to the pool of water that lay at the center of the garden. He walked into the water and began praying. The pain subsided as the wounds began to heal. Clarity returned, and he knew what he had to do.

"I must find a way to warn them!"

CHAPTER 1
THIRTEEN DAYS: WARNING

Many philosophies and scientific principles try to explain the concept of opposites and why they exist, reasoning that without a comparison or contrast, how would we know one thing from another? How would we know life without death, light without darkness, and good without evil? This may be a condition of existence: that something doesn't exist without its opposite. True as this may be, there is no proof that opposites must exist in balance. That is a myth, a superstition. Humankind extended day by creating light. We created heat where there was cold and cold where there was heat. We have caused death where there is life and extended life where there was death. It is the gift of intelligence, of knowing, that has allowed us to become what we are: the image of the Creator. Every day, our actions have an impact in the world. We can choose to make a positive impact or be negative. Let there be no doubt that evil exist in this world largely because it is allowed to exist.

Samar Hamish tossed and turned in his bed for the fifth night in a row. The whispers he muttered in his troubled state echoed off the plain white-painted walls in the small apartment he'd called home for the last nine months. He was staying in the Rechavia neighborhood of Jerusalem, a place close to the university that sponsored the dig he was working on. The dig centered on trying to find the city of Bethsaida, the lost city of the apostles, which was important to Samar because the more physical evidence he found of the past, the more his beliefs could be confirmed.

The apartment, on loan from the aforementioned university, had once belonged to a professor who taught classes on religion, which had been Samar's minor in college. A degreed archeologist, Samar had traveled to Israel from his home in India with his fiancée, Ira, to work on a project. It wasn't the team or the project that inspired him, but a calling he had inside of him. The neighborhood, complete with shops and coffee bars, appealed to his fiancée.

From the earliest time he could remember, events in his life led him to be fascinated with the concept of good and evil. He had turned to the study of religion to try to understand the origins of the concepts, hoping this would help him understand what he had seen. His obsession with finding meaning had led him to make world religions his second degree. He had hauled Ira, who was a self-proclaimed sensitive— someone who considered herself intuitive and in touch with powers beyond the physical world—halfway around the world on his quest to understand his personal experiences.

He whispered in his sleep as the dream continued and he made his way down a familiar path through a garden, grayscale and void of color, that opened up into a picturesque view of tall grass and large trees full of leaves. There was no air movement, and the leaves draped down as though frozen. In this dream, Samar had learned he had limited control. He couldn't see the source of a light behind him, nor could he go to it. He could look up, but there was no sign of a sky, stars, or roof—only endless black that he couldn't see beyond. The only direction he could move was forward.

He traveled down the known path, which led to an outcropping of large rocks. There, he would see a man, one he'd spoken to before, sitting on the rocks with his face turned away. In the distance, the vegetation gave way to a barren and rocky landscape. The man on the rocks always faced the barren landscape as he sat on one of the large boulders. Samar couldn't go any farther and always came to a stop just a few steps behind and to the right of the man whose words he could hear but who never turned to face him. He tossed back and forth between his hands what appeared to Samar to be a hand-carved wooden cane, but he never stood or walked. He simply sat on the rocks, looking forward into the surly landscape.

"You've come back. Why?" the man asked, still looking ahead.

"I don't know. I keep having this dream," Samar said. He looked down at his bare feet in the grass and wondered why his shoes were always missing in this dream.

"You believe this is a dream?"

"I know it is; this is not my life. I suppose this dream is a sign that I'm dwelling on something and trying to sort it out."

"I wish it were that easy," Samar's dream companion said. "Why have you come to this place, to Israel?"

"See, that's how I know it's a dream in my own head. Otherwise, how would you know I'm in Israel?"

The man didn't answer.

"I'm part of a new dig, a project that interested me. I have been provided with a place to stay and expense money. It suited me."

"You dig to find answers, to find something to confirm what you think you believe. Is that it?"

"Yes," Samar said. "I seek evidence. Why are you here?"

"In your dream?"

"In this place," Samar said, pointing to the surroundings. "What place is this?"

"This is where it all began, the battle."

"Battle?"

"Between good and evil."

"What happened?"

"I'm not sure it's something we can comprehend, but the forces still exist in this place, and the war continues. That's what has drawn you here, isn't it?"

"Yes. Things have happened to me, and I need to know that they were real and I'm not crazy. Why are you here?"

"This is where I stand watch."

"What's out there?" Samar asked.

"Out there"—the man pointed to the dark areas—""are the shadows, forces of evil that seek to drive us to ruin. Here, in this place, I help people who are in pain or suffering or who have lost hope. I go to them. You are the first to visit me. Perhaps you were sent to help me."

"What do you mean?" Samar asked.

"I have a message I need to get to someone. You have something inside of you that you don't understand. You know it comes from something greater. You're here trying to prove that there is something beyond. You're looking for evidence, but what you search for, you won't find here by digging in the dirt. You have power that you'll need to use."

"You're a philosopher," Samar said. Again, he tried to move forward, and he managed one step.

Samar was still looking down when the man turned slightly, reached out his hand, and grabbed Samar's right arm. He felt the hand grasping him as though it was not a dream, and the man who looked at him spoke with a deep voice that echoed through him, imprinting the words on his mind.

"You must stop searching in the past. I need you to get a message to someone for me. It's time for you to reach out, time to make a positive change in the world. Follow the signs and find the author. Now wake." He released his grip on Samar.

Samar woke with a shudder and sat up in bed, startling Ira beside him.

"You were talking in your sleep again," Ira said as she turned over to face him.

Samar could see the outline of her face in the light filtering through the window from a streetlamp.

"It's still night," she said, "when most people sleep."

"Sorry I woke you. What did I say?"

"You were talking about removing your shoes because you were on holy ground. And then you kept talking about going somewhere to find the author."

Samar looked forward into the darkness of the room, trying to visualize the landscape from his dream.

"You know," Ira continued, "there's a condition that some people get when they travel to the Holy Land. It's called Jerusalem syndrome."

"No, no," Samar said, waving his index finger back and forth. "You think I'm delusional? I know the term. I am not a religious person and not subject to such conditions."

"Why are we here again?"

"You told me to follow what was calling me," Samar said. "You told me the things that were happening to me meant something and I should look for signs and follow them."

"Yes, I did do that, didn't I?" Ira said. "I just didn't know it would delay our wedding."

"Well, we can't very well take time off now when I am in the middle of a project—unless you want to give in to a smaller ceremony."

"My family would never agree. Why this project again?"

"In my studies of where the concept of the battle between good and evil first manifested, I found it was here, in this very valley. This is the place where three of the world's most influential religions were born. It was only natural that the path I seek would lead me to such a place. Even my dreams are telling me this is where I should be."

Ira sat up and ran her hand through her long black hair. "Was it the same dream again?"

"No, it changed this time. It seemed more like the man in my dream was real and like he was trying to tell me something. He knew about the dark forms."

"The dark forms?"

"It's hard to explain," Samar said, "but when I come into contact with certain people, I see an aura around them, and sometimes it's very dark, but they don't seem to notice it's there until after I touch them. There is something I need to find here—proof that there are forces of good and evil."

"To affirm you're not going crazy? You expect to find that by digging up old relics and proving what? That ancient people were superstitious too? Why are you here, really? Why are you looking at me like that?"

"That's what the man in my dream kept asking me: 'why are you here?'"

"Maybe you should listen to him," Ira said. "Too many people get lost in the past, and in it they lose the ability to see the path to the future."

"That's sound advice. The man in my dream told me to 'reach out, make a positive change, and find the author.' I don't even know what that means."

Samar got up from bed and looked out the window of the second-story apartment to the narrow street below. He went over to the television and turned it on. "Do you mind?"

"No, you've got me up now too. Maybe we can find something to watch that will get your mind off things and help you go back to sleep."

After flipping through multiple stations airing infomercials and late-night action shows, Samar settled on a talk show where the host was interviewing a best-selling author.

"Welcome back to *A Brighter Tomorrow*, the talk show that highlights good stories," said the young, black-haired female host. She sat on a small white couch on a set in front of a live audience, and the title of the show was displayed on the wall behind her. "Our next guest is best-selling author and psychiatrist Dr. Claudia Walden, author of the book *Reaching Out: It's Time to Make a Positive Change in the World*." The host stood to greet her guest and shook her hand as the woman sat down on the couch beside her. "Thank you for being on our show today."

Samar glanced at Ira to see if she had heard the same thing he had. Ira didn't seem to have noticed. He increased the volume.

"Thank you for having me, Naomi," Claudia said. The blonde-haired author was dressed in a red-and-white medium-length dress.

"What an attractive lady," Ira said.

"Why do you say that?"

"Other than being a little pale, look at the tone in those arms and legs—definitely a fellow kickboxer," Ira said. "Or else she's an aerobics instructor. You don't think so?"

Samar smiled and tapped Ira on the nose. "I just didn't want to appear to be looking at other women."

"She's on television in another country," Ira said. "I think I am not jealous."

They shared a laugh and moved closer together to watch the show.

"Your current book has sold over ten million copies worldwide. Did you expect such a reception?" the host Naomi asked.

"At first, I was astonished, but then I analyzed the reason the book was so popular," Claudia said.

"Analyzed," Naomi said, facing the audience. "For those in our viewing audience who may not know, Dr. Walden is a degreed and certified psychiatrist who worked with troubled youth in one of the nation's most-renowned clinics." She turned back to her guest. "I'm sorry. Please continue."

"There is so much negativity in our daily lives. I think people are looking and longing for some healing. Hollywood does a poor job of putting out any movies or shows these days without using the F-word every other sentence or worrying about action and blood more than meaningful stories and dialogue. And the internet is full of yahoos who want to deliver their message through what I call 'shock value,' using obscene or racy material to attract an audience."

"I agree," Naomi said. "Perhaps we can start a GoFundMe drive to buy some dictionaries for the screenwriters."

The two laughed.

"Today's news—pardon me if I offend you—thrives on the tragedy and drama," said Claudia. "Don't even get me started on social media and the lack of decency that thrives amid unregulated and uncensored mass postings and poorly screened comment sections. The book I've written is something people long for and need to hear, a positive message that doesn't get overly political."

"Yes," Naomi said. "It's about healing and making positive choices. If you don't mind me asking, I would think someone with your background, a scientific one, would be more logical and calculating in your approach and outlook. But your writing is full of passion. Am I missing something? Was there something in your background that inspired you?"

"Actually," Claudia said, "I used to work with, well, a group that solved problems. I often found myself being the voice of reason in our decision making, the psychiatrist looking for cold reason. But then I met someone who inspired me to take a different approach."

"This is the Father Frank Keller that you mention?"

"Yes."

"The book makes some critical points about how we expect to live our lives and the consequences, not just for us but for society in general," Naomi said. "What would this friend tell you about why your work is winning people over?"

"Frank showed me how to have courage and that I was being called to action. As I told you, I think the reason the book is finding such a good following is that it's something people have longed for—to know there is hope in the darkness. And those who don't reach out in faith need to understand that they can still make a difference in how the world works by what they do. You don't have to be religious to make a positive impact. Each day, we have a choice to make: do we make the world a better place with our actions or spread evil?"

"I understand you have brought us a sample from your upcoming book to share?"

"Yes, of course. As you know, the book is not yet finished and doesn't have a title yet, but I will share with you one part—another passage from Father Frank Keller's last sermon: 'Our actions don't just affect ourselves but start a ripple that continues in the world around us, in the world we leave behind that others will inherit. And it is our right to demand this action of others, to tell them it is not okay to turn away and let darkness exist. It is not okay to let injustice exist. Whether they believe in God or not, they are not alone in the world and must act as responsible parties to a larger agreement: that we all share this place. And each of our decisions has an impact that can last well beyond our time into the everlasting, which is the legacy we leave for those that come after us.'"

"Powerful words," Naomi said as the audience applauded. "So it follows the same theme as your first book in promoting having a positive impact on the world we live in."

"Yes," Claudia said. "It will continue to follow the same premise but go further in asking for more involvement in the world around us. The message in it will be very clear that it's time to quit asking for help and be the help. As a person very close to me once taught, the actions we take today echo and have impacts that reverberate longer than we think."

"Well," Naomi said, "we wish you the best of luck on your new book and thank you for joining us."

"Thank you for having me."

The television screen went blank as Samar hit the power button on the remote.

"I think I have that book," Ira said. "I've been meaning to read it. But these trips back and forth to see you have caused me to be a little less organized."

Samar stared forward at the empty screen. "What she said—it's time to reach out and make a difference. The man in my dream said I need to reach out and make a positive change in the world. I wake up and see this author, and he said to find the author. What are the chances of this?"

"Maybe you heard the show earlier today and your mind is playing tricks on you," Ira said.

"It's a live talk show," Samar said. "Remember the time difference?"

"I'm supposed to be the spiritual one, but it's clear you have some intuition. I've known that from the day I met you."

"That's why you love me," Samar said.

Ira reached over to a small dresser, pulled a cell phone off the charger, and handed it to Samar. "The man in your dream told you to find the author. Maybe it's her."

"I can't just up and leave. Besides, I'm not sure I have enough money to do this."

"We must embrace this. Your spiritual side that you refuse to believe in is trying to communicate with you."

"We?"

"Yes. My father will send me money. This quest of yours is important. Whatever you are trying to find, you must find, or you will never have inner balance."

Samar pulled a small notebook out from the dresser that the television sat upon and started writing notes. "Claudia Walden. That was the author's name."

"I think you need to find out why you are having these dreams.

This author is a psychiatrist, so maybe she has the answers or can help you," Ira said, "if she'll meet you."

"Yes, and how do you suppose we get her to meet me?"

"She's an author who does appearances. We just need to find out where she is going next." Ira reached over again to the small dresser next to the bed and grabbed a blue notebook computer. After typing a few things into the search engine, she turned the screen to face Samar. "New York on September 22."

"That's only two days from now."

"I have an aunt who lives in New York that I used to stay with when I was going to school. I haven't seen her for some time, and it would be good to visit. We can stay with her," Ira said. "I can arrange a flight out tomorrow."

"You sure you are not just doing this because you are bored?"

"If it helps you find the answers you need, we can get on with our lives."

Samar looked into her big brown eyes and stroked the bangs of her long black hair from her eyes. "I'll tell the others tomorrow that I am taking a break from the project, and we will go to New York to find this author."

<hr />

On the other side of the Atlantic Ocean, Claudia Walden had just finished her final talk-show appearance and was looking forward to some long-awaited time off.

"Thank you, Dr. Walden, for you time," Naomi said. "I wish you the best on your new book. Perhaps when it is a success, you can come visit us again. I'm sure your positive message will reach millions. I know it gave me a lot to think about."

Claudia wasted no time exiting the studio and getting to her rental car in the parking lot. She had only one more book-signing appearance in two days, and then she would be on her way back home to Chicago.

She pulled her car around to the door of the hotel and let the valet driver take it. When she entered through the double doors, the desk clerk waved at her and handed her several messages, which she grabbed but had no intention of reading right away. She headed to the elevator and up to her suite. "Rosie?" she called as she entered the suite. "Rosie? There you are."

A medium-haired tabby cat rested on the bed and flicked her tail back and forth as Claudia approached.

"You know, I had to pay extra to have a room where they'd let us stay together. Just one more night, and we can head home. I bet you'd like that." She sat on the bed and petted Rosie. Her smile faded as Rosie started to purr, and she put her face next to her friend's soft, furry head. The cat nuzzled her back.

Tears fell from Claudia's eyes. "Every time I do a presentation, I can't help but think back to the past, Rosie. I know Frank would think I'm silly. It was his choice. And Adnan, he knew what he was doing." She lay down and drew closer to Rosie, who continued purring. "I just miss the group and the times at the Kozy Tavern. It was the closest thing I had to a family after my father passed."

Claudia slipped off her shoes and heard them hit the floor. She reached for the remote, which she'd left on the nightstand next to the bed, and turned the television on to a classical music station. As the sound of soft violins entered the room, Claudia was soothed to sleep and found herself in the land of dreams.

"David?"

"Yes, Dr. Walden?"

Claudia was in her counseling room in the psychiatric wing of the hospital. David Jenson, a patient of hers who had killed his parents and his sister, was lying on the couch, facing away from her. "What were you telling me?" she asked.

"I was apologizing for being late to our session. I've been working a lot of hours lately. You know, it makes the time pass."

"It's okay, David. I'm glad to hear you are working." Claudia looked at the notebook in front of her: the pages were blank. She flipped back to the beginning, but there were no notes in the book. Claudia became confused without a reference for what they had they been speaking about. She didn't remember the start of the session or when they had started meeting in her office. She had no recollection of David being released from the institution where he'd been held after being convicted of murdering his parents and sister.

"Did you say you were working?"

"Yes, I have a job. Are you okay, Dr. Walden?"

Claudia moved her eyes from the blank pages to see that David had changed his position on the couch and was now facing her.

"Did you forget what we were talking about? You didn't forget what happened back at the hospital. You didn't forget how Father Frank saved me. He freed me from the shadows."

She glanced around the room and noticed that much of it was out of focus, with the exception of the couch and the patient before her. She didn't remember coming back from her tour, let alone going back to her practice that she'd quit three years ago.

"David, how long have we been meeting?"

"We haven't been meeting, Dr. Walden. You've been out of town. This is a dream you are having, and I am in it because we are connected."

"Connected how?"

"Frank, Father Frank. He still helps me. See, the shadows had me, and they know I am weak. Father Frank keeps them out of my life. He comes to me in my dreams, and now so do you."

"You think this is a dream?"

"I know it is," David said. "I also know why I am here in your dream. Frank told me. He says he can't get to you because he can only get to those who the shadows touch, so he had to use me—that's what he said. They're evil, you know. He said he would help me try, but I didn't know how."

"Didn't know how to what?" Claudia asked.

"I didn't know how I would get you the message, the message from Father Frank. But your mind is dwelling on me because you want to help me. But you must go now. You must go now."

"Go where?"

"Claudia." The voice that came from David was now Frank Keller's voice. "Claudia, you're the only one I could reach. You must stop them—you must tell them not do it. Find Jimmie. You only have thirteen days."

She woke in a sweat. Rosie was sitting on her hind legs at the foot of the bed, watching her. Claudia could always tell if she'd slept restlessly because when she rested well, Rosie lay on the bed beside her through the night. When she was restless, Rosie would often leave the bed. Claudia put her hand out, and Rosie moved closer. Claudia stroked the soft fur of the black, white, and brown-colored cat. She ran her index finger around a small pattern of black hair on Rosie's head that resembled a rose; it was how she'd gotten her name.

"It's okay," she said. "I had a bad dream. It's probably all of the traveling."

Claudia lay back on her pillow and stared at the ceiling. She wondered what the others were doing. Was Chic still running the Kozy Tavern? Was Kanuik still working with the Council of World Religions, and was Professor Jimmie Barnes still teaching? She decided that after her book appearance it was time to find out—time to track down the others and get back in touch.

CHAPTER 2
TWELVE DAYS REMAINING

*Look away from the light for too long, and you will
find yourself living in the darkness you've created.*

"We are going through these measures for your protection,"
said the man who had blindfolded Mike Delgado as he
settled into the back seat of the car.

Mike had received a note offering him work related to his expertise
in research, but he had to be discreet. Desperate to do anything that
would get him out of his cable installation job, he had decided to take
the offer even if it meant meeting late at night.

"You guys work for the government or something?" Mike said.

The men in the front seat remained silent. Suddenly, Mike wished
he had told someone where he was going. After about twenty minutes,
the car came to a stop.

"Our associate wants to meet with you. He's willing to pay you if
you can help him, but you've got to keep this meeting secret."

As they exited the car, Mike could hear various street sounds in the
background, but nothing that would distinguish a particular location.
The men led him down a set of stairs and placed him in a chair. One
man removed his mask. Mike moved his hands over his eyes to clear
his vision and brushed aside his thick red hair. It felt out of place, but
he was too nervous to comb it.

Mike found himself in a dimly lit concrete room that looked like
the basement of an old manufacturing shop, with thick floors full
of leftover anchor bolts where machinery had once been mounted.
In front of him was a desk with papers on it, and to the left stood a
set of tables holding bottles of chemicals, lab equipment, and various
electronic equipment, some of which he was familiar with. As his eyes

adjusted from the blindfold, what caught his attention the most was a cell against the far wall with five or more teenagers locked inside.

"Don't worry about them." The deep voice came from behind the desk, from a man who sat still and blended in with the shadows so well that Mike hadn't noticed him until he'd spoken. "And whatever you do, I warn you not to engage in conversation with them. They have … issues and can't be trusted."

Mike took a moment to make sure none of the men who had escorted him in were carrying weapons or seemed threatening. He checked his pocket and noted that his cell phone was still there. The man behind the desk was dressed in black, just like the men who had escorted him. He was a thin man with medium-length black hair that came down in sideburns and a beard that was cut to frame his face. A long scar lined the left side of his face.

"You noticed the scar," said the man behind the desk, moving the bangs of his hair out of his eyes. "This scar made me what I am today." He ran his finger along the scar. "A gift from my father."

"I didn't mean to stare."

"It's okay. I'm used to it," the man said.

"Who … who are you people?" Mike asked. "If this is about a cable bill or something, I don't work in billing. I just install the stuff."

"Mike Delgado," said the man, whose black attire resembled that of a priest, "you have a dual degree in physics and chemistry. Yet you are a cable installation man by day and ghost hunter by night."

"Yes, well, the college and I had some disagreements about research money and stuff like that," Mike said. "So we parted ways. Cable installation is more of a freelance job. I don't have to be confined to an office."

"It's no coincidence that you are here. We could put your full set of skills back to use."

"You contacted me," Mike said. "What do you have in mind?"

"I have an offer for you. I understand you used to be involved with researching the supernatural. How would you like to make it more than a hobby? I could pay you for your work, and you would have considerable autonomy."

"Why would you do that? Didn't you hear what I said about the college? My research wasn't exactly met with approval."

"We believe, like you do, in the supernatural. Besides, it may not be what you know now but what you remember. I am interested in finding out what you know about Professor Jimmie Barnes and a machine he created, a machine that is more important than you think. In fact, you could say it might save the world."

"Who are you?"

"I am Father Thomas, a servant of the church. If you join my team, I promise you revelations unlike anything you've ever seen before. All you have to do is agree to secrecy; everything we do here is confidential."

Mike sat back in his chair. "Secrecy is not a problem. I mean, I don't exactly have a huge social life. You said you could pay me?"

"Yes, to do research again," Thomas said. "Much better than your cable job."

"Why the secrecy?"

Thomas moved his hands in front of him and tapped all five fingers of each hand together. "Let's just say that there are those in society who are not ready to accept what we are dealing with. More will be revealed if you agree to my terms."

"Which are?"

"I am in charge," Thomas said. "You will not question my direction, and you will not tell anyone else what you are doing here."

"You said you are a servant of the church?"

Thomas nodded.

"I guess it can't be too bad then. Agreed," Mike said as he stood and reached across the desk to shake Thomas's hand. "Where do we start?"

Thomas leaned forward and put his arms on the desk, his hands together. "Do you believe in evil?"

High above the desert plains in northern Arizona, Kanuik, a descendant of the Cherokee Indians, sat in a small hut, waiting to meet with the council of warriors. A man dressed in ancient ceremonial skins and feathers entered the doorway and motioned for him to follow.

It was twilight, and the air grew still on the plateau as Kanuik was escorted to a large kiva, where he stood and waited. A short, stocky, elderly Native American man emerged in ceremonial dress with an eagle feather and smoke pipe. Following tradition, he used the smoke coming from the pipe to purify Kanuik by moving the pipe around him and immersing him in the smoke. Then he brushed Kanuik with the eagle feather. Kanuik knew this man, Alo, as his guide from when Kanuik had been recruited as a member of the warrior tribe whose mission was to fight tricksters—another name for what Kanuik had come to know as shadows. Alo had taught him how to use holy fire, how to use different herbs in his pipe, and the important chants, dances, and rituals for fighting, cleansing, and focusing.

Kanuik knew he was not allowed to speak until he was addressed and invited to do so because he was not a member of the elder council. With the cleansing ritual complete, Kanuik entered through one of the thirteen doors to the kiva and continued to a place in front of four men who were seated on the ground on the opposite side of two lit firepits. The men sat toward the north side of the room while Kanuik stood on the opposite side. Other than a few blankets on the floor where the men sat and cups for drinks, the kiva was empty. One of the men motioned for Kanuik to sit down. He took a position on a well-placed blanket facing the men and waited patiently until he was addressed.

"We are pleased that you have come to visit us again," the eldest of the four said.

Kanuik knew the head of the council of elders, Kwanu, a representative of the ten tribes, from the time he had trained with the Hopi on how to battle the shadows. Kwanu had already been old when Kanuik was just a boy. The wrinkles of age and wisdom were set on a weathered face. Framed by flowing white hair on both sides, his eyes of kindness and vision appeared to stare beyond the person he was looking at. Kanuik marveled at the power and strength emanating from such a small, humble man.

"It is great to be here and see my old friend, the Eagle," he said, referencing the meaning of Kwanu's name, "doing so well. It is an honor to be here among the elders of the ten tribes."

"I am sorry to hear that your friend Adnan passed from this world," Kwanu said. "I wish we could have met. He was a great warrior in the battle against the trickster spirits of this world, and he joined with us as one among us."

"He was a great man and helped many," Kanuik said. "He reminded me of you, Kwanu, because he had no prejudices and knew it was up to all of us to defeat the evil among us." During the conversation, Kanuik looked periodically to his mentor, Alo, for any nonverbal clues to whether or not he was behaving appropriately. He knew Alo would remain stoic if Kanuik was addressing the council with respect. If Kanuik were disrespectful, Alo would lower his eyes and look at the ground.

"Word of your triumphs over evil has spread far. Your representation of the tribes in the Council of World Religions has done much to advance our causes. I understand the leader of your group, Adnan, was not the only person you lost in your battle."

"No," Kanuik said. "There was another, a priest of the church named Father Frank Keller. He entered the world of the shadows and fights them there."

"We have heard of this man," Kwanu said. "Let us take time to remember your friends and honor their courage."

The men sat in silence for about twenty minutes before Kwanu opened his eyes. "Now, great warrior, tell us why you have returned."

"I have traveled long and fought evil as directed by my power. I heard the calling to be with the ten tribes. That calling led me to a quest beyond these shores and back. I found my spirit warrior and served with the strongest man to ever go forward and battle the shadows. Since his passing, my calling has been for rest and peace. I have no son to whom to pass my legacy as a warrior, and I desire to find my wife and retire from this way."

No response came, but the men shifted about, as though uncomfortable, and glanced at each other. Alo remained still and undisturbed, and this gave Kanuik confidence. Kwanu put his right hand out, face up to his right side and then to his left. The men around him stood and left the kiva so that only Kwanu and Kanuik remained.

Kanuik caught Alo glancing back before he exited the kiva, and he hoped his mentor would be waiting for him to give him advice after the meeting ended.

Unlike the representatives from the plains tribes who wore headdresses, Kwanu and Alo each wore a simple headband and clothing that was not as colored or decorative as that of the other elders. Kanuik appreciated the simplicity that was reflected not only in the dress but also in the speech and deeds of the men. He watched the man before him close his eyes in a tense moment before opening them and taking a deep breath.

"It is not often that one with your power asks to stop in the battle. The warrior call remains even in the ancient men in our tribe, men like me," Kwanu said.

"I am sorry if I have offended you," Kanuik said. "My path took me from the tribes to another way, and now I can't find it. I have tried to be content with serving the Council of World Religions and going back to my wife."

"But you are restless," Kwanu said.

"Yes."

"You suffered loss and did not grieve with those who shared your loss."

"Our group went separate ways," Kanuik said. "There was no time to grieve."

"Yes, I see," Kwanu said. "From the first breath of men, the war has been with us, a battle of deeds. We know that before our tribes, there were others in this world that walked about and were not men. These others were at times evil. The battle for control of our deeds is one that goes back centuries. Evil walked in the thirteenth month. The thirteen doors on the kiva represent the thirteen cycles of the moon. We know how one battle changed the thirteenth month and how men turned the cycles into twelve. The battle between good and evil goes back in our history as long as stories have been told. You mentioned the shadows— tricksters, as we have known them throughout our history. We fight them and come here together to cleanse ourselves of the remnants of battle and to remember our promise to the earth: to take only what is needed without destruction and give back."

"Yes, I remember the stories," Kanuik said.

"You know that a warrior is chosen by the path," Kwanu said.

"Yes," Kanuik answered. "Many say it is a calling that we cannot turn from, something that forges our spirit."

"Then you know the calling is not something that ends. Once you enter the path of the warrior, it is a lifelong journey."

"I served with a group of people, as a warrior against the evil forces. Our group is no longer; our leader, a great man, has passed. The man he mentored, Father Frank Keller, entered the land of the shadows and is no more. Since this time, my senses have been ... dulled. I haven't found a spirit who complements my power. I feel that the journey you speak of has ended for me. I wish for your blessing to put down my spear and become what I am, an old man."

Kwanu closed his eyes for a moment. Then he reached in front of him, picked up a long pipe, and lit it. He moved the pipe up and down to let the smoke go about the room.

"Sit and meditate with me," Kwanu said. "We shall think of these things."

Thousands of feet above the Atlantic Ocean, Samar sat with his eyes closed and his hands, white-knuckled, grasping the armrests. He listened to the hum of the plane's engines and tried to relax. Ira sat in the window seat beside him and casually glanced out the window. He felt her hand as she gripped his and squeezed it.

"Don't worry. We are perfectly safe," she said.

"Unlike you, who had a rich father who flew her all around the world when she was young, this is only my second plane ride. And both of them have been very long rides—first from Chennai to Jerusalem and now from Jerusalem to New York City." He looked out the window.

"At least now the sun is going down, and you won't be able to look out the window and see how high up we are," Ira said.

Her words caused him to glance out the window once more. Samar felt tightness in his stomach and a pounding in his head. He leaned forward.

"You sure you won't have anything to eat? It's an awfully long flight, and food might make you feel better."

"I won't feel better when it comes back up because of how my stomach feels." He grabbed Ira's hand tightly and sat rigid in his chair.

"What is it? Do you need one of these bags?" She hurriedly pulled one of the bags from behind the seat and unfolded it.

Samar brushed the bag to the side. "You know that feeling I described to you that I get when something bad is about to happen?"

Ira didn't respond to his comment, but as she gazed past Samar to the aisle, he saw her eyes widen, and her hands went up to her mouth. Time seemed to move in slow motion for him as he heard screams and turned his head to see what had frightened Ira. A man, dark-haired, with sweat running down his face and a determined look in his eyes, was coming up the aisle with a small gun in his hands. As people noticed, more screams rang out.

A feeling overtook Samar that he had experienced numerous times before—when playground bullies hurt others at school, when boys harassed his sister in the street and he had to intervene, and when corrupt government officials extorted a bribe from him on his first archeological dig. As before, he knew he had to act, to do something, and just like before, he spotted the black, legless form hovering around the man who was nearly parallel to him in the aisle.

When the man with the gun started to pass him, Samar reached out and lightly touched his arm. The man stopped walking. He looked down at his arm where Samar had touched him before he made eye contact with Samar, who rose from his seat. Everything around the two men seemed to be silent, and as Samar spoke, not even the sound of the jet's engines could be heard over his words.

"I know this is not what you want to do," Samar said to him. "You are in control, and this is not right." He felt the internal struggle, a wrestling within the man before him. He felt the power lash out at him, and the shadowy creature came at Samar, diving at his chest. For a moment, he couldn't breathe, and his heart pounded, but he kept hold of the man's arm. "Help me," Samar said. "Help me fight it, for your future." As Samar pleaded, the man started crying.

"I have to," the man said.

"No," Samar said. "These people around you are not responsible for your pain, and what you are doing will only make it worse. It is the easy way but not the right way." He put pressure on the man's arm and got him to lower the gun as he continued sobbing.

Samar felt darkness overtake him as the pain in his chest increased. He lost his breath and closed his eyes. Some men tackled the terrorist, causing both him and Samar to fall to the floor. He tried to open his eyes and saw people standing over him, looking down, before he lost consciousness.

Day had turned to evening high on the mountain where Kanuik sat in meditation with the head of the council elders. He was progressively less sure of what Kwanu would say to him the longer they meditated. He just wanted to live in peace the rest of his life, if he could find it. He had been a part of a team and at his age couldn't see joining a new one and traveling about.

Kwanu opened his eyes and started talking. "Many other races, not just the whites, haven't understood their place under the stars. Without your representation on this new religious council, how will our voice be heard?"

"My wife and I will continue to be part of the Council of World Religions, but I no longer desire to travel or fight."

"And she has agreed to this?"

"We are not together very often, but yes. This is what she wants."

Kwanu picked up a different pipe and lit it. He blew the smoke toward Kanuik, who inhaled it deeply. "Tell me about this man you followed, Adnan."

The fire in the pit provided warmth and light. Kwanu passed the pipe to Kanuik, and as he took a smoke from it, he thought back to the time he had spent with Adnan and how they had met.

"You know I was brought up on the reservation," Kanuik said. "It was when I was just becoming a man that the power I had inside of me was noticed. I was an outcast in my tribe, fighting against those who stood by and took no action. I wanted to leave.

"Alo came to visit; it was he who knew I had the calling. He taught me great energies and power. His medicine was strong. He gave me a mission to leave and help another group who were also warriors, but not of my tribe. It was during my travels that I met Adnan. He had joined a group fighting evil in Africa. It was rooted there amid years of bloodshed and suffering.

"Adnan could see the shadows. He had a mirror from the Dark Ages that somehow revealed them. He was older than I and had tremendous power, and soon, I looked up to him. During one of our battles, he somehow trapped a shadow inside of him. He used his power over the shadow to detect others of its kind prior to their mischief. We joined with others—a psychiatrist, a priest, and a science professor—in order to further our cause and research."

"A great story," Kwanu said. "He was a teacher and friend to you, this I can see."

"The story does not end there," Kanuik said. "Adnan felt we were losing the battle against the evil forces. He wanted to enter their realm and take the fight to them. He thought he could use the creature he had captured inside of him to do this. In the end, the shadow found a way to trap Adnan and used a person he was helping to kill him."

"You did not take his place after and continue leading the warriors in your group?"

Kanuik thought about the group that Adnan had led: Jimmie, the college professor; Claudia, the psychiatrist; and Frank Keller, a priest. "We were not prepared to continue," Kanuik said. "In my writings to the council, I wrote about the man who Adnan wanted to take over, Father Frank Keller, and how he crossed over to the world of the shadows. This left the group confused, with too much tragedy to overcome. Dr. Walden and Professor Barnes were more advisors than warriors. Both of them had other careers."

He thought about what he had just said and remembered how he had tried to find meaning in the quest, but without the companionship of Adnan and the team they had put together, Kanuik no longer felt complete, even with his wife, whom he loved but had not been around for years, back in his life. He had stumbled for the last three years, helping the council but still feeling lost. He noticed the intense brown eyes of Kwanu studying him.

"I understand," Kwanu said. "This group you were with became your family. But you dwell upon the past, and that has blocked you from the new path that calls to you."

"I think about times that have passed, yes," Kanuik said. "I haven't heard or seen any path that calls to me. The journey forward is not the same without those who have shared it with me."

"You have come to me and this tribal council not because you need our permission to step away from your journey. You did not need our permission when you joined a group outside of the tribes. You look to us as the teachers, but it is you, Kanuik, who have furthered our cause and helped us see that the battle between good and evil is a cause for all races. You have become our teacher. We must spread this message to the tribes of all races."

"So you don't accept my withdrawing from the path?" Kanuik asked.

"If it were but that simple," Kwanu said. "We are just men, and we don't always control what guides us. It is not my decision. If I were to tell you today that you are free to go on the path you choose, you would not find the peace you seek."

"Tell me then, what is it you see for me?"

"Your time as a warrior is not done. I see another great journey in front of you. Every race I see is battling for possession of the relationship with nature and each other. We rage against each other, we rage against nature, we rage against God, whatever we believe God to be. There is a call for healing that goes unheeded, and so, with great momentum, the world is headed for upheaval. There is not much time. I am sure of this. All warriors must be ready."

"Then I'll stay here with you and search for what is calling to me."

Kwanu stood, which signaled Kanuik to stand. The elder walked to Kanuik, who towered over him by two feet, and patted him on the shoulder. "As much as I would like to have you around and add new blood to this tribal council, that is not your path. You must continue to spread the message that all share the same blood, that we are one people that must unite against evil. More than that, the group you served with is not through. I sense in my spirit that someone searches for you. This priest who has gone to the world of spirits wants you to go to her."

"Father Frank," Kanuik said. "He wants me to find Dr. Walden?"

Kwanu put more wood on the fire and took his seat opposite Kanuik. "Yes, he is the one the tribal council has spoken about, the man who walks in the world of spirits where we can only visit. You must find a way to help him."

"Then I must go." Kanuik turned away and then realized his error. He immediately returned to his position, knowing he had to wait to be dismissed.

"I see a great strife in the future of all men," Kwanu said. "And you, you are in the middle of it." He stood and walked out of the kiva and returned with the other members of the tribal council. Many returned with drums and war paint. They gathered in a circle around Kanuik. The drums and dancing began.

Kwanu danced and chanted words that Kanuik understood to mean "Awaken your soul and be true in what you must do before you go. Be strong, warrior, and beware of the coyote. The power of the tribes is with you."

Samar opened his eyes and moved his head side to side as a strong smell permeated his nostrils.

"Sorry," a man's voice said. "I had to use the smelling salts to wake you up. Just wanted to make sure you were okay. He's awake."

Samar heard clapping as he struggled to stand with the help of two men. He suddenly realized he was still on the plane, in the aisle by the flight attendants' station. The man he had confronted was bound with handcuffs and seated on the floor of the plane, crying. The applause came from several flight attendants and two men dressed like pilots.

"We've landed?" Samar asked.

"You are safe on the ground," said one of the men who had helped Samar to his feet. The man was about five foot nine and balding, with a little bit of gray hair left on the sides, and as he bent down to pick up a jacket that Samar had been lying on, Samar noticed his shoulder holster and weapon. "I'm Dusty Muller, a federal air marshal of the United States. I would like to ask you a few questions." He helped Samar into a seat and stood beside him.

"Ira?"

"I'm here, Samar," Ira called, and he saw that she was just up the aisle. Several men dressed in security uniforms stood between him and the front exit of the plane where Ira stood.

"Do you know this man?" the air marshal asked Samar, pointing to the terrorist.

"No," Samar said. "I've never seen him before today. Where are we?"

"Your plane was diverted to Dover Air Force Base due to the security concern. We've kept you on board until we can assess the threat. All of the other passengers have been evacuated and are being questioned. So far, they are saying that you're a hero."

Another man approached them. "Here," he said, handing papers to the air marshal. Samar recognized his passport among the papers. "Everything seems to be in order. This man is not on our watch list. Also, he's from India, not the Middle East."

"What were you doing in Jerusalem, Mr. Hamish?" Muller asked.

"I am an archeologist," Samar said. "I was working on a project there."

"And why have you traveled to the United States? What is your business here?"

"I am traveling with my fiancée." He glanced to Ira, who nodded. "We have come to visit her aunt," he continued, looking again at Ira.

"Doris," Ira said. "Doris Klawson, New York. You need her address?"

"No," Muller said. "That won't be necessary. Well, what you did today saved a lot of lives." He handed Samar his passport. "I don't know how you got him to lower the gun, but it allowed the flight crew to restrain him and get the plane down safely. You must have been in shock and passed out yourself. These officers will escort you off the plane and arrange transportation to wherever you need to go."

"May we please arrange transportation that doesn't involve flying?"

"Sure thing," Muller said. "We can arrange a car to take you to your next stop."

After Ira and Samar exited the plane, the air marshal guided them to baggage claim and then outside, where a black limousine was waiting for them.

"Mr. Hamish, keep yourself and that lovely lady safe and enjoy your visit to the United States of America," Muller said, shaking Samar's hand.

Once inside the car, Samar breathed a sigh of relief.

"Do you have an address where I can take you?" asked the driver.

Ira provided the address, and the car started down the road.

"Why did you do that?" Ira said. "What were you thinking to grab that man?"

Samar looked forward at the driver. The man seemed to be paying them no attention, but he looked fit and muscular and was dressed like the air marshals. Samar suspected that the man was a law enforcement or security officer of some type.

"I don't know why I did it," Samar said in a hushed voice. "The feelings are getting stronger, and it was as though I was compelled to reach out to him to help. I had a sense that the man was in trouble—influenced by something he didn't really understand."

"Now I don't understand," Ira said. "You mean he was possessed by something?"

"No, that's not what I mean."

"Good. For a moment, I was going to remind you of the Jerusalem syndrome that you deny you have, but I don't know. Maybe there's something deeper here."

"I am sure we are on the right track, going to see this author," Samar said.

He decided not to share any more with Ira about what had transpired on the plane. She was already worried, and he didn't want to tell her about the dark form he had seen around the man he had helped or that it had attacked him and made him pass out. He was still trying to make sense of it, and this wasn't the first time he'd run into one of the dark forms. What he knew was that it was evil and intended harm. That's what had driven him to the Holy Land in the first place. Samar wasn't sure if he believed in God or religions, but he believed in evil because he had seen and felt it.

"How far is Dr. Walden's author appearance from where your aunt lives?"

Ira pulled out her phone and looked up the addresses. "Not far," she said. "She lives in a nice neighborhood where there are a lot of new shopping centers. The bookstore is located in one of the centers close by, less than an hour given traffic. I hope they don't start checking too deeply. The person we are going to see is really more of an adopted aunt. She used to work with my father. Her name is Doris Klawson."

"Yes, I believe you told me that. I think we are in the clear," Samar said. "But we are traveling from the Middle East, so we should naturally expect some suspicion."

"That's just prejudice," Ira said.

"Not so," Samar said, increasing his volume a little, hoping the driver might overhear him. "People with our profiles have been killing Americans—how can you blame them for being cautious?"

"Well, I don't like it," Ira said.

"You are sure your aunt won't mind us staying with her?"

"Oh no, not at all. She's the friendliest person. She has a beautiful yellow canary named Ladie that sings, and she lives in this New Age building that uses cats to keep out the rodents. It really is a beautiful place."

"Cats?"

CHAPTER 3
GATHERING: ELEVEN DAYS REMAINING

We search for an all-powerful source to ease our
pain and solve all of our problems. I say that source is
waiting for us to make the right choices.

K anuik stood outside the door of the Kozy Tavern, a place he
used to frequent. Located in a run-down part of Chicago, it was
surrounded by the dilapidated shells of buildings that once had
housed manufacturing companies that made automobile parts.

The name, "Kozy Tavern," was painted in white lettering against
a blue, faded background. Kanuik pushed on the heavy wooden door
to enter. After his eyes adjusted to the dim lighting, he looked to his
right across a rectangular room. Two pool tables sat in the middle of the
room with widely spaced dining tables on either side. There was no one
seated at the tables, and Kanuik shifted his eyes to the left as the door
closed behind him. There he found the bar and the barkeep, still as he
remembered: a short, balding man, with two streaks of silver hair on
either side of his head, who wore thick glasses and looked well into his
sixties, drying a glass with a white towel. A cigar, not lit, flicked back
and forth in the man's mouth as he looked to the doorway.

"Well, what did you expect, a disco?"

"It is like time has stood still here," Kanuik said as he approached
the bar.

"It's part of the mystique of the place," Chic said, raising his hands
and gesturing at the room. "It's good to see you," he said as he shook
Kanuik's hand. "I knew when I saw a raven in the park today that you'd
be coming around."

"You mean you actually left the bar and went to the park?"

Chic chuckled and pulled out two cups and then a pot and poured a black, hot tea into the cups. He served one to Kanuik and kept the other for himself.

"To old times and old friends," Chic said as the two men toasted.

"Speaking of old friends," Kanuik said.

"I am fine," Chic said. "But I know that's not what you are interested in. I haven't seen Claudia for over a year. Mark has returned and taken up Frank's parish. He rarely visits. Professor Barnes, or Jimmie as he prefers to be called, comes in here quite often. Still doesn't have a girlfriend, though. Frank's nephew Connor helps Jimmie at the college and is living with him."

A mirror behind Chic gave Kanuik a view of the entire place behind him. "I see business is booming," he said with a smile.

"Yes," Chic said. "It's a regular party down here. If I hadn't won that lottery, I wouldn't have enough money to keep this place in business. The job growth may be up in other areas, but around here, nothing. I take it you're not just in town to ask me how I'm doing."

Kanuik put his cup on the bar. He didn't know how to tell Chic about his meeting with the elders or the confusion he was experiencing over returning to a place that stirred such strong feelings in him. He knew this was where he needed to be to try to find a way forward.

"You still have my room?" Kanuik asked.

"Yes. Cleaned and waiting for you."

Kanuik raised an eyebrow. "You knew I was coming?"

The cigar shifted in Chic's mouth. "I've kept that room ready for you since you left. I didn't expect you to take so long to find your way back. The war isn't over, you know, just because you lost someone. That's why I keep working to keep this place open."

"Hmm," Kanuik said. "You and Kwanu would get along fine, I think."

"What?"

"Never mind," Kanuik said. "If you don't mind, I have traveled a long ways. I'll be resting in my room." With a single bag in hand, Kanuik walked to a hallway in the middle of the bar that led first to the restrooms and then to the basement door. "Please wake me if Jimmie comes in. And don't tell anyone I am here. I wish to reveal myself when I am ready."

"Oh, by the way," Chic said, "there's a box on your bed—a gift from Claudia."

"How is Claudia?"

"I don't know," Chic said, returning to his work wiping glasses with his towel. "Like I said, I haven't seen her for a year. She's been on her book tour."

Kanuik went down the hall to a door that read "Employees Only" and opened it. He descended the stairs to an antiquated basement whose masonry predated the bar that stood over it. Ancient holy symbols from different religions adorned the stone walls.

Stepping off the stairwell and entering the hall below was like entering the past. He had stayed in the room below the bar many times over the years to rest, to collect himself, and to wait for the next battle. Many times, he had depended on the strength of his youthfulness and visions or, when this faded, on the knowledge and courage of himself and his fellow warriors. This time, he lacked faith in the vision the elders had seen for him, and he was tired. Although seeing Chic had brightened his mood, he felt isolated, especially being in the last place where he had stayed with Adnan, his friend and a warrior he had revered, before Adnan died.

Kanuik continued down the hallway to his room and put his bag by the door but didn't stop there. He traveled farther down the hall to another room—Adnan's. Like Kanuik, Adnan had largely traveled alone and kept to himself. The common thread that had brought them together was the fight against evil. Both men had been called to join the battle and because of it had been doomed to a life off the main grid. A warrior Kanuik thought greater than himself, Adnan had fallen in battle, and soon after, the group had disbanded. Now he was back at the place where it had happened.

Kanuik put his hand on the doorknob but couldn't bring himself to go inside. He turned away, went back to his room, and opened the door. It was a very plain room with stone walls, a wooden two-door closet, and a single light in the middle of the stone ceiling. A wood-framed full bed with sheets and wool blankets and a small table by the head were the only furniture in the room.

Kanuik walked across to the closet and opened the door to find some clothes that he'd left behind still hanging inside. He hung his jacket and sat down on the bed to remove his boots. A white box with a ribbon around it was on the bed. After he removed his boots, Kanuik lifted the box and removed the card from under the ribbon.

The card's message was written in eloquent handwriting: "I thought you could use this to keep your handsome nose from getting a sunburn. Love, Claudia." He opened the box to find a black El Presidente Stetson cowboy hat. He put the hat on and went to the closet, opened the door, and looked in the mirror. On many occasions, he had told Claudia he would not wear a hat, but she had insisted because he was always getting a sunburn, and she kept warning him about skin cancer. "Your nose is one of your defining characteristics," Claudia had told him.

He looked at the reflection of his dark-skinned face, at his long-bridged nose that stuck out like an arrow, his broad chin, and his high cheekbones, and a smile appeared. Kanuik liked the hat, and for a moment, his feeling of isolation was lifted.

Claudia reached into her purse and pulled out her cell phone, dialed the number to the clinic in Chicago, and waited for someone to answer. Her hand trembled as she picked up her chai latte and guided it to her mouth to take a sip. It was midmorning, and her feeling of nervousness was normal, or so she reasoned; it was part of her preparation for her presentation at the bookstore, which was to begin in less than thirty minutes. She tried to ignore the man staring at her from a table near the door of the small coffee shop. She was used to being recognized in public at times and tried not to let it bother her. In her private life as a psychiatrist and as a secret member of a team that had fought evil, she had learned to be discreet. With the success of her book, her personal life was often on hold.

"Northwestern, psychiatric ward," said the male operator who answered the phone.

"Yes, is Dr. Pool in?"

"Let me put you on hold while I ring his office," the operator said.

"I'll hold."

"This is Dr. Pool."

"Yes, Dr. Pool, this is Claudia Walden."

"Dr. Walden, how are you?"

"I'm fine, thank you. I wanted to check on David Jenson. I just want to make sure he is still doing fine since I've been out of town and haven't been able to see him for a while."

"He's fine, Dr. Walden. I told you I would take good care of him."

"Yes, I know you are. It's just that I promised him that I would keep coming by and not lose touch. Without any family members left, I think it's essential that he have someone to maintain contact with outside of the facility. I've been away for some time now and just wanted to make sure there was nothing going on."

"Perhaps you're right," Dr. Pool said. "I am just now looking at a briefing from David's nurse. He was asking for you this morning and seemed a bit anxious. Any idea why?"

"Not that I know of," Claudia said, not wanting to reveal the dream she'd had with David speaking to her. She suddenly wondered how much David knew and if he was conscious of the dream. She returned her attention to the conversation. "It may be because he hasn't seen me for a while. I am planning to be back in town within the next two days. I can come and see him then. If you can let him know, that might settle him down."

"I'll let him know."

"Thank you, Dr. Pool."

As she took another drink of her latte, she considered her plans to check out of her hotel after her book signing, which would take place across the street. If the signing didn't go too late and she wasn't overly tired, she could catch a flight to Chicago. The call she'd just made gave her more reason to go home soon. She was tired of traveling and needed to see some familiar sites and faces.

The bookstore where she was appearing had a coffee shop inside, and the manager, Deanna, had told her she was welcome to whatever she needed, but Claudia had needed a moment to herself, so she had stopped at the coffee shop across the street, hoping for a chance to collect her thoughts. She was still thinking about the dream she'd had the night before and trying to determine the meaning; the psychiatrist inside of her told her that the cause was the stress of traveling and that she needed a break, a true break from the world of bookstores, talk shows, and fans. She could sense the man near the door still looking at her. Although she had gone out of her way to stay out of the bookstore so that she wouldn't be recognized, it appeared someone had recognized her anyway. She looked in his direction and tried to smile back as the man and now a woman sitting beside him stared at her.

The man was young, and he and his attractive female companion sat between her and the exit. *Be nice*, she thought. *You need your fans.* She smiled again at the man and decided it was time to go to the bookstore. She took one last drink of the chai latte and started toward the door, expecting him to stop her or say something to her as she passed the table, but he didn't. Once outside, she took a deep breath and walked to the crosswalk, where she waited for the light to change. She was starting to cross the street when a man's voice called out to her.

"Dr. Claudia Walden, I have traveled a long way to see you. Please, if you have a moment." It was the man from the coffee shop.

"I'm sorry," Claudia said. "I have an appointment I have to get to."

"You mean your appearance at the bookstore," the man said. "We were hoping to find you there later, but I guess we got lucky and found you sooner."

"Yes," Claudia said. "If you want to come, I would be more than happy to speak to you there. I don't carry any books on me."

"Yes, of course. May we walk with you?"

Claudia didn't object to his request and started across the street.

"I am Samar Hamish, and this is my fiancée Ira."

Claudia nodded politely as the three walked together across the painted lines to the bookstore.

"I haven't read your book, but I feel that I am supposed to meet you."

Stalker alarms immediately sounded in Claudia's mind, but it would be highly unusual for a male stalker to bring his fiancée, so she tried to remain calm. "Why is it you think we should meet?'

"I've had a recurring dream, and a man in that dream said some things to me that led me to you."

The group stepped onto the sidewalk, clearing the street, but Claudia went no farther. "A man in your dreams? What was he like?"

Samar described the man to Claudia. She knew from the description that it was Father Frank. The dream and warning from David the previous night and now the arrival of this man who spoke of Frank could be no coincidence; something was happening, and she needed to find out more before it drove her crazy.

Claudia looked at her watch. "I really have to go now," she said. "They're expecting me inside. But if you are willing to wait a few hours, I'll make time to speak with you."

"I am staying at this address." Samar grabbed a pen that Ira offered him, wrote the address on his receipt from the coffee shop, and handed it to Claudia. "It's an apartment complex right down the road. If you just go in and ask for Ms. Doris, they will call for me. My number is there as well. It would be a great pleasure, and I promise not to take much of your time."

He held out his hand, but Claudia had both her hands full. She took the piece of paper with her finger and held it against her cup.

"Look, if you don't trust me, don't worry. See that car over there?" He pointed to two men sitting in a car across the street, watching them. "On the flight over here, there was a disturbance on the aircraft. I think those men are still suspicious of me. It appears they have decided to escort me wherever I need to go. The best thing is that they are saving me a fortune in transportation. I think they're from your government and would be available to rescue you. But I assure you, I am not dangerous."

Claudia smiled. "I didn't think you were. I'll come by as soon as I am done." The shape of his face and his polite tone of voice reminded Claudia of someone she had known before, someone who had been special to her. She studied Samar's face, and the resemblance was there.

Although a much younger man stood before her, she couldn't help but think about Adnan.

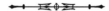

"Shut it down!" Professor James Barnes shouted across the basement of St. Therese Church.

The lights flickered and then grew brighter as the machines that had been taking the power came to a stop.

"What is it, Jimmie?" Connor called out. He stood in the middle of the rectangular room along with twenty-five men dressed in khakis and armed with high-powered walkie-talkies, holy water, religious relics, and crosses, all of them waiting to enter the portal that Professor Barnes was trying to create.

"The readings aren't right," Jimmie said. "We are going to have to recalibrate again."

Several of the soldiers headed toward the stairs.

"Where are you going? Sergeant Lee?" Connor said.

"Look," said a short, black-haired man with a mustache and the name "Lee" embroidered across his shirt, "we've trained all day. It's time to take a break. Don't worry, kid." He patted Connor on the shoulder. "We're going to go through with it, and we'll make sure you're the first one in." The men continued up the stairs, and Connor heard the door above close behind them.

"See you tomorrow, Sergeant Lee," Jimmie said belatedly.

Bishop Tafoya, head of the diocese and leader of the offices that sat above the basement, stood beside Jimmie. "Why don't we all take a break until tomorrow?" the bishop said.

The rest of the soldiers exited, leaving only Jimmie, Tafoya, and Connor in the room.

Jimmie continued to check the machine that looked a lot like a large moving camera. It was pointed toward two giant electrical coils in the middle of the room, where Connor remained. Cords were strewn about everywhere in the concrete basement, and Connor carefully crossed over a jumble of them as he came up beside Professor Barnes.

"What do you need me to do?" Connor said. Dressed as one of

the soldiers, he was the youngest on the team. Like the others, he had volunteered to go through the portal that Jimmie was trying to open.

"Nothing," Jimmie said, running his hand through his hair. "I need to check the readings."

"Check the readings?" repeated a voice that both Jimmie and Connor hated to hear. The two men looked up to spot Father Christian Thomas, their number one critic, at the doorway.

Father Thomas stepped into the room. "Can you get the opening to work or not?"

"It's not the opening I'm having trouble with," Jimmie said. "I'm trying to calibrate a retrieval system."

"A retrieval system? That's a bonus, not a requirement," Thomas said. "These soldiers know what they've signed up for. We've been delayed more than a year. The time frame has been set, Professor Barnes. While you have delayed, our streets have become overgrown with hoodlums, gangsters, and a new breed of terrorists who have no problem killing innocents. Poverty and drug use are out of control. A record number of refugees are fleeing conflict, and church attendance is down. We need a solution."

"Father Thomas, we know the timetable is set," Bishop Tafoya interrupted. "Until that time, Professor Barnes is authorized to do his work in the manner he sees fit. Now is there something you needed?"

Jimmie was glad that Bishop Tafoya was present to keep Thomas in check, but he knew the delays were intolerable. He just didn't know how to get the results he needed.

"I am just here to say what needs to be said," Thomas replied. "As a representative of the Council of World Religions and spokesperson for the church, I am here to report back on progress. It has been over a year since the tribal council approved funding for this project, and the funding grows short. We need to hit the target this time."

"Well, having to move locations cost me at least six months in my test data," Jimmie protested. "And I'm sure not making enough money doing this, so I've had to keep teaching, which does not allow me to give this project my full and undivided attention."

Thomas walked over to the far wall across from Jimmie. On the wall hung an old chalkboard and an eraser. Thomas picked up the eraser and examined it. "Did you know, Professor Barnes, that this basement was once a classroom when the church was popular and Catholic schools were everywhere? Now there are but a few left in rural towns where faith is still alive." He slapped the eraser down, causing a pile of dust to float up from it. "You think I am here to criticize you, but to the contrary, I fully support you. However, you need to understand that our position grows weaker with each delay. And I'm not just talking about our financial position."

Thomas marched across the room and stopped at the door. "I have a report due in two days. If there are no new results to share by that time, we go forward with the original plan and send the soldiers through in eleven days."

Jimmie watched the door close behind Thomas and turned back to his equipment. Bishop Tafoya and Connor were still watching the doorway.

"Can't you do something about that guy?" Connor said. "I mean, he's only a priest, and you're a bishop, right?"

"He is not in my diocese," Bishop Tafoya said. "Besides, he reports directly to the Council of World Religions on the cardinal's orders, and the cardinal outranks me."

"He just drives me crazy," Connor said, hitting his fists together.

"But he's not wrong," Jimmie said.

Connor's blue eyes widened at his remark.

"We aren't getting the results we need."

"Why?" Bishop Tafoya asked.

"Maybe it's because we are trying to open up a portal to someplace evil, and we are doing it from the basement of a Catholic church?"

"I was under the impression that you could overcome that somehow with your technology," Bishop Tafoya said.

"I was joking," Jimmie said. "I don't know what's wrong. I've been crunching data and trying stuff, but what we are dealing with is so far beyond the realm of what we know, it's like we need someone who specializes in quantum physics or something. I mean, I don't even know if we are dealing with other dimensions or wormholes that go to other places in this dimension."

"Is there anything we can do in the meantime? If this place isn't the right location, what place would be a right location?"

Jimmie thought for a minute. He held a stylus up in the air and pointed it at Bishop Tafoya. "You know, for not being a scientist, you're a pretty smart person. What we need is someplace where we know there has already been a portal without our having to create it," Jimmie said. He clapped his hands together as the idea struck him. "We need to move it to David's house."

"David Jenson's house? But why?" Bishop Tafoya asked.

"Because it was a confirmed portal. Besides that, the house has been left vacant since the tragedy. David's been under Claudia's care ever since. No one would care that we are there."

"I'm afraid I cannot authorize that," Bishop Tafoya said.

"Why not? If it works," Connor said.

"We have to remember," Bishop Tafoya said, "that we know the truth of what is going on. Outside of these walls, there are many people not ready to hear about it. Going out there into a neighborhood is risky. If something were to go wrong, how would we explain it? Trust me." He put his hand on Connor's shoulder as Jimmie watched. "I am on the front line of this thing, and I am in front of people every week. All peaceful faiths are struggling for followers while those religions that accept violence are gaining daily. Father Thomas has a point that we are losing ground."

"Then maybe it's time to take the battle out of the closet," Connor said. "Tell the public the truth about what we are doing, the truth about the shadows."

"That's what Adnan used to say," Jimmie said.

"I know you want to perfect your technique," Bishop Tafoya said. "No one has ever been asked to do what you are doing; you are getting ready to send a thousand men through a portal that may lead to the gates of hell, and you want to send them with a rope so that they have a way to get back. But you may not have a choice, and at least we have told those men the truth—that they might not come back."

"I just need a few more tests," Jimmie said.

"It's not my decision," Bishop Tafoya said as he started toward the stairs. He took two steps and then turned back to Jimmie. "You know, this is an old building with lots of entrances and exits, and we don't really have security or anyone watching the back door. Rachelle, my secretary, leaves by four thirty. I leave later than that and lock the door. But I stay in my office most of the time, where I can't see the hallway."

As Bishop Tafoya left, Jimmie turned toward Connor.

"What was that stuff about security and staying in his office?" Connor said. "Is he worried someone's going to come in here and try to take our stuff?"

"No," Jimmie said. "I think he was giving us a hint of how we could go through with what I want to do. He can't authorize us to go to David's house, but he won't stop us either. If he doesn't see us take the equipment out, well …"

"I can help you," Connor said. "We can get some of the other guys from the college and a few vans and have this stuff moved in no time. Didn't you say you opened a portal at the hospital where David Jenson was staying?"

"Yes," Jimmie replied.

"Then is the portal at the house or the hospital?"

"I'm not sure there's one at either," Jimmie said.

"What do you mean?"

"The portal might have been caused by David himself, and that's why it opened at the hospital. But we'd never get back in there after what happened."

"So we need David?"

"He's locked up in an asylum for life," Jimmie said. "Remember, he murdered his parents. Besides, David no longer has the shadows about him and would be of no use to us now. However, the house he was in—a traumatic event happened there. Kanuik and I witnessed a portal opening upstairs even when David was not upstairs. Just as in hauntings, the portals these things operate through might leave a residual effect—something I learned from my ghost-hunting days. That may be our way in."

"I don't know, Professor. The longer I work with you, the more confused I get."

"What do you mean?"

"You were part of the group, and you talk about it all of the time. You've told me the story of how my uncle, Father Frank, went through the portal to the other side. He wasn't a scientist. It doesn't seem like it should be so difficult. I don't understand why we are struggling to do it. Are you sure you're not forgetting something about that night?"

"Believe me, kid," Jimmie said. "I want to get at the shadows and eliminate them from this world more than anyone." Jimmie shivered upon remembering his encounter with the shadows and how they had managed to warp reality. He was not a man of faith, but his encounter had led him to join in the cause to eliminate the threat. He just didn't know if he could. He'd been trying for some time but lacked one ingredient that he was afraid to tell the others: a secret regarding how Frank had opened the path for the shadows to come. Frank had pushed David to the brink of sanity, and David had nearly committed suicide. Suicide was a draw for the dark creatures. Frank had stopped David at the last minute, but that was how he had tempted the shadows and opened the portal big enough for him, Frank, to enter—a risk too high for Jimmie to repeat.

"Come on, kid. Let's get a beer," Jimmie said.

The two men headed to Jimmie's Subaru and got in. It was after eight and dark outside. Although they hadn't eaten, Jimmie figured they could get both food and drink at the Kozy Tavern, a place he still frequented. He was about to put the keys in the ignition when he noticed Thomas down the road, standing with someone next to the open back door of a van.

"That looks like some of our equipment," Connor said.

"They couldn't have loaded it that fast," Jimmie said. "We just left. It must be more stuff he's bringing in."

"Doesn't look like they are unloading it to me," Connor said.

Jimmie held the keys, ready to start the car in case Thomas noticed them watching, but he didn't do anything to draw attention. "I guess it won't hurt to sit here for a minute and see what he's doing."

"So you don't trust him either?" Connor said.

"I've worked in colleges for a few years. You would think that it's all about education and just getting students to learn. Well, there are a lot of things about teaching I enjoy, but dealing with the political hacks who decide who's learning what and what department gets what money for what is probably the worst part of my job. Thomas is up to something. He hovers over our research, over us. He's always in the background, and I don't think he's used to that. He's up to something."

Jimmie and Connor continued to watch from Jimmie's car and were startled for a moment when Thomas looked around, as though checking to be sure no one was watching.

"Keep low," Jimmie said, and he and Connor crouched down in their seats.

Jimmie waited a few seconds and then peeked. Thomas entered the back of the van and closed the door behind him. The other man with him went to the driver's side and got in. The taillights came on, and the van pulled away.

"We should follow them," Connor said.

Jimmie pulled out from the parking space and followed the van. Twenty minutes and three turns later, they watched from a distance as the van stopped in a run-down part of town next to an old warehouse.

"What is this place?" Connor asked.

"This area used to house a bunch of manufacturing and shipping companies," Jimmie said. "Auto parts, mainly. Then the economy went to heck, and the unions wouldn't budge, so everything went south or overseas." Jimmie noticed people on both sides of the street, some with shopping carts full of stuff, others with duffel bags. "I wouldn't doubt that some of these homeless people once worked in these buildings."

One man approached Jimmie's car. "Can you spare some change?" the man asked as Jimmie rolled down his window.

"Can you tell me what that building is?" Jimmie asked as he pulled out a five-dollar bill and showed it to the man.

"That's machine shop number five. But it's closed now because nobody comes down here anymore, nobody that matters anyway."

Jimmie handed him the bill. "Thank you."

The man tipped what was left of a hat upon his head and walked away.

"Why would he be taking equipment into an old machine shop?" Connor asked.

Jimmie suspected that Thomas was using the place as a backup location for the plan. It would make sense since this place was out of the way and, as an old machine shop, probably had the wiring to support the equipment. His only question was why Thomas was keeping it a secret.

"Like I said, he's up to something. Come on, kid. Let's go get that beer," Jimmie said.

Thomas entered the alley to the side of the abandoned machine shop, no longer concerned about whether anyone was watching. He had picked the building carefully; it was near a homeless shelter, and after a few months, the locals had come to assume he was part of the clergy helping the shelter and homeless people and didn't pay any attention to him. The area also allowed him a supply of thugs he could bribe to keep anyone from going into the building. He unlocked the large door with a key, shut it behind him, and headed down the stairwell to the basement. He could hear two of his workers talking as he neared the last step.

"I only took this job to get money to stay in school," said a female voice he recognized as Kaitlyn Drew's. "I'm really glad you offered the chance to me."

"I figured you would like it, since you were into the paranormal and all of that," a man said.

Thomas entered the basement to the surprise of Mike Delgado, who immediately stood and distanced himself from the young intern. With his red hair and fair complexion, Mike blushed easily, and Thomas could tell he was embarrassed now. Kaitlyn was a short, attractive blonde-haired woman with blue eyes and an athletic build. Thomas had hired her for her strength and ability to use computers to log information. He also had counseled her once for a drug problem and knew he could trust her to keep his secret lest hers be told. Although Thomas was sworn to celibacy, he understood why Mike was attracted to her; she was young and pretty and had a lot of energy.

"We need to increase our efforts, Mr. Delgado," he said as he entered the large, well-lit room full of lab equipment. The deadline for the other project, Jimmie's project, was eleven days away. In the event that project failed, Thomas needed a backup plan.

"Hi, Father Thomas," Kaitlyn said.

"Miss Drew, I hope you are well," Thomas said. Then, turning to Mike, he asked, "Are you ready to proceed?"

"Yes, of course," Mike said.

"Kaitlyn, get the boy," Thomas ordered and threw her the key to the cell.

Kaitlyn went to the other side of the room and unlocked the cell, where a boy of seventeen sat among other captives. She helped him to his feet, marched him over to a medieval-looking metal chair welded to the floor, and began strapping his arms and legs to it.

While Kaitlyn was on the other side of the room, away from them, Thomas decided to make sure Mike was keeping his mind on the job at hand.

"I know you have a thing for Kaitlyn," Thomas whispered to Mike, "but try to remain focused."

Mike turned red, but Thomas's comment worked: Mike turned his attention back to the screen where Thomas needed him to pay attention.

"Is that thing around him like last time?" Thomas asked. "I don't see it."

"No," Mike said. "If it was, I would be able to see it through that camera over there." He pointed to a hand-held device that was lying on a portable table with other equipment. "Sometimes it has to be provoked." Mike went to the boy and attached monitoring straps to his head and arms. "What is happening with Professor Barnes's experiments?"

"He is still failing," Thomas said, "which is why it is important for us to succeed. We must find these creatures and learn how to destroy them."

Suddenly, the boy in the chair stirred and started to jerk back and forth. His right arm came free, and he swung it at Mike, who dodged it but fell backward into a table of tools in doing so. The boy undid his other arm and then his legs, but Kaitlyn jumped on him and tackled him to the ground, where she subdued and restrained him.

"Are you okay?" Kaitlyn asked Mike as he retrieved the tools that had fallen.

"I'm fine," he said.

Thomas remained behind the table, watching the scanners. "I think one of those creatures was around his head when that event happened," Thomas said, "especially at first when he lashed out at you. That is the camera that I am seeing hooked up to this monitor, right?"

Mike nodded. "Here, let's get him back in the chair," he said as he leaned down and helped Kaitlyn get the boy positioned. With renewed effort, the two made sure the straps were tight.

Mike went over to the table where Thomas stood. "Now get back, Kaitlyn," Mike said. Kaitlyn moved away from the chair, and Mike put his hand on a control that administered electric shock to the boy. "See, my theory is that these things are made of energy and can be stimulated by a pulse of electricity." He turned the control and watched the subject, who shuddered in the chair.

"Are you sure the dosage is strong enough?" Thomas asked.

"Anything stronger, and we could do permanent damage," Mike said.

"He's a drug addict," Thomas said. "His family has abandoned him to the street. He doesn't have much left to damage or lose." He watched the monitor as Mike hit the control again. "There," Thomas said, spotting the black form on the monitor as the boy reacted violently. "The creature emerged," Thomas said. "It appears that this theory of yours about the electrical shock is sound."

"These creatures, as you call them, may be attracted to violence or something of that nature, but they must be composed of energy," Mike said. "That is the only way they could exist in our world. Somehow, the thing is feeding off this boy's energy—it's plugged into him, if you will. If we find a way to separate them and isolate it, we might learn more about what gives it power."

"How do you do that?" Thomas asked.

"If we can find the right frequency, we should be able to shock it right out of him," Mike said.

"And once you do, we can capture it?" Thomas said.

"I haven't really figured out a containment field yet, but that's the plan," Mike said. "Then we can figure out how to destroy it. Look!" Mike pointed to the screen. "There it is again."

Thomas looked at the screen and could see the red highlighted figure around the boy's head. The technology Mike had devised allowed them to see the creature through a modified lens on the camera. "Why is it out now?" He noticed that Kaitlyn had neared the boy to pick up tools and instruments from the table that Mike had toppled over.

"I could have found the right frequency," Mike said. "Hold on a minute. Kaitlyn, don't get too close." He left his spot and went to help her.

Thomas reached over, turned the control switch higher, and noticed that the boy jolted when he did so. He also noticed the shadow react, so he turned the charge higher to see what would happen.

"What are you doing?" Mike said in a stern voice that startled Thomas and caused him to accidentally turn the switch farther. The boy in the chair yelled out and convulsed. Thomas immediately turned the switch off.

Mike yanked the electrodes off the boy. "Kaitlyn, help!" The two quickly undid the straps and lowered the boy to the ground. They administered CPR but were unsuccessful. Kaitlyn stood, but Mike remained sitting on the floor next to the boy.

Thomas walked over to him. "Looks like your subject was too weak," Thomas said. "Don't worry. I'll have someone take care of him."

"What are we going to do for more subjects?" Mike asked. "The others in that cage are younger and even weaker than he was."

"Leave that to me," Thomas said. "Do you think we killed the creature in him with the shock?"

Mike stood and walked over to the monitor and moved some switches, causing the camera to pan in and out about the room. "I don't know. Were you watching the screen when it happened?"

"Unfortunately, no," Thomas said. "It was a mistake. You startled me." Thomas could tell that Mike's hand was shaking by the vibration of the instrument he held. "That boy would have overdosed on drugs long ago if I hadn't brought him here."

"Exactly where are you going to get more subjects?"

"Don't concern yourself with such things, Mr. Delgado. We are in the middle of one of the largest homeless districts in the city. Opportunity will present itself, and no one will care what happens to these people. Remember the greater good we are doing."

Claudia pulled her rental car into the parking lot of the building where Samar said he and Ira were staying. She parked her car, went inside to the front desk, and noticed how clean and new the complex appeared.

"Can I help you?" a lady behind the lobby desk asked.

"Yes, I'm Dr. Claudia Walden, and I am here to see Samar Hamish."

The lady picked up a phone and made a call. "Mr. Hamish, there is a Dr. Claudia Walden here to see you ... I'll let her know." She hung up the phone and turned to Claudia. "He will be down shortly. We have seats over there if you'd like to be more comfortable."

Claudia took a seat in the lobby and positioned herself to face the elevator and stairway down the hall, hoping to see him approach. While watching, she noticed something peculiar: a small black-and-white cat at the edge of the hallway where it intersected with the lobby. The cat was watching her. The small, fluffy cat soon came over to her and rubbed against her leg.

"Well, aren't you just a little darling," Claudia said, reaching down to pet the cat on the head. "You must know I like cats."

"Pretty amazing."

Claudia was startled by Samar's voice as he approached her from a hallway in the opposite direction of the elevators.

"Sorry, did I startle you?"

"Yes," Claudia said as she stood and faced Samar. "I expected you to come from the elevators, not from behind me." She looked down at the cat.

"The entire complex is patrolled by cats. There are pet doors on every apartment, and the cats keep all the vermin out. At least that's what my fiancée's aunt Doris says. She calls that one Mouse." The fluffy little cat turned as it recognized its name. "There's a cafeteria here if you would like to sit and talk. Ira and I were just getting something to eat ourselves."

"That would be nice," Claudia said.

Samar led Claudia to a set of double doors to the rear of the lobby desk. They entered a busy cafeteria with twenty or more tables set around a large buffet section in the middle. Samar led Claudia to a table where Ira was sitting.

"Would you care for something to eat?" Ira asked. "The food is really good." She pointed to her plate full of fresh fruit.

"No," Claudia said as she sat down. "I would like to be on my way as soon as possible. I'm heading back home today, and there are people there I need to see."

"Forgive me," Samar said. "I would not have troubled you so, but—"

Ira reached across the table and touched Claudia's hand. "You must help him, please," Ira said. "What he is going through is driving him crazy. He sees things and has dreams. He has taken us thousands of miles from our home, all the way to Israel, to find these religious icons he has visions of, seeking proof that the evil he is witnessing is real."

"Ira." Samar raised his voice, glanced about the room, and then put his fingers to his lips. "Not so loudly."

"She needs to know," Ira pleaded. "In order to help you, she needs to know."

"What is it that you see?" Claudia asked.

Samar leaned in and in a quiet, calm voice relayed the story of what had happened to him on the flight from Israel. He described the dark form that he had witnessed surrounding the man and what had happened.

Claudia knew that Samar was battling the same thing Adnan, Kanuik, and Frank had battled: the shadows. Although Claudia hadn't been able to see the forms like the others, while with the group she'd had her own encounters that let her know they were real. "Is there some place more private we can speak?" she asked.

Samar and Ira led Claudia down the hall to the elevators. With a ring of the bell, the door opened, and the trio entered. An elevator attendant asked, "What floor?" Claudia didn't quite hear Samar's answer because she was distracted by the little fluffy cat from the lobby who came into the elevator. She noticed the attendant back away from the cat as it took its place in the elevator just like it was a person. The cat turned around to face the door as though watching the numbers for the floor it wanted. It exited on the same floor as they did. Claudia followed Samar and Ira to the apartment, glancing back to see the cat going the opposite direction.

Claudia entered the apartment behind the young couple, and Samar gave her a quick tour. The apartment had a comfortable living room, an adequate kitchen area, and two bedrooms.

"Ira's aunt Doris is out playing bridge, so we have the place to ourselves right now," Samar said.

They went to the living room and sat in two cloth-lined chairs adorned by decorative afghans. Claudia felt secure in the living room, which looked like an appropriate place for a grandmother or aunt.

Ira sat on a small, light brown couch, next to a cage holding a yellow canary . The canary sang a tune that echoed through the quiet apartment and gave Claudia a moment's pause. Samar stepped into the kitchen, came back with coffee for her and him, and sat down.

"That was quite a performance," Claudia said as the bird finished its song. "Almost makes me want to get one, but I don't think my cat would agree with me."

"My aunt named the little bird Ladie," Ira said. "And from what I understand, she is quite social with the cats in the complex."

Claudia smiled and took a sip of her drink and then another as she tried to come up with a way to start the next conversation. She wasn't sure how to start telling Samar the story behind what he was dealing with and the world of the shadows.

"I am sorry, Dr. Walden," Samar said. "What we are telling you may seem crazy, and here you are a psychiatrist."

Claudia took a drink of the coffee and contemplated what she should do next. She could simply pretend not to know anything and offer her regrets that she couldn't help. That would be simple and less complicated. *Let the nice couple go on their way*, her conscience called out to her.

"What you have witnessed is evil, and it is all too real," Claudia finally said. "Although others may not be able to see them, the forms you have seen exist. I worked with a group that used to fight these creatures. We referred to them as shadows. The Native Americans referred to them as tricksters, and there are stories about them from many cultures throughout the world. I cannot see them, but they have attacked me in the past, and I know they are dangerous. I can't explain how or why you see them, but it must be connected to something you are doing—maybe your work. You said you're an archeologist working on religious digs?"

"Yes," Samar said. "I can see what you are thinking—that my work has caused me to somehow become a witness to these things and experiences. But I tell you, my experiences with these things go back to my childhood and are what led me to my studies, not the other way around."

"That does lead to questions about why you are able to see them then," Claudia said. "That is something I can't explain. Before my writing career, I was a practicing psychiatrist who treated mental illness. There were things I couldn't explain about the behavior in some of my patients, and that led me to interactions with the group I joined and exposed me to their mission. For the most part, I was a skeptic until the very end."

"What changed your mind and made you believe?" Samar asked.

Claudia shivered when she remembered her experience with the shadows and how they had attacked her and warped her reality, making her see things that weren't there. Her expression must have been enough for him to understand.

"I see," Samar said. "You've had an experience with them as well. Who is the man I keep seeing in my dreams, the one who told me to find you?"

Claudia took a sip of coffee to warm herself. "The man you are seeing in your dreams is from our group. His name is Frank Keller, Father Frank Keller to be precise. He was a priest and a very successful one at that. He had a reputation with the local youth, who admired him. A member of his parish, David Jenson, killed his family in a horrible act of violence. Because of the shadows' connection to this tragedy, Frank joined our group to learn the truth about the battle that exists, a battle that you are now taking part in."

"Maybe it is this Frank Keller I should be talking to. How did he get in my dreams?" Samar asked.

Claudia noticed her hand shaking and put her other hand on the cup to steady it as she sat forward in her seat. "This is where you're going to think I sound crazy," she said. "The group believed that the only way to defeat the shadows was to cross over to where they come from and fight them on their own ground. Frank crossed over to where these entities come from, a place I cannot pretend to comprehend and still don't understand."

"Crossed over … to where?"

"I don't know," Claudia said. "Members of our group were doing an intervention with David, the young man I spoke about, and something happened. I wasn't in the room when it happened, but when the others came out of David's room, Frank was no longer there. He had vanished. His body was never found, and soon after, reports came in about a man fitting his description helping people—through their dreams."

"How is that possible?" Samar said.

"Some in my group spoke about a battle between good and evil that existed in ancient times," Claudia said. "The place these things come from is where they were banished when they lost the battle. I don't know much more about it."

Claudia watched as Samar and Ira exchanged glances.

"This is exactly what you have been trying to study," Ira said. "See, I was right that we should come here and find her."

"Why do you think he is appearing in my dreams?"

"He has been reaching out to people in need since he disappeared," Claudia said. "There have been reports from all over the world. With what you are telling me about your experiences with these shadows, maybe he thought you needed help."

"That's interesting," Samar said.

"What?"

"He has been asking me why I keep coming back, like it's my dream that's leading me to him, not the other way around."

"Almost as if you two are connected somehow," Claudia said. "But you've never met him?"

"No," Samar said.

"Could you have read about him in my book?"

"I didn't know about your book until I saw you on television, and that was after I'd been having these dreams."

"There must be a connection," Claudia said. "We just haven't thought of it yet."

Ira went into the kitchen and returned with another cup of coffee, which she handed to Claudia, taking the empty cup from her.

"Thank you," Claudia said.

Ira stood in front of her for a moment, causing Claudia to look up at her.

"You were close to this man, Frank Keller, weren't you?" Ira asked.

"Yes," Claudia said. "We were close. I didn't know him for very long, but I admired him. In fact, a sermon he gave was the basis for my book and my success."

"He didn't tell you what he was going to do?"

"No," Claudia said. "But he thought it was the right thing to do." She sniffled and wiped a tear from her eye.

Ira went back into the kitchen, returned with some tissues, and handed them to Claudia.

"I'm sorry," Claudia said as she wiped her eyes. "It was a very tough time we went through."

"I am going to get us some snacks," Ira said. She went back into the kitchen, and Claudia heard cabinets opening and shutting as she busied herself.

"This group you are speaking about," Samar said. "Do you think they can help me?"

"There isn't any group, not anymore," Claudia said. "We haven't stayed in touch. But there are people I know who were continuing the work we did. We can try to contact one of them and see if they can help you. We would have to go to Chicago."

"When do we leave?" Ira said from the kitchen, provoking a smile between Claudia and Samar.

The agreement that Claudia had made with Jimmie and Kanuik was to always leave a contact number and address with Chic, the owner of the Kozy Tavern, where the group used to meet. She only hoped the other members had kept in touch with Chic and could help her. She thought about her own dream that seemed to beckon her home, and now she had met Samar and heard his story. She knew that it was no coincidence and she needed to go home.

"Do you have transportation?" Claudia said.

"Yes," Samar said, and he started to walk to the window. He hesitated and then stopped a few steps from it. "Did you just see a yellow crested cockatoo at the window?"

"Sorry," Claudia said. "I didn't notice."

"There." Samar pointed down to a car parked in front of the complex.

Claudia came to the window to see what he was pointing to.

"There are two men down there in that car who I am assuming work for the US government. Remember I told you about an incident on the flight over here?"

Claudia nodded.

"They have been following me since I arrived. I helped stop a terrorist attack, but I don't think they trust me. Since it is easier for them just to take me where I want to go instead of trying to follow me, they have been doing just that. The big vehicles they have are very comfortable, and they are polite men. Let's just say we have transportation, and we can take you as well if you don't mind driving instead of flying."

"I suppose it wouldn't hurt to go with you," Claudia said. "I can check my rental car in and cancel my flight. Then we could talk on the way there."

"Tough day?" Chic asked from the serving side of the bar as Jimmie and Connor entered. As always, Chic was well dressed in slacks and a nice shirt, with a white apron around his waist.

"You could say that," Connor answered as he headed to his stool at the bar.

Jimmie quickly glanced around the bar and stopped at the familiar table he used to sit at with the group. He was sure something about the table had changed. Chic had hung Adnan's homburg hat on the back of one of the chairs, which caused the rare visitors to the bar to sit elsewhere, leaving the table habitually unoccupied. The hat was still on the chair, but something else was different—a different chair stood out of place, as though someone had been sitting at the table. There was no one at the table now, and Jimmie continued to the bar and sat down on a stool by Connor.

"Well," Jimmie said, "since I can see there is absolutely no one here who would care what we are talking about, I guess I can tell you. The experiments aren't working like they should." He always enjoyed talking with Chic. His years of experience behind the bar gave him a great perspective on life, and he usually had good advice.

"No?" Chic responded.

"No," Jimmie said. "Set us up please. First round's on me."

Chic put a beer in front of Jimmie and a soda in front of Connor.

"Oh, come on, Chic," Connor said. "I'm getting ready to go through a portal to hell. Doesn't that qualify me to drink?"

"I just have to wonder about your training, young fellow," Chic said. "Aren't they supposed to be teaching you the ultimate self-control, so when you do cross over, you won't be tempted? Think of me denying you a drink, which could get my license revoked, as just another step in your training." He grinned at Connor, and Jimmie laughed.

"I'll be right back," Connor said, walking toward the restroom.

"He's the youngest in the group," Jimmie said.

"I've asked you this before," Chic said, "but are you sure he's ready?"

"He's a witness, one of the first to see Father Frank in his dreams. That's a powerful connection. His youthfulness also gives him the ability to withstand extreme pressure, and that's what we need. We have no idea what they may face once they go through the portal, but it's bound to be a physical strain."

"If you succeed in opening the portal to that dark place, do you think you can get them back?" Chic said.

"That's exactly what is not going right and not in the plans currently." Jimmie removed his sport coat and set it on the barstool next to him. He took a drink from his beer and wiped his mouth. "I am trying to develop a retrieval system, but it's complicated. Right now, it's a one-way trip, and I've been reminded that that's what they signed up for—you know, end of the world and all of that if they don't succeed; sin and evil rule and the suffering just keeps getting worse. So whether I can bring them back or not, leadership has set a deadline, and we are going through, full speed ahead."

Chic broke eye contact with Jimmie and picked up some glasses. They were already clean, but he started wiping them out again.

Jimmie took another drink and sighed. "I need something stronger than a beer."

Chic served Jimmie a whiskey. "Did you ever think the reason you can't succeed is maybe you don't really want to?" Chic asked.

"What? You think I don't want to succeed?"

"I think you are one of the smartest people I know. So what's holding you back?"

"I don't know," Jimmie said. "I can't seem to get the portal to open up wide enough. I can send a signal through, but I can't trace it."

"And what does that mean?" Chic said.

"It means I don't really know where they are going—another

dimension or just somewhere far away. It means I can send them through just like Frank, but they may never be able to come back." Jimmie picked up the shot of whiskey and spun around on his barstool as he drank it, throwing his head back. He closed his eyes and felt the burn as the liquid hit his throat. As he slowly opened his eyes, he noticed someone watching him from the table across the room—the table he'd focused on when he first entered the Kozy. Jimmie blinked several times before standing and walking toward the table.

"What was in that shot?" Jimmie said as he approached the table and tried to focus on the man seated next to the chair reserved for Adnan's hat. The person looked familiar, but Jimmie couldn't quite make him out under the man's own hat and through the cloud of smoke that surrounded his face.

Jimmie thought he could see a familiar face through the smoke—that of Kanuik. "You remind me of someone," he said, pointing at the man. He squinted and tried to get a better view. "But the man I know would not wear a hat like that."

"And why is that?"

"Something about blocking his power," Jimmie said.

"But it is me, and I am in your vision. I have come to give you an important message," Kanuik said.

Jimmie shook his head and looked at the shot glass still in his left hand.

"You must listen to what I have to tell you. It is very important that you do what I tell you."

Jimmie glanced back at the bar, where Connor had returned to his seat. Both he and Chic had turned to watch him. Connor shrugged his shoulders while Chic went about cleaning glasses as though there was nothing going on. Jimmie wasn't sure the others could see the man who appeared so clearly to him. "What is it you need to tell me?" Jimmie asked, sure he was speaking to a spirit and worried that Kanuik had passed. He heard the shot glass hit the floor as his trembling hand released it.

The smoke over the table was thick and flowed from Kanuik's

mouth as he began to speak again. His lips moved, but Jimmie couldn't hear him. He motioned for Jimmie to come closer, so Jimmie leaned in.

"I am hungry. Bring me food," Kanuik said as he raised his hat so that Jimmie could get a clear look at him. A deep, low chuckle came forth as Kanuik leaned back in his chair and smiled at Jimmie.

Chic smacked Jimmie in the back, snapping him out of his haze. Jimmie remained still, not sure what was taking place.

"Sit down, Jimmie," said Chic. "You're not having a vision. He's really here." Chic put a plate of bread down on the table. "He came in earlier today and has been waiting for you."

"It is okay that I smoke?" Kanuik asked as he wiggled his pipe.

Chic nodded. "Smoking has been all but banned indoors, but no one complains around here, unless it's one of those electronic cigarettes. You're not going to smoke one of those sissy things, are you?"

Kanuik grinned. "No, just my pipe."

"I'll bring you some good old-fashioned pasta and some tea," Chic said. "How about you, Jimmie? Are you hungry?"

Jimmie nodded.

"Me too," Connor said.

"You're always hungry," Chic said. "I'll bring a few plates, and we can all eat."

Jimmie noticed that Chic was walking with a little more spring in his step and appeared happy. He assumed this was because Kanuik was back and Chic finally had someone to talk to again. He turned back to the table.

Kanuik put out his pipe and continued smiling at Jimmie. "Please, Professor Barnes, sit down."

"You're really here," Jimmie said as he slowly took a seat at the table. He looked over his shoulder and waved Connor over.

"This is Connor Dietz, Father Frank's nephew."

"Yes, we met at the conference last year," Kanuik said.

Connor sat at the table.

"I see you are still comfortable at our old place."

"Actually, we haven't been in for a few days," Jimmie said. "But I'm glad we came in—it's good to see you. Have you seen Claudia?"

"Only on television," Kanuik said. "Are you still working with the conference?"

"Yes," Jimmie said, "although we have moved operations here now, and we are working at St. Joseph's, in the basement. If we get the equipment working, we are going to use the old youth rec center to execute the plan. Guess it helps being in a city with lots of abandoned buildings."

"No luck getting them through then?" Kanuik asked.

"I think we can get them through, just not sure how many. The problem may be getting them back."

"If there is a way back," Kanuik said.

"I'm assuming since the shadows are able to come through to our side, there must be a way," Jimmie said.

"Yes, but they are not the same as us—they are spirit," Kanuik said. "You do not know what it is on the other side that you are sending these men to deal with."

"The risk has been explained," Jimmie said. "We continue training soldiers to go through the portal, and I'm trying to perfect the ability to open it wide enough to send multiple people through at a time. It's rather exciting but very complex." He grabbed a piece of warm bread from the middle of the table and took a bite. "Mm, that's good stuff. You know, I wouldn't doubt that those damn things are on the other side somehow plotting against me and blocking me."

"No one truly knows the mind of the shadows. And you"—Kanuik looked to Connor, who was eating as well—"you look a lot older than the last time I saw you."

"It's the training," Connor said. "Both physically and mentally intense. It can wear you out. But I plan to go through to this other side where my uncle is supposed to be and help him out."

"I'm sure he would be proud of what you are doing," Kanuik said. "He is a brave warrior."

"If you stay awhile, you can witness it," Jimmie said. "I think we had a breakthrough tonight, and we're going to move to a new location and try something different, but either way, we are going soon. What are your plans now that you're in town?"

"I have been traveling," Kanuik said. "But something has brought me back to this place. I think I'll just sit here for a few days and see what comes through that door. Tonight, it brought us back together. I am curious to see what happens if I just sit here and wait." He started packing his pipe with tobacco.

"You still smoke a pipe?" Connor said. "I thought that went out of style."

Kanuik chuckled. "You say 'smoke' like I do it for sport. You think too much of current culture and the recreational uses. The ancient peoples have used the smoke of many herbs, sacred to them, to perform rituals. We use it to cleanse the air of evil spirits, to heal and purify our bodies, to protect others, and even to tell when someone is being false."

"I didn't know," Connor said.

"Maybe I came back this way to help teach you more before you charge into battle with the shadows," Kanuik said.

"That's not a bad idea," Jimmie said. "Our training has been one-sided. We do have a handful of Native Americans in our group of soldiers, but we haven't really shared these types of things. Maybe we can arrange a session for you to talk to the group."

Chic brought out four plates and sets of silverware. While Jimmie set the table, Connor glanced at Kanuik's pipe. Connor then followed Chic back to the kitchen at Chic's beckoning. The two emerged with bowls full of steaming pasta and red sauce.

The smell of tomatoes, garlic, and onion permeated the air, and Jimmie felt better. He reflected on the day's events and found himself focusing on this potential new breakthrough. Maybe the change in location really was what he needed to open the portal. It was a place that he knew had opened before, and remnants of the portal might remain, making it easier to get a return signal. He knew the upstairs room in David Jenson's house was a portal. He felt better now that Kanuik was back in town too; he took it as a good sign.

Jimmie raised his glass as Chic offered a toast. "To old friends."

CHAPTER 4
REUNION: TEN DAYS REMAINING

False words are not only evil themselves, but they infect the soul with evil.

—Socrates

"That's it right there," Claudia said as the driver pulled up to her house.

Samar and Ira sat behind her in the large black SUV. The three got out and unloaded the luggage from the back, including the cat carrier that held Claudia's cat, Rosie.

"Thank you for the ride," Claudia said to the man who sat behind the wheel. "If you need anything during the night, feel free to knock."

Claudia led the way to her door and unlocked it, allowing Samar and Ira to enter. They stopped right inside the doorway. Claudia put the cat carrier down and let Rosie out. The cat immediately went to Ira, who picked her up.

"How did you come up with her name?" Ira asked.

"She's Frank's cat," Claudia said. "I just inherited her. You see"— she stepped closer and pointed to Rosie—"that patch of black on her head looks a little like a rose. That's how Frank got the name. Come on, I'll show you to the guest bedroom."

She walked Samar and Ira through the living room and pointed out the kitchen. "There's not much to eat. I haven't been home much this past year. We can take a quick trip to the store once we get settled."

"Well," Ira said, "your house looks very well kept and clean."

"That's because no one is ever here," Claudia said. They continued down a hallway that led to a bathroom and three bedrooms. She directed them into a large bedroom with a queen bed and dresser. "This room would probably be best. The bathroom is right there," she said, pointing. "The other bedroom is where my dad used to stay and still has some of his stuff in it, so I'd appreciate it if you didn't go in there. The room at the end of the hall has exercise equipment in it. Feel free to use it if you're in the mood."

Ira and Samar set their luggage in the bedroom while Claudia remained at the door.

"When can we go to meet your friends?" Samar asked.

"It's pretty late," Claudia said. "I need to check my email for messages. How about we take the rest of the night to settle in, and then we will go meet them tomorrow?"

"That sounds fine," Ira said, stepping in front of Samar. She hugged Claudia. "Thank you so much for your hospitality. We will be fine. Have a good night."

Claudia went to her bedroom, located on the other side of the house, and started unpacking. She took care of her bills online, so she just needed to check her mail for any unexpected letters and her email.

Rosie came into the room and hopped on the bed, purring. Claudia stroked her back. "Yes, we are finally home," she said.

After she fed Rosie and took a long bath, Claudia checked on Samar and Ira one last time before settling into bed, happy that she was in her own bed for the night.

Frank stumbled toward the garden, barely able to walk. In his latest battle, the shadows had latched onto a large group of young men, and Frank had tried to help them, but they were too far gone, convinced of the blind cause they had adopted. He knew bad things would come of this. Only when he felt himself fading had he withdrawn from the men, unable to convince them to turn away. He had fallen back through the portal, and the attack had come immediately.

He had defended himself and scrambled to the light, but the shadows were relentless; in a change of tactics, they didn't let go even when he was in the light. He could tell as he continued toward the garden that the creatures were in pain, which grew greater as he neared the garden, yet still, they latched on and kept attacking him.

He considered that having grown tired of his interference, they had adopted a greater resolve to get rid of him. He recited scripture to block his mind from the attacks.

"'Finally, be strong in the Lord and in the strength of his might. Put on the whole armor of God, that you may be able to stand against the schemes of the devil. For we do not wrestle against flesh and blood, but against the rulers, against the authorities, against the cosmic powers over this present darkness, against the spiritual forces of evil in the heavenly places. Therefore, take up the whole armor of God, that you may be able to withstand in the evil day, and having done all, to stand firm. Stand therefore, having fastened on the belt of truth, and having put on the breastplate of righteousness,' Ephesians 6:10–18.'"

This seemed to help, and momentarily, the attacks stopped. He reached to his chest, where he could see one of the dark forms, and tried to grab hold like he'd done before. He found the place to grab, and though he was weak, the creature was weaker. He successfully flung it off him. He grabbed another, and this one was stronger, but he still managed to throw it clear of him. It came back and kept attacking, but as he got closer to the garden, the creature grew weak, and its claws were unable to pierce his skin.

The battle was taking a toll on him this time, and he considered that he might be pushing his strength too far; without day and night, he had no way to truly measure time. It seemed to him that there had been a shift recently in the number of attacks and people calling to him for help. The shadows were attacking more aggressively and repetitively than in the past. The voices crying for help were numerous, and he couldn't keep up with them. Even as he crept along the path, holding his gut, which felt like it wanted to come out of him, and trying to remain focused and to ignore the pain, he could hear the calls around him. He felt too weary to reply as his strength faltered.

He had left his best weapon, a cane given to him by Adnan, at the edge of the garden. The wooden cane came from the cross of Christ. He didn't take it into battle at times due to the ferocity of the attacks and the fear he would lose it. Many times, he had made it to the boundary of the garden and used the cane as a last resort to ward off the shadows that followed him. The only other relic he had was a metal cross around his neck. The cross was not only a religious relic but also a weapon; if he clicked down on both sides, a four-inch blade emerged from the bottom. Father Mark Uwriyer, a priest whom Frank had mentored to take over his church, had brought it from his home in Israel. He remembered when Mark first showed him the cross.

"Where I come from, Christians are never really safe," Mark had said. "There are those of us who believe we must be men of peace but defenders of faith as well."

Frank had regarded his young friend as impulsive, but it was actually a sound philosophy and one Frank himself had taken up.

Frank could see his goal—the perimeter of rocks that lined the garden. He headed for it with all his strength and fell to the ground once past it. The shadows that remained let go as he crossed this final border. He looked back and could see the black forms slithering away slowly. He wished he had enough strength to try to finish them off, but he simply remained in his position, trying to catch his breath.

Finally feeling strong enough to walk, he lifted himself to his feet and followed a familiar path that he'd worn into the grass. He stretched out his hand to feel the tips of the long grass that lined both sides of the path. He often walked in the garden, where the sounds of those who needed help were silent, when he needed a break or needed to reflect. He enjoyed the garden even though it lacked color. The long grass, the trees, and the flowing water soothed him. He made it to the base of the small waterfall where the stream originated. Here lay a pool where the water collected before running down across the garden. He lowered himself into the water. This was where he gained strength and where the tears in his flesh healed to the point that he couldn't even tell they had been there. Frank closed his eyes and remembered when he had first arrived.

He had been in David Jenson's hospital room with Jimmie and Kanuik, fighting the shadows that tormented the boy. Once he'd enticed them in and had the portal open, Jimmie had sent a pulse of energy through it to widen it big enough for Frank to go through. It originally had been Adnan's plan, and Frank believed it had fallen on him to see if it would work. Upon stepping through the portal, he had immediately fallen to the hard ground and couldn't move. His muscles wouldn't work, and if not for his mind, he would have succumbed to the shadows.

He had crawled into the light, not knowing its power but finding that the creatures would not attack him when he was in the light—not then anyway. They would get bolder the more he interfered, and he soon would learn that the garden was the only true safe place.

Surrounded by a formation of rocks, the garden was the only place he'd found completely free of the dark creatures. At the top of the rock formation was a waterfall. Frank tried to go up the rocky precipice to the top of the waterfall but couldn't climb it without equipment. The hill it formed blocked out some of the brilliant light. On both sides of the garden, the landscape gave way to the grassy plain. On one side of the plain was light that grew brighter the closer he got to it. On the other side was darkness. There was no day or night in this new world he had found, only light on one side and darkness on the other. Frank spent most of his time between the two extremes. He had traveled outside of the light and tried to walk into the dark areas, only to be attacked by the shadows. It was only by luck that he had made it back to the garden the first time he'd ventured out. He once had tried to pierce the light by walking in the direction from which it emanated, only to find that it grew too bright for him to see and too uncomfortable for him to bear. He had closed his eyes and tried to keep walking but soon found it was impossible; his body froze and would not go forward. A force of humility, of compassion, had so overwhelmed him at the time that he had simply knelt and wept.

All of this, he had managed to find out quickly, and he had soon realized he was stuck in this place. That was when he started learning how to fight the shadows and intervene on the behalf of those they tormented. Since that time, he'd been battling them as much as possible.

Frank walked out of the pool healed and refreshed. He turned to the light and walked toward it. It was soon hot enough to dry him, and he stood until the drying was complete. Then he slowly made his way back to the boundary of rocks that circumscribed the garden in a semicircle. He'd learned that this location was where he could sense those who needed help. He looked out at the darkness: the landscape went from lush grass to rock and dirt; barren trees and shrubs stood void of life. Out there, where he looked, were the shadows. They never crossed the boundary and were weaker as they moved into the light. Since the garden remained lit, that was where he stayed.

Frank had noticed a recent change in the behavior of the shadows, which he could sense in the darkness; they were communing just outside of the garden more, as though watching him. When he had first arrived and experimented with going into the dark areas, the shadows had attacked him when he encountered them, but then after he left the area they occupied, they appeared to pay no attention to him. This had changed when he started to intervene; then they continued attacking him until he returned to the light. Now this too had changed, and he could sense their presence all of the time just at the boundary of the garden. At first, only a few watched him, as though curious. Now he could feel their presence everywhere along the border, a cold, bitter hate that was directed at him.

He grabbed the wooden cane and stepped out from the line of rock, swinging the cane in the air. "I'm not going anywhere! I'm right here!" he yelled toward the darkness. He stepped back to the barrier and started to take his usual seat on the large rock, which was flat and provided a perfect place to sit. He wondered if he'd see his visitor today, the man who came to ask him questions. He hoped the man had gotten his message and was seeking Claudia. Frank knew this man was special, but he didn't know how the man had managed to communicate across to where Frank was at or how to control the communication. Frank took his position on the rock, but his thoughts were restless and turned to Claudia and the group.

He worried about his friends. He wasn't sure his warning through David Jenson had reached Claudia, so he decided he must try again. He stood and headed out to the path where he'd communicated with David. The portal opening Frank used to communicate with him was always in the same place, but it had started to fade and grow smaller over time. Frank suspected the portals remained open only by the will of the shadows and the host on the other side. Since he'd helped David free himself of the shadows' influence, the area where Frank could reach out and communicate had grown weaker, and it was harder to reach David.

Frank felt the dark forms edging toward him, though he remained in the full light. He swung the cane around his body, letting them know that he had brought the powerful weapon with him. He took a deep breath and measured his strength. It hadn't been long since his last battle, and although his bath in the water had healed his body, his mind was still distracted. He knew he needed more time before he engaged the creatures again.

Suddenly, Frank came to a halt. He looked around to make sure he was on the right path. He was, but the path ended prematurely, and in front of him, the light stopped. Before him rose a wall of darkness. He studied what was in front of him carefully. It wasn't the normal lack of light that caused the darkness, and there was nothing solid about it; the darkness moved fluidly. The shadows themselves had formed a barrier across Frank's path. He gripped the cane firmly in his hands and closed his eyes, reaching forward with his mind. Thoughts here were different and could travel when he focused. He sensed chaos in front of him.

"What do you want?" Frank said aloud. He waited patiently, but his nerves were tested when he felt something brush up against him. He prepared himself for an attack, but the forms moved away. He stepped closer to the wall of darkness and opened his eyes for a moment; he looked up, and the darkness seemed to reach as far as he could see. He sensed the creatures—pain, rejection, hate. It was overwhelming, and Frank stepped back.

"My God," he said, "how can there be so many?" Frank knew he couldn't let the creatures get through to the other side, but he wasn't sure how to stop them.

As the thought "stop them" crossed his mind, he felt something reach out and sense this thought. He opened his eyes and looked again at the swirling mass of darkness in front of him. Even as he was tempted to charge in and do battle against the mass in front of him, to show the shadows they couldn't block his way, he felt an ominous message directed at him: *Something is about to happen, and we are setting a trap for your friends. Give up. All hope is lost.*

Claudia stirred in her bed and sat up. She listened but didn't hear anything out of place. Maybe she was just restless because of the current situation and the fact that she hadn't slept in her own bed for some time. She went into the kitchen and made some hot tea before taking a seat on the large, black plush couch. Rosie had just settled in beside her, purring, when Claudia heard a sound down the hall and spotted Ira coming toward her.

"Having trouble sleeping?" Ira asked.

"A little," Claudia said. "And you?"

"Oh, I sleep fine. It's the other one." She flicked her head in the direction of the bedroom where Samar was sleeping. "He dreams constantly and keeps me awake talking in his sleep."

"I have another bed if you need it."

"No, I'll be fine in a moment."

"Do you want some tea? It's decaf."

"Sure, tea sounds good, thanks," said Ira.

Claudia went to the kitchen and brought back a cup of tea for her guest. "When did he start having these dreams?" she asked.

"Oh," Ira said, "these dreams are new and just started the last few weeks. But he's always seen the black things. He has since he was a little boy. At first, he didn't understand and was taken for medical examinations. They found nothing wrong with him. He started understanding the incidents more as he got older, and he also understood that talking about them got him in trouble. So he learned to hide his gift."

"Understandable," Claudia said. "In my practice I couldn't help but wonder how many people like Samar were misdiagnosed because there is so little we understand."

"His gift led him on a quest to understand it. This involved the study of religion and the histories of supernatural things. That led him to archeology. Now he thinks that somewhere in the past is his answer to what is going on today." Ira sipped her tea slowly.

Claudia pulled a blanket from one of the chairs and handed it to Ira, who put it over her shoulders.

"Did anyone else in his family have this ... ability?"

"Not that I know of, but he never knew his father. He sent him money all of the time, but there was never a location or way to contact him. His mother told him that the work his father was doing would endanger him. Then one day, the money stopped. He assumes it's because his father died."

"A tough upbringing then," Claudia said. "I'm surprised he doesn't have more issues. Sorry. I shouldn't have said that last part."

"It's okay," Ira said. "He is a good man—very dedicated to his work."

"And you? How did you come to have an aunt here?"

"She's more of an adopted aunt. She used to work with my father. When I came here to go to college, she let me stay in her house before she retired—that's when she moved to this apartment where she lives now. While I was here, I became very American-like—my father says 'too much' like an American girl because I believe in the equality of the sexes. That's why it's so good to meet you, an actual author who is also a doctor."

"Of psychiatry," Claudia said. "I don't do brain surgery."

"Still, that's incredible."

"That's what you get when you have no social life or family to slow you down. I'm an only child."

Ira moved closer to Claudia on the couch. "Do you have regrets?"

"It would be nice to have someone around at times," Claudia said. "But I have Rosie."

"Have you always had cats?"

"No, work took precedence over everything. If I wouldn't have inherited Rosie from Father Frank, I wouldn't have a pet."

"I can sense when you speak about him," Ira said, "that there is more to your relationship than business—a sadness, a loss. Were you in love with him?"

"He was a priest," Claudia said. She examined the back of her hands as though there were something there to find.

"That's not what I asked."

Claudia examined her palms next and then rubbed her hands together and clasped them, carefully weighing her words before she replied. "Frank Keller was not an ordinary priest. He was somewhat of a hit with the youth around here and very motivational. He did not start as a priest but was turned to God by an event in his life. This gave him a unique perspective, perhaps one I found attractive."

"So he was handsome?"

"For a priest, yes. We had a bond beyond that of friendship, a mutual attraction."

"What happened to him? How did he go to this place you speak of?"

"Something surreal. Something I can't explain. All I know is that he is no longer here, and no one knows how to find him." She reached for the box of tissues on the coffee table.

"I'm sorry. I didn't mean to bring it up," Ira said.

"No, it's fine. I haven't had anyone to speak with for so long that it feels good to get it out. Besides, I believe he succeeded in what he wanted to do."

"How's that?"

"About a year after the incident, I was allowed to attend a secret meeting held by an organization representing multiple religions from all over the globe. They had testimonies from around the world about a man matching Frank's description who was helping people, most of the time appearing in their dreams. He even managed to reach out and help his own nephew."

"That's an amazing story," Ira said. "And to think Samar may have spoken to him through his dreams."

"I'm envious," Claudia said. "He has appeared to all these other people, but I have never seen him."

"Because you don't need his help," Ira said. "You should be grateful—it means you are strong."

Claudia shifted in her seat. She knew Ira was correct in her observation. "I would just like to see him once, to know he is really out there."

"Would that really change the fact that you still can't be together?"

"No," Claudia said. "Can I get you anything else?"

"No," Ira said. "I'm ready to go back to sleep. If Samar is still talking too much, I might just sleep out here on the couch. I've enjoyed your company. I hope these friends of yours can help us sort this out." She folded the blanket that Claudia had given her and set it on the couch before heading back to the guest bedroom.

Claudia sat for a minute, trying to decide what she should do first the next day—go see Chic at the Kozy, in the hope he can help her get hold of the others, or go see David. Knowing that Chic probably had stayed up or still was up late and wouldn't enjoy an early visit, she decided she'd see David first.

CHAPTER 5
NINE DAYS REMAINING

This is what the Lord Almighty said: "Administer true justice; show mercy and compassion to one another. Do not oppress the widow or the fatherless, the foreigner or the poor. Do not plot evil against each other."

—Zechariah 7:9–10

Claudia drove her 1972 AMC Ambassador into the parking lot of the state mental facility. Driving the mint-condition, classic car that her father had left her was one of the things she enjoyed. The engine, full of more power than she needed, hummed and vibrated in a manner that soothed her. She pulled her car into a spot close to the wing David Jenson was kept in, a wing she had rarely visited when she had her practice because it was for wards of the state, those patients who were not to be released. Claudia had prided herself on a reputation for helping people with mental illness, but most of her practice had been outpatient care. Her flashback to her past was interrupted by a knock on her window from a handsome, young black-haired doctor. She rolled her window down.

"Good morning, Dr. Walden," the young man said. "You're here early."

"Yes, Dr. Pool," Claudia responded. "I just got back into town last night. I have some people visiting today and figured we'd get busy later, so I wanted to come by before I got sidetracked."

"Well, if you walk in with me, there'll be less hassle with security," Dr. Pool said.

Claudia rolled up her window and took her keys with her as she exited the vehicle. She walked with Dr. Pool to the double-door entrance.

"I think it will do David some good to see you. He's also been talking about a priest he knows; he speaks of him all of the time. I haven't met the guy personally, but he seems to be good for David."

"Father Mark Uwriyer," Claudia said, referring to the priest who had taken over Frank's parish.

"No, not that one," Dr. Pool said. "Father Frank. I believe that's what David called him. He said he just visited him a few days ago. I've never met him, but David speaks highly of him."

Claudia felt the blood drain from her face at Dr. Pool's comments. He apparently had the impression that Father Frank had recently visited David—a good trick for someone who'd been declared dead.

"Are you okay?" Dr. Pool asked.

"I'm fine," Claudia said. "Probably just the last day of travel getting to me, that's all."

"Your reputation as a therapist is well known here, if you ever want to return to practice."

"Thank you," she said. "I'll think about it." Claudia knew she did not intend to return to practice with all the rules and regulations she'd have to follow. As long as her book continued to sell and she had a message to spread, that was where she intended to spend her time.

Dr. Pool signed Claudia in at the front desk and then gave her an access card for the ward where David was housed. "Well, let me know if you need anything, and please don't forget to leave that key at the front desk. My offer stands if you want to come back to work."

"Thank you, Dr. Pool," Claudia said. She proceeded down the white, sanitized halls of the ward. She had never thought much about the layout when she worked in the clinical environment, but now that she was a visitor, the stale coldness of the place was apparent and left her feeling detached. "No, I couldn't return to work in a place like this," she said to herself as she scanned the badge at David's door and knocked.

"Come in," a young male voice said from the other side.

Claudia stepped into the room to find a young, thin, blond man with blue eyes sitting on his bed. The room had a small desk with one chair and a locker. There were no pictures or other personal items that would give a hint to the identity of the person who resided there. David was dressed in jeans and a blue-collared shirt. He had work boots on his feet and looked like he was ready to go somewhere.

"How are you, David?" Claudia asked as she pulled the chair out from the desk and moved it close to the bed and sat down.

"I saw you drive in," David said. "They don't let me out much, but I often look outside my window and wonder what it would be like to live out there again. I miss my room and being able to go down to the store and get a soda and a snack."

"Yes," Claudia said, "it's easy to miss those things we too easily take for granted. But you're doing so well in here, and there's so much support around you. I hear you are working a job now."

David walked to the window and pointed. "Yes, I'm working in a weld shop close by. They take me there and pick me up. But I'm not allowed to leave the building." He raised his leg and displayed an ankle tracker. "If I go too far from the shop, I get in trouble. Funny thing is, several other guys in the shop have these same things on, so they think I'm just being monitored for something simple like drunk driving. They don't know that I killed my family. Only my boss does. They had to tell him, you know, so he could decide if he wanted to trust me."

Claudia didn't know what to say immediately. She was glad to hear David admit so freely what he had done without breaking down. It was a sign that he had dealt with it the best he could. "Do you enjoy what you are doing?"

"I have a station that's my own, and I don't have to talk to anyone much. My boss says I make a good employee because I'm always quiet and get my work done." He turned and fixed his eyes on Claudia as he went over to his bed and sat down again. "I haven't seen you for two months and three days."

"Yes, with my new work I've been traveling. Did you read the book yet?"

David nodded. "It was very inspirational."

"Thank you." Claudia chose her next words carefully because she didn't want to lead him in his answers. If he had experienced the same dream as her, she wanted him to tell her. "Did you have anyone else visit you?"

"Yes," David said. "Is that what you came to talk to me about?" Claudia nodded.

"If I tell you about him, you can't tell Dr. Pool. If you do, he'll give me medicines that will make me unable to work. I don't want to lose my job."

"It's our secret," Claudia said.

"Okay," he said, nodding. "You are here to find out something … if the dream you had was real. Am I right?"

"Yes."

"I thought so." David seemed pleased and smiled.

"Do you really see Frank in your dreams?"

"I hadn't seen him for a long time. I think it's because I'm getting better, and there're other people he needs to help. But we have a special bond, and I think that makes it easier for him to communicate with me than others. He came just last week and had a message for you. He said time is short. I saw you in my dream too."

"Yes," Claudia said. "Do you know what he meant?"

"I don't know," David said. "I was hoping you would know."

"Thank you, David."

"Are you going to find Jimmie? Maybe he knows."

"Why?"

"The message he sent you—he told you to find Jimmie and that you only had thirteen days."

"Yes, I suppose I should find Jimmie, if for no other reason than to find out how he's doing."

"Not just to visit." David leaned forward to grasp her hands, startling her.

She tried to draw back, but David was too strong.

"Time was short four days ago. You only have nine days left!"

Claudia relaxed, knowing that struggling would only upset David. He let go of her hands, stood, and walked back to the window. She moved the chair farther away from the bed.

"Nine days before what, David?"

"I don't know," David said. "That's just what he told me to tell you."

There was a knock on the door.

"I have to go to work now," David said. "You don't have to come and see me anymore if it's too much trouble."

"It's no trouble, David."

"I think sometimes seeing you brings back memories," David said, "memories that I no longer want to have. I'm not that person anymore." The two exited the room, and Claudia went down the hall to the front desk while David went the other way with his escort. She briefly watched him and wondered if he was right about her visits. She exited the facility and considered that seeing him was only stirring up bad memories for her as well.

Claudia opened the door to her car and sat down. She was glad to be in her own car and not a rental after so much time spent traveling. She stretched her arms out behind the wheel of the light blue Ambassador and let the purr of the powerful engine soothe her. It reminded her of secure days when her father would take her places. Her moment of calm was interrupted by the memory of the message David had given her—that she only had nine days left. She wondered what it meant. Was her life or Jimmie's life in danger? She needed to find the answer.

Her first step would be to go back to the Kozy Tavern. It was where the group used to meet and where they would go if anyone was trying to get hold of her or if she needed to get hold of them. She pulled up in front of her house to see Samar waiting at the door. He approached the car and got in the passenger's side.

"Is Ira coming?" Claudia asked.

"Her father owns a small outlet shop here, and he asked her to stop by and give him a report. I think she might also go shopping," Samar said.

"Did she need a ride?"

"Oh no. She called one of those rental car places—you know, the kind that pick you up. She said I was safe with you and that she would see us later. Where are we going?"

"We are going to a place where I used to hang out with some friends. Perhaps we might find some answers for you there."

"As long as you don't mind the federal agents tagging along," Samar said, pointing at the car that sat in front of Claudia's house. "They stayed there all night. I thought maybe one of them would follow Ira, but they both stayed for me, I suppose. I didn't realize you Americans were so paranoid."

Claudia and Samar waved at the two men in suits who were watching from the car. The men waved back and followed them to the Kozy Tavern.

"This is a fairly run-down part of town," Claudia said, exiting her vehicle. "Maybe those men will help keep an eye on my car while we're inside." She laughed as they exited the car and headed to the door of the Kozy Tavern.

"What does 'run-down' mean?" Samar asked.

Claudia scratched her head. "It means an area that used to be vital and new but is no longer important, meaning investors no longer put money into the area, and the buildings don't get fixed."

"Oh," Samar said. "You mean a slum. We have those in India."

"I guess that's the proper name for it," Claudia said. "Just don't tell the owner of the Kozy Tavern that I said that about his location."

Samar put his fingers across his lips, zipping them shut.

Claudia stepped in through the large wooden doorway, with Samar following her. She hesitated as her eyes adjusted to the dim lighting inside. Samar stopped a step in front of her. Her eyes went to the left of the room, where she spotted what she was looking for: there, like a steadfast painting that glorified a room, was the bartender, Chic.

His eyes lifted from his duties, and the unlit cigar flicking about in his mouth came to a stop. After an uncomfortable period of waiting in which Claudia felt she needed to say something but couldn't figure out what to say, Chic broke the silence. "You're the spitting image of him. I suppose you've come to get his stuff?"

Claudia put her hand to Samar's back and urged him forward as she stepped to his side in full view of Chic.

The bartender smiled. "Well, I'll be. If this week just hasn't been turning up one surprise after another." Chic put down his cleaning towel, came out from behind the bar, white apron about his waist, and hugged Claudia.

"I am glad there is someone here," Samar said. "For a moment I thought the place was closed."

Chic broke his hug and faced Samar. "Well, this place isn't what it used to be, that's for sure. The parts companies died out years ago when everyone started buying foreign cars. Then when they did start building cars back here in the good old US, the companies relocated to the south. It is what it is. So, Claudia, how did he find you?"

Claudia raised an eyebrow. "I don't know what you mean. Who found me?"

"This has got to be Adnan's son—he's the spitting image of him." Chic walked back toward the bar. "Adnan told a story about how he'd tried to give up the fight and settle down with a woman once. Nevertheless, his calling wouldn't let him be. So he finally left the woman, pregnant and all, behind. He didn't tell many people, but I guess the story is out now."

Claudia and Samar followed Chic to the bar, and as he went to the other side, they both sat down.

"Now I hope you know he sent you and your mother every cent he could spare. As soon as Kanuik gets back, I'll take you to his room. Now what can I get you two?"

Claudia and Samar were speechless as they glanced at each other and then back to Chic, whose cigar was now in full swing as he chewed on it.

"By the way, how did you find out? Was it something in Claudia's book? Is that why you two are together?" Chic stopped what he was doing. "Someone say something. You two are making me feel awkward here."

"Chic," Claudia said, "this is Samar Hamish. He is an archeologist from India."

Chic shook Samar's hand. "Pleased to make your acquaintance. Now what can I get you two? I know something you will both enjoy." Chic turned and started making a drink, facing the large mirror at the back of the bar.

Claudia couldn't help but stare at the young man sitting next to her.

"Why are you looking at me like that?" Samar said.

"I noticed a resemblance before, but never did I consider …"

"I don't know who this man is that you are speaking about," Samar said. "Is there a restroom I may use?"

Chic pointed to the restrooms, and Samar left the bar.

"Here you go," Chic said. He set three glasses of a warm brown liquid on the bar. "It's the tea Adnan used to drink. I found this great honey from Colorado—it makes it taste spectacular." Chic took a sip. "Ah, perfect."

"You really think he's Adnan's son?"

"You don't? Why are you with him then?"

Claudia took a drink from the glass. "You're right, this is good."

"Claudia!" Chic pleaded. "What's going on?"

"All I know is that I was at a coffee shop in New York, right before a book appearance, and this man, Samar, and his fiancée Ira approached me and knew things about Frank. He says he talks to him in his dreams."

"Wow." Chic looked down and rested his fists on the bar. "You mean that kid had no idea what's really going on?"

"He's got Adnan's ability, I think," Claudia said, "from what his fiancée has told me and the incident on the airplane."

"Incident?"

"Apparently, he stopped a terrorist attack on his way over here. By the description he gave, a shadow was involved."

"If you didn't know who he was, why did you bring him here?"

"There's something going on," Claudia said. "He"—Claudia pointed in the direction of Samar as he made his way back to his seat—"is not the only one who has seen things. I had a dream related to Frank, and David Jenson is telling me that Frank has given him a warning, and it concerns Jimmie. I was hoping to get back in touch with Jimmie and Kanuik and see if they can help me. Do you know where they are?"

Chic smiled. "Kanuik just arrived yesterday. He's staying downstairs in his old room."

Claudia immediately stood.

"But he's not there now," Chic said. "He went out to see Bishop Tafoya. That's why I can't let you into Adnan's room yet, not without Kanuik here."

"I don't need in his room," Claudia said.

"I didn't mean you." Chic nodded toward Samar.

Claudia shook her head. She wasn't as convinced as Chic that Samar could be related to Adnan. "What about Jimmie—Professor Barnes?"

"He's with Kanuik. Jimmie is still working on the experiment to send soldiers through to where Father Frank is. He and Connor live together. They should all be back in a couple of hours if you want to wait."

Samar sat down and took a drink from the glass in front of him. At first, he only sipped, and then he drank the whole glass down. "This tastes just like the honey tea my mother makes back home."

"Need any more proof?" Chic said, smiling at Claudia.

A noise from the doorway caused all three of them to turn. Claudia recognized the three men who came through the entrance: Kanuik, Jimmie Barnes with his shaggy hairdo and sport coat, and Bishop Arthur Tafoya, the shortest, eldest, and baldest of the men. All three men greeted her with outstretched arms, especially Kanuik, who hugged her tight.

Claudia introduced Samar to the group. "This is Bishop Arthur Tafoya of the Catholic church. This is Professor James Barnes."

"Call me Jimmie," Jimmie said as he shook Samar's hand.

"And this fellow over here with the great hat on"—Claudia winked, having noticed that Kanuik was wearing the hat she had bought for him—"is Kanuik, no last name. Kanuik is from the Cherokee tribe."

Samar had to look up to meet Kanuik's eyes. "I did not know Native Americans were so tall."

"Most aren't," Kanuik said.

"He comes from a tribe that can trace some of their ancestry to the Knights Templar," Chic chimed in, "if you know who they were."

"Yes," Samar said, "from my studies."

Kanuik's eyes narrowed.

"Oh, don't worry about him," Chic said. "He's an archeologist from India and, I believe, Adnan's son."

Claudia watched Kanuik's eyebrows rise at Chic's comment. "We don't really know that yet," Claudia said.

"I see a resemblance," Kanuik said. "Have you come to get his father's stuff?"

"He doesn't know anything about Adnan," Claudia said. "He is here because Frank appeared to him in his dream and told him to come and find me."

"For what reason?" Kanuik asked.

Claudia shook her head. "I don't know."

"Let's take him down to his father's room," Chic said, coming out from behind the bar and gesturing for Kanuik to join him. "The rest of you, make yourselves at home. We'll be back in a moment." Grabbing Samar's arm and escorting him away from the group, Chic said, "This place has been used by your kind for a long time. My family has owned the pub for over a hundred years and has helped in the cause. However, the battle has changed over the years. Fewer believe in it."

"In what?" Samar asked.

"Oh, we have a lot to tell him," Chic said.

Claudia gave up on reasoning with Chic and Kanuik as they led Samar away. She couldn't hear the rest of the conversation as the trio disappeared down a hallway opposite the front door that led to the bathrooms and the basement area.

"What brings you back into town?" Jimmie asked, taking a seat at the bar next to Claudia.

"Would it make you feel good if I said it was to see you?"

"Yes, it would. But how did you know I was back in town? Did one of these guys call you?"

"It would amuse me to see Kanuik actually use a phone, but no, in truth, it is a great surprise to see both of you. I was hoping I would find you, but this worked out better than planned. How are you?"

"Surprisingly well," Jimmie said. "I'm working both at the college and with the church."

"Still on the project," Claudia said. She knew about the project

Jimmie was working on to send soldiers through the portal to Frank's location.

"Yes, still on the project," Jimmie said.

"He doesn't give himself enough credit," Bishop Tafoya said, entering the conversation. "Do you mind?" He took a seat next to Claudia. "Without him, our plan would be failing. Instead, we are now ready to go in ... how many days?"

"In eight days," Jimmie said. "Eight days from tomorrow."

Claudia felt blood rush to her cheeks and a sensation of butterflies in her stomach when Jimmie mentioned the timeline. She looked at the counter for something to drink and spotted some bottled water behind the bar, but when she stood to get it, she stumbled.

Jimmie reacted and caught her as she fell.

━┿ ▆◆▆ ┿━

"Thank you, Chic," Claudia said as he changed the cold washcloth on the back of her neck. She had nearly fainted when Bishop Tafoya and Jimmie mentioned a deadline that matched the number of days in Father Frank's warning. Now she just needed to find out more from them. The group moved to their old table, where they all sat together except for Chic, who was busy about the bar.

"You're saying that Father Frank has been trying to communicate something to us about our operation?" Jimmie asked.

"I think it's very likely," Claudia said.

Samar and Kanuik returned from downstairs and took a seat at the table, leaving the chair with Adnan's hat hanging on it vacant.

"I believe he is Adnan's son," Kanuik stated to the group. "When we went in Adnan's room, he recognized several items that were his father's. His aura is the same as Adnan's."

"Then it is no coincidence that you have all been brought back together," Bishop Tafoya said. "There must be a reason."

"This is the group you were telling me about then," Samar said.

"Yes," Claudia said.

"Exactly what do you do?" Samar asked, glancing around the table.

"Mr. Samar Hamish," Bishop Tafoya said, "what I am about to

tell you may cause you to doubt my sanity. Nevertheless, it is time you knew the truth about who you are and what you are getting into. Have you ever wondered why it seems like moments go slower when things are going wrong or why bad days seem to last forever? Have you ever experienced a bad dream, a nightmare, that seems so real that you know it must be happening, but you wake up? Have you ever felt pain or loss after one of these dreams that you couldn't explain away or found out that a dream you had was really a vision of something that has come to pass? Or have you witnessed people display extreme changes in behavior and then snap out of it as though they didn't really know that what they were doing was real?"

"Yes," Samar said. He moved around in his chair and put his hand to his chin and then back on the table. "I have experienced this all of my life."

"Negative moments," Bishop Tafoya said, "yours or those of others that you are dragged into—those are what I am alluding to. When we are happy or experiencing pleasant moments, it seems we only want them to slow down. But the negative, painful moments—they seem to pass by slower, as though something is manipulating time.

"Consider the violence that is going on in the world today, the inhumanity of acts perpetrated by parents on their children, neighbors on their neighbors. How is it that normal people whom we see every day all of a sudden snap and perform such malevolent acts? You hear people talk about how they were shocked that the person they knew could do such things, and at the same time, you often hear of other people who gave warning signs that they weren't quite themselves."

"I have seen this up close," Samar said.

"Yes," Bishop Tafoya said. "What if I told you the battle is more in our minds and in our actions than we know? Have you ever wondered why there are texts that speak of demons, of physical forms of evil in the past, but none walk the earth today?"

"History is full of superstition," Samar said. "That is why I have studied religion—to try to understand what is happening to me."

"So from your studies, you know that there was a time when evil walked upright among men in other forms that are no longer here today? They became extinct—lost the battle of existence somehow."

"Or they never existed," Samar said.

"What if I were to tell you that what you have been experiencing is evil interacting with humans and that you are able to sense it and fight it somehow? Would you believe me?"

"Are you asking me to believe that demons are real?"

"That evil is real." Bishop Tafoya looked around the table. "Evil is among us, not in a physical place where we can find it, but hidden in moments of time."

"In time?" Samar questioned. His eyebrows drew low on his forehead as he quickly glanced at Claudia.

Claudia nodded to Samar and listened as Bishop Tafoya continued his story.

"I don't think the church knows the specifics, but evil was among men on earth. Some say it was fallen angels who spread evil. Others say that we were born in sin because without bad, there couldn't be good— the theory of opposites, yin and yang. Whatever the case, our free will gave us a choice. Church historians say the first attempt to purge evil from the world was the flood of Noah. The second time God tried was in the time of Enoch. Do you know of the legend of Enoch's sword? It was a weapon, given to a servant of God to fight evil beings. The weapon was supposed to be so powerful it could defeat any being, even demons. But using it comes at a price, a sacrifice of one's own soul."

"What happened to the sword?" Samar asked.

"Many scholars think the text refers not to an actual sword, but to a person of power."

"Oh," Samar said. "But I didn't think your church considered Enoch an accurate text."

"You're correct. It is in the Apocrypha and not accepted by most. There are many writings the church decided were too full of the fantastic to be worth including. The truth is that some of the books not included in the Bible may have been referencing things we couldn't explain but that make sense in terms of what we face today. Evil was driven from physical form to spiritual; demons that walked upright could no longer do so, except for one period in the year, known as the thirteenth month.

"There is debate on when the final battle of good and evil happened, but many believe it was in the time of Christ, when he drove evil forces completely out of men. All that was left of evil then was the ability to influence, but not control."

"Is that why the number thirteen has such superstition about it?" Samar asked.

"The shadows made themselves known in the early twelfth century," Bishop Tafoya said. "They infested weak men and attacked believers who traveled to the holy city. The Templars were formed to protect the travelers."

"What does this have to do with the number thirteen?"

Bishop Tafoya held up his hand. "Give me a minute. The rebellion against the Knights Templar that resulted in the execution of their leaders happened on a Friday, the thirteenth! That led the number to be associated with evil, as is the force behind it. The evil we fight today hides in moments of time."

"The evil tries to make those brief moments longer and attempts to influence its human hosts," Jimmie said. "A brief whisper becomes a constant nagging."

Claudia listened intently to the conversation around her. Although she knew of the shadows, she hadn't known the history behind them. She noticed Samar folding his hands together, as though he was trying to grasp it all.

"All of you believe this?" Samar asked.

"I had trouble at first," Claudia said. "I was raised going to church, but my education took me into the world of science, psychiatry, and the study of mental illness. I could not explain all of what I have seen, so I joined the group and helped them."

"It is an age-old battle in all histories," Bishop Tafoya said, "a battle that your father was a part of and that has now touched you."

"So," Jimmie said, "ready for that plane ride back to wherever you came from yet?"

"Here, drink this," Chic said as he put one of the glasses full of honey tea in front of Samar and passed out various drinks to the others. Judging by the look on Samar's face when he took a drink, the tea had a little something extra in it. Samar wiped his mouth lightly with a napkin.

"It's okay," Claudia said. "I'm driving tonight."

"From what I've seen and felt," Samar said, "I believe that there is evil. In addition, there are forces of good. My fiancée Ira is an intuitive, and she senses this stuff all of the time. If you know about these things, then that is exactly why I've come, to understand better."

"Ironically," Jimmie said, "the time of Christ is also the time when the battle between good and evil started being written about more as an internal conflict, as a matter of the morality of men. Evil lost its physical form and became spiritual as portrayed by Christian writers of the time. Also ironically, I must point out that if you research history, you'll find that the Catholic church had a hand in controlling the calendar and finally made it into its current twelve-month form. They had to account for the time shrinkage where evil was no longer present in the thirteenth month. See"—Jimmie held out his hands wide with his palms facing each other and then moved them in closer—"time expanded and contracted, much like the force of gravity. The leaders of the church wanted to make sure the record of a thirteenth month was buried in the past so that evil would never be remembered as whole."

"But they are still there," Samar said. "Correct?"

"Yes," Jimmie said. "It's like when scientists knew there was a ninth planet: they couldn't see it, but it was there. There is another dimension inhabited by these shadows. We are trying to stop them from coming back into ours."

"And my father was part of the group fighting them?" Samar said.

"Yes," Bishop Tafoya said. "He was the leader."

"Ironically," Jimmie interjected again, "religions that were forged to fight evil and give humankind moral direction have been the cause of much of the evil."

Chic came to the table and put a drink down in front of Jimmie, who jumped in his seat, startled by Chic reaching over him in the heat of the discussion.

Chic raised his eyebrows as he looked down at Jimmie. "All causes, good or evil, can be turned around by the will of humans. That is the point. You need a drink," Chic said. "You used the word 'ironically' three times in all that philosophizing you just did. You're going to have a heart attack if you don't relax a little."

Claudia and Kanuik laughed.

"I'm just trying to clarify everything here," Jimmie said, "so he understands what's going on a little bit better than I did when you guys were all running around, battling these things."

"I understand," Samar said, "more clearly than ever before in my life now. I thank you for telling me this. I have studied all the histories of the religions and have tried to find meaning in what I have seen and felt. Now I have found that. You must let me join your group and allow me to be part of this."

Jimmie picked up the drink in front of him, turned to Claudia, and drank it down. "I think I'll get another drink." He stood and went to the bar, where he sat down on a stool in front of Chic, who had returned to his post.

"Was it something I said?" Samar asked.

"No," Claudia said. "It's just … we aren't really a group anymore."

"Then become one again."

"It's not that simple to go back to a life we all walked away from," Claudia said.

Her comment silenced the table.

She stood and went to the bar and sat down by Jimmie. "I should have made a better effort to stay in touch with all of you."

"That's not it," Jimmie said. "I am a scientist. Granted, with my paranormal adventures I might live on the edge. However, what I experienced with the group that night in the hospital in David Jenson's room … well, let's just say I'm still trying to find an explanation that makes sense to me. You weren't the only one who left town. We all did. I just came back first."

"Yes, and that's why it was so hard on all of us," Claudia said as she reached out and put her hand on Jimmie's shoulder. "We shared an extreme set of experiences together and then parted too soon. We lost two people who were close to us in a matter of days. We should have helped each other through the trauma."

"We're here now," Jimmie said. "That's got to mean something."

"It does," Claudia said. "And it's good to be back in familiar surroundings with familiar friends." She looked at Chic and Jimmie, who returned her smile.

Chic went back into the kitchen. In the mirror behind the bar, Claudia could see the entire place behind her. Other than their group, no one else was in the bar. "How does this place stay open without any customers?"

"Remember?" Jimmie said. "Chic won the lottery."

"Oh, right."

"So you believe Samar has the same ability as Adnan to track these shadows?" Jimmie asked.

"From what he and his girlfriend have told me, his ability seems very similar to what Adnan used to do," Claudia said.

"How do we know?"

"Let's take him out on the town," Claudia said. "See where he takes us. That's the only way to be sure."

"And then what? Are we going to start meeting every night like we used to?"

"I think we should celebrate our reunion first and let that sink in. Maybe we can go out tomorrow—see what happens and take it from there."

"What about the message from Frank? Do you really believe he has survived for all this time and is trying to warn us?"

Claudia didn't respond right away. The group knew Adan had died; they had the body. In Frank's case, no body had been recovered, and then the reports had come from all over the world—a man fitting Father Frank Keller's description was helping people through their dreams.

"My biggest fear in all of this is that I'm about to send a thousand more to where he is," Jimmie said. "They know what they've signed up for; it's just the thought of them being stuck there."

Claudia gasped. "A thousand soldiers?"

"Yes. We only have a hundred active at any time. However, we've trained over a thousand soldiers to go through. Once we start, they'll be bused in from all over the country."

"I only hope Frank is really out there and he's okay," Claudia said. "If he is trying to get a message to us, whatever it is, we are running out of time to figure it out."

Thomas looked to his left and right to make sure he hadn't been followed as he entered the old building and went down the stairs to where he had set up a second lab—a step he felt necessary due to the indecisiveness of some of the church leaders.

Once again, he could hear Mike and Kaitlyn talking as he descended the stairwell. He knew the two were attracted to each other, a setback in his mind because it distracted them from the work they needed to get done. The two went in different directions when they spotted him. Mike Delgado approached him as he exited the stairs while Kaitlyn went to the chair and checked the straps.

"You've taken more teens," Mike said, pointing to the cage across the room. "How many do you need?"

"That is none of your concern," Thomas said as he continued to the table that held the computer and all the data Mike was gathering.

"Aren't you worried about the police?"

"The parents of these kids aren't worried about them. In their respective homes, they are a threat, now cast out and forgotten. What I need you to do is focus on a cause that matters and get results." Thomas hated getting angry because it not only made his blood pressure rise but also turned the scar on his face purple, making it more noticeable. He ran his fingers across it and noticed Kaitlyn and Jimmie watching him.

"Let me tell you a story from my childhood, about how I got this scar." Thomas pointed to the mark across his face and moved a few paces so that he was between Mike and Kaitlyn. "You see, the battle against evil was revealed to me at a very young age when my father, a laborer for Vatican City, became obsessed with exploring dark powers. You may or may not believe in these things, and at that time as a young boy, I wasn't sure either. But believe me, the evil manifests itself and makes those who welcome it or who are weak-minded do its bidding. The church calls them shadows.

"My father continued his work and one day succumbed to the influence of the evil we are trying to fight. In a fit of rage, he almost killed me. This scar"—Thomas ran his fingers across it again—"is a reminder of how close I came to death."

"What happened to your father?" Kaitlyn asked.

"A young priest, Father Denaro, came to my aid and took me into his care. My father was too far gone, and he died in the fight." Thomas knew this experience had led to his dedication to the church, a dedication that often overpowered his loyalty to any leader. "So you see, that is why we need to get to work."

"That's a powerful story," Kaitlyn said. "Right, Mike?"

Mike didn't say anything but walked over to the table and started going through the pages of data. "I don't know if there is a way to separate these things without killing the host."

"If needed, we must accept that," Thomas said. "Have you found a way to detect them?"

Mike didn't respond and just stared into space.

"Mr. Delgado, the reason you are here is because of your experience with the group, with Professor Barnes. The church supports you and your research, but if at any time you can't handle what is going on, you are free to go. Now do you have the equipment working yet?"

"I'm still making adjustments," Mike said. "If this doesn't work, I might have to find Professor Barnes."

"Do what you must, but don't expose what we are doing here," Thomas said. "I'm not sure the world is ready for the revelation of the shadows. We could start the next Salem witch trials, with people assuming everyone around them is infected with these shadows—which is why you need to come up with a way to detect them and destroy them, don't you think?"

Mike glanced up momentarily and then fidgeted about, adjusting his monitoring equipment, and nodded. Thomas handed Kaitlyn the keys to the cage. She went over to the cell, retrieved a young man who was barely able to walk, and strapped him down to the chair. Thomas waited until Kaitlyn had checked the straps before he approached the boy. He had long, unkempt black hair, earrings all throughout his ear, and tattoos all over his arms.

"Let's try another method of provoking the things," Thomas said. He went to the chair where the boy was strapped down. "You are worthless. You are selfish, dirty, always up to no good. Look at yourself." He held up a mirror. When the boy didn't look into it, Thomas grabbed him by the chin and forced him to look in the mirror. "You have degraded your body. You have turned from your family, and you worship drugs. You are nothing."

"It's working. I'm getting readings," Mike said, smiling. "I think we're about ready, Father Thomas."

"Just call me Thomas." Thomas turned back to the boy and continued to torment him and degrade him. "You are filth, not worthy of your mother's care or her bearing you into this world."

"Do you need to be so harsh?" Mike asked.

Thomas stood slowly. He walked to where Mike was sitting and extended his arm, clasping him on the shoulder. "Look, our enemy is ruthless. I understand your hesitation, but it is only delaying results. We need to step up our efforts. We are losing at every turn. Our new techniques have proven effective, and we are learning more and more about these creatures. We need to keep attracting the shadows so we can study and learn how to defeat them. These subjects are what we have to work with. Do you think they would be any better out on the streets where society has let them rot? Are you going to save them?"

"I guess not," Mike said.

"So tell me what you have."

"This scanner here lets me see brain patterns," Mike said. "It appears the force—the shadow, I mean—interacts with the medial orbitofrontal cortex and somehow heightens both aggressive and sexual drives, and at the same time I can see strands of the black form pulsing in and out of the hypothalamus."

"What purpose does that achieve?"

"In addition to confidence issues, the shadow seems to be affecting the part of the brain that regulates self-control. My theory is that it makes the host weaker and more susceptible to feeling insecure. Research in this area is still very hypothetical. But from the abnormal patterns in this scan, I would guess that boy in the chair doesn't even know where he is right now."

"How can these things affect him this way?" Thomas asked.

"I haven't determined that yet. I don't know if the subject hears voices or if it's subliminal impulses or some other form of energy control. I do know that when the affected subjects act out, they have heightened levels of melatonin, a sleep enhancer. It's almost as though the subject gives up control."

"Are you saying the shadow possesses them?" Thomas had moved over to where a teenage boy and girl sat in a cell.

"Not exactly. You know, like when someone uses a drug, they make a conscious decision to use it but then lose control of themselves."

"Yes," Thomas said. "I've seen where the subjects take back control very aggressively. However, others remain dormant, as if not caring what happens to them. So how can we stop the shadows before they activate again?"

"If we can figure out the motivation, what makes these things interact the way they do, maybe we can block them. But you're way beyond my expertise."

"Then it may be"—Thomas put his index finger in the air—"that they choose the subjects like we have here because they are already damaged and easy to influence."

"It's likely," Mike said. "It may be that the only reason we aren't affected is because we have normal, strong brain patterns."

"Thank you, Mr. Delgado," Thomas said as he headed toward the stairs. "You have learned a lot. I leave you and your assistant to continue and find out how to control these things. Time is of the essence. I'll expect results."

CHAPTER 6
EIGHT DAYS REMAINING

The very world we live in—our society, our cultures—has grown to allow a certain number of problems to exist: poverty, war, corruption, racism, hunger. Moreover, for years upon years upon years, we have seen plans, committees, subcommittees, and all sorts of combatants try to solve these problems. You can see that these ways will always fail because what is wrong has nothing to do with papers and policies. These problems are moral issues and must be dealt with on a moral basis. But how do you enforce moral conduct?

After spending a day resting and catching up on household chores and bills, Claudia met the group at the Kozy Tavern for dinner. After dinner, they decided to test the theory that Samar had the same ability as Adnan, that he could sense the shadows. They headed out on the town in Jimmie's car. Not wanting to take two cars, they decided that Ira would stay back at the tavern to visit with Chic.

Claudia sat in the front next to Jimmie. Kanuik and Connor sat in the back seat, with Samar in the middle. She watched in the rearview mirror as the expression on Samar's face changed from excitement to boredom. He caught her looking at him.

"Is this what you used to do?" Samar asked. "Drive around until something happened?"

"No," Kanuik replied. "Your father had a way of sensing where the shadows were. We didn't drive around long before he would sense something and we would go into action."

"After hearing your story, we thought you might have the same ability," Jimmie said.

"I don't even know how I have this ability," Samar said, "let alone how to control it like you are asking."

"I may be the only one who knew Adnan had a son," Kanuik said. "He was a very reserved man and did not talk about his personal life much. I think he was from the same village where your mother lived. After the experience he went through where a shadow became trapped inside of him, he took some time to go back to his roots. This was when he met your mother and conceived you. Perhaps the ability runs in his family, or maybe it's because the shadow was in him, and that affected your birth in a way that allows you to sense them as he did."

"I'm sorry," Samar said. "But I must admit to you that I don't really know how to control what I have."

"It's not your fault," Claudia said. The psychiatrist in her wondered how much of what they were doing was for Samar's sake compared to the sake of the group. Connor was just happy to be part of something. However, she, Kanuik, and Jimmie were trying to replace something lost—a sense of belonging with others in a purpose. Through Adnan's leadership, they had made a difference. Father Frank Keller was the one Adnan had picked to take his place, but both men had exited the group within a week of each other—Adnan was killed, and Frank disappeared through the portal. After the tragedy, Claudia had lost herself in her work, a book inspired by Frank's last sermon, and she had lost touch with the others. Was tonight all about recreating a past that she hadn't let go of?

Jimmie interrupted her thoughts. "Where should we go?" he said as he stopped for a red light.

"Are you asking me?" Samar said. "I cannot tell you where to find these things."

Jimmie pulled over at a gas station. He got out of the car and started filling the tank while the others remained in their seats, waiting for him.

"It doesn't matter if we drive around all night," Connor said as Jimmie settled back into his seat. "Maybe what your group used to do was important, but the army we are getting ready to send through to the other side will be able to do a lot more. Jimmie, why don't we go show them the setup we have?"

"I wouldn't want to take you to the church basement," Jimmie said. "If Thomas discovered us, he would freak out. However, we could go to David Jenson's house, where we were experimenting yesterday."

No one protested, so Jimmie headed to David's house.

The car came to a stop in front of a white-and-red two-story house. The double-bulb motion light on the outside of the garage came on. As the light streamed down in front of them, they could see a blue Dodge pickup with peeling paint parked by a small Ford Escort in the driveway.

"It looks the same," Claudia said. "The electricity is still on, and they've left the cars in the driveway."

"The house is paid for," Jimmie said, "with insurance money. It belongs to David, but he will never be able to live here."

Claudia opened her door and exited the vehicle. "It's like it's been frozen in time."

Jimmie exited the driver's side and fiddled with some keys as he approached the front door.

"How did you get the keys?"

"From David," Jimmie said. "He donated the house to Father Frank's church. But they won't use it for anything because of what happened here."

"What happened here?" Samar said.

Claudia turned to see Samar staring at the house, his arms down at his side; he looked different somehow—pale. He stepped forward as though he was dizzy, and then suddenly, he bent over a patch of grass and vomited.

Claudia rushed to him. "Are you all right?" She put her hand on his back, then reached in her purse and pulled out a few tissues. "Here," she said, handing them to Samar.

"Must be the food I ate," Samar said, wiping his face and blowing his nose. His eyes were bloodshot as he faced Claudia. "Sorry."

"Door's open," Jimmie called out and headed into the house.

"You sure you're okay?" Claudia asked.

Samar nodded, and they headed toward the doorway.

Kanuik met them at the entrance. "I must warn you," he said. "I have cleansed this house many times, but what happened here left its mark deep in the energy that surrounds us, and evil still remains. Keep on your guard."

Before them was a stairway to the right that led up to the second floor and a hallway that led to the kitchen and living room. Claudia was starting down the hallway to the living room when Kanuik grabbed her arm.

"I'm worried about you the most," he said. "Don't trust anything you see in this house."

"I was here before," Claudia stated. "I remember what happened. I'll stay close."

"What happened here?" Samar asked again. He, Claudia, and Kanuik moved down the hallway.

"We should have prepared you," Kanuik said. "This is where your father was attacked by the shadows. During the attack, they had the ability to change what we were seeing—our reality—and make some of us see things that were not real. This is their power, the power of deception, lies."

The three entered a large living room that contained a brown leather four-piece sofa and a black leather recliner. Both were facing a fifty-five-inch television that sat atop a huge entertainment cabinet with DVDs and CDs on both sides. The only light in the room streamed in through the half-open blinds of the opposing wall's windows. To the left was a kitchen area. Dishes, cutlery, and all the appliances made the house look inhabited.

Claudia paused in the hallway, looking down at her shoes. She was sorry she had worn open-toed heels. The memory of stepping in blood at the very spot where she stood came back to her.

"Do you need to step back outside?" Kanuik asked.

"No, I'm fine. Part of my dealing with this is being back here—to put to rest what happened and caused us to go our separate ways."

Samar stepped around Claudia and looked to the ceiling. Claudia also heard the footstep above her.

"Jimmie and Connor are upstairs," Kanuik said. "We should go there next." He stepped out in front of them by the couch.

"Samar, this house is where David Jenson killed his family, under the influence of the shadows," Claudia said. "In order to combat them, your father brought us back here. He thought he could trick them and create an opening into their world and defeat them on their own ground."

"What happened?" Samar asked.

"The plan went horribly wrong," Kanuik said. "The creatures seemed to know what we were going to do and swarmed him. His power was great, but he did not survive the attack. It happened right here." He pointed to the location in front of him where Adnan had fallen.

Samar went to the spot and looked around. He turned and sat on the couch. Claudia moved to where she could see his face. His eyes were closed, and he took deep breaths, as if meditating. She wondered what he was seeing, what he was feeling. The psychiatrist in her warned her about the pace they were taking. First, they had suddenly revealed to him that he had unwittingly tracked down his father, Adnan, whom they had known as a great man in a secret battle between good and evil. Then they'd revealed that his father had been killed, and now they had taken him to the place where the event had occurred. She considered that having Ira along for support might have been a good idea. It startled her when Samar suddenly opened his eyes.

"I sense nothing here," Samar said. "But there is something upstairs." He pointed.

Claudia turned to Kanuik.

"That is where Jimmie and Connor have set up the equipment," Kanuik said.

"Why up there?" Claudia asked.

"When we were here before," Kanuik said, "the portal opened there. It was in David's room. That is where Professor Barnes thinks he can get it to open again."

"Open?" Samar said. "You are saying these creatures can come through this portal to control us and you are opening it?"

"No, it is important that you understand that they don't control, only influence," Kanuik said. "Control would be if they could take over at will. The host has to relinquish control and is able to fight back. The shadows try to expose any weakness. The more you give in, the closer their power comes to control."

"Why would anyone want to open a door for them to come through?" Samar said.

"Why do we follow any leader or rules? Sometimes it's just easier to give in," Claudia said.

"Like being numb—you just give in instead of fighting," Samar said.

"Yes. But the advantage is that the door goes both ways," Kanuik said. "Father Frank went through, and he is helping others, but we don't understand how. The Council of World Religions has approved research to try to send others through, to fight the shadows where they come from."

"Time to go see," Claudia said, and she headed down the hall with Samar and Kanuik following her. She went up the stairs, where pictures of David's family and some artwork still hung on the walls. The house itself had remained largely in the condition it had been in the night of David's crime, other than removal of the evidence and the cleaning of the room. There were three bedrooms on the second floor; the first to the left was David's, then down the hall to the right was a small bathroom, followed by another bedroom, and at the end of the hall was the master bedroom.

Claudia found Jimmie and Connor working with some electronic equipment in what used to be David's room. Jimmie was seated behind a small desk in David's room, while Connor was across the room, where he had pushed the bed against the wall to make space for two large mechanical devices he was setting up. The devices stood about five feet apart and slightly leaned into each other.

"What are those?" Claudia asked, pointing at the machines.

"Those are conductors," Jimmie said. "When we opened the portal at the hospital in David's room, I was able to shoot a pulse of energy into it and keep it open while also preventing the shadows from coming through. They consist of energy, just like everything else in the universe. However, Frank is the one who got the portal open. Since he's not here, I needed a way to open it—therefore the coils." He pointed. "The rest of this stuff is all kinds of energy and temperature sensors. I have them placed all over the house to monitor changes in motion and changes in temperature. Heck, I can even tell how many cockroaches are in the kitchen."

"You said Frank opened a portal in David's room? How did Frank open the portal?" Claudia asked. She caught the glance between Jimmie and Kanuik, and Kanuik shook his head once. She was about to ask them what was going on but didn't get a chance.

An alarm went off from the equipment in front of Jimmie, and he looked down. "Don't touch anything!" Jimmie hollered to Samar, who was standing by Connor around the conductors.

"He didn't," Connor said. "What is it?"

"I don't know," Jimmie said. "Probably nothing."

Claudia went over to where Connor and Samar stood. "So somewhere on the other side of these things is Father Frank, if we can open the door?"

"I don't think it's quite that simple," Jimmie said.

"In my dreams he said he was close to the place I was at. I think he meant Israel," Samar said.

"Why there?" Claudia asked.

"The mythology is that the battle between good and evil started there," Samar said. "It's just so hard to believe that you somehow sent someone to this place you say these shadows come from and that he is still alive."

"In the Council of World Religions," Kanuik said, "we have had testimonies about a man who resembles Father Frank Keller helping people. They see him in dreams and sometimes when they are awake. These reports come from all over the world, not just the Holy Land."

"Well, if Frank really is in another dimension, space and time could be completely different where he is," Jimmie said. "For all we know, he went to a different place that is in our own time connected by wormholes that open here on earth through energies we have yet to explain."

"Enough of your theories," Claudia said. "How do we get him back?"

"We've only been able to send things one way," Jimmie said. "And we can't really tell where they go. We have yet to achieve any retrieval, which is why we are still doing tests."

"So the mission is one-way?" Samar asked.

"Yes. Regardless, there have already been multiple delays," Jimmie said. "The council is dead set on going forward with the plan this time."

"That's what we've signed up for," Connor said. "I just hope there's something to eat over there. There must be—otherwise, how has my uncle been able to survive?"

"If the shadows can go back and forth, why can't you?" Samar asked.

"I have no explanation," Jimmie said. "Sometimes I think they are on the other side blocking us and know what we are attempting to do."

Claudia watched as Jimmie typed on his computer and continued looking at the screen.

"All I know is that it's dangerous to leave this equipment on," Jimmie said. "When we first started experimenting, some things came through. They might have once been people, but they were bent over, their arms and legs twisted and contorted, and they were covered in a black mold. None of them survived. I'd rather not talk about it."

"How long are we going to be here?" Claudia said. She bent over and put her hand to her stomach. "I think I ate the same thing Samar had. First, he threw up, and now I don't feel so good."

"It may not be the food," Kanuik said. "It may be the energy of this place."

"I think I need to lie down," Claudia said, grabbing her stomach.

"The other bedrooms have been completely cleaned," Jimmie said. "The parents' room is just down the hall if you need to go lie down."

"Maybe I'll just rest for a moment." Claudia headed down the hallway. All the bedroom doors were closed. When she opened the last door, a whisk of air went by her, as though the room, closed for three years, had held its breath.

"Let me check the room," Kanuik said, surprising her as he stepped around her and entered the room. He walked around, looking in the closet and out the window. He sat on the bed and closed his eyes for a moment while Claudia remained at the doorway. "It is clear. But I'll be back to check on you."

"I'm just going to lie down for a moment," Claudia said. "Jimmie said he had monitors all over the house. He probably has a camera in this room watching us right now. I'll be fine."

She started to doze off after Kanuik left the room. When she found herself back in David's room, where Jimmie, Kanuik, Connor, and Samar were still working, she didn't know how much time had passed and didn't remember waking up or walking back down the hall. They seemed distracted as she walked in. Samar sat on David's bed, and Kanuik sat on a short wooden desk chair while Jimmie and Connor continued working with the computers and monitors.

An alarm went off that got everyone's attention.

"What are you doing?" Jimmie said. "Don't touch anything." He glanced at Kanuik and then Samar, who was the closest to the conductors.

"I didn't touch anything this time either," Samar said. "It just came on by itself."

"Why would it do that?" Jimmie said. He looked down at the monitors. "That's strange. I'm getting readings I've never seen before. There is an energy source, faint but close by. The reading looks like an EEG."

"Jimmie, our language please," Kanuik said.

"Electroencephalogram," Jimmie said.

Kanuik shook his head.

"It's a scan of the electronic neurons of the brain. The energy is in two locations and is emanating from there." He pointed to the coils, where a small round ball of blue light was visible.

"Can you locate where it is going?" Connor asked.

"It's going down the hall where Claudia went." Jimmie pointed out the door.

Kanuik jumped to his feet, and Samar joined him as they ran past Claudia to the back bedroom.

"Stay away from the coils," Jimmie said. "They are going hot for some reason. Connor, get ready to shut them down."

Claudia moved closer to the conductors that Jimmie had also referred to as coils. She could see the blue light, very faded but there in the middle. Jimmie didn't scold her, so she went closer. She felt a breeze touch her cheek and reached out with her left hand to feel the air passing between the two conduits.

"We couldn't wake her," Kanuik said as he entered the room.

Claudia turned and was shocked to see Kanuik holding her body in his arms.

He laid her body down on the bed. "She still has a pulse but seems to be in a deep sleep."

"What do you suggest we do?" Jimmie said.

"I don't know. She's the doctor, so I would normally ask her," Kanuik replied.

"You don't suppose that there's something trying to reach her from the other side?" Samar said.

"I knew there was a reason we brought you along," Jimmie said. "It could be. This is why we came here—because the portal was already open here once. The veil between worlds is very thin. That could be why I'm getting readings."

"Claudia told me about the dream with David," Kanuik said, "how David told her Frank was trying to reach her. Do you think he is trying to tell her something?"

"Who knows what is possible at this point?" Jimmie said. "We are in uncharted territory. We need to be careful."

Claudia called to Jimmie and Kanuik, but they didn't hear her. The breeze coming from the other side of the two conductors brushed against her face, and she stepped back in front where she could see the light and reached out her hand. She touched the light and felt a quick, moving sensation. All was bright for a moment, and Claudia reasoned with herself, *Something went wrong, and I've passed. I'm in the tunnel everyone talks about.* But the light faded, and then all became dark.

She stepped forward and noticed that she was on a path, in a garden filled with trees and flowers. There was light enough for her to make out her surroundings, but she could see no colors, just black and white and grays. Water ran in the background, a stream of some sort, and as she got closer to one of the trees, she could see fruit hanging from the branches. She took a few steps and noticed that there was an opening in the trees and, beyond that, a clearing. She headed past the trees, and as she emerged into the clearing, she found herself on a slight downward slope and facing a ring of rocks that bordered the area from which she had come. Down the path in front of her, there was someone, a man from what she could tell from the person's profile, sitting on one of the rocks, with his back turned. Claudia headed toward the man. The closer she got, the harder it became for her to move forward, until she came to a stop, just out of reach of the man.

"Where am I?" she said.

"I thought you were someone else, but that voice is not the same," the man said without turning to face her.

Claudia thought she knew the voice. "Frank?"

"Yes, it's me, Claudia." He turned to face her.

"How? Where are we?"

"I don't know how you are here. You must be in a dream. I've been trying to communicate with you or someone close to you to warn you and the others. But I couldn't reach anyone."

"You reached David and Samar. Samar is with us."

"Samar?" Frank asked.

"He said you told him to find me—the author. He did."

"I didn't know his name," Frank said.

"We are all back together again—Kanuik, Jimmie, and me. Jimmie has set up some equipment, and he's getting ready to send you some help, maybe even get you out of this place."

"You must warn them not to come," Frank said. "You must tell them it's dangerous. There are more shadows than I ever knew. If they somehow get through to your world, all may be lost. Go back, Claudia—wake while there's still time."

"Not without you," Claudia said. She managed to reach forward and touch his shoulder, and he flinched at the physical contact.

"How did you do that?" he said. "This is only a dream." He reached out to her and tried to grasp her.

She tried to embrace him, but as soon as they made contact, all went blank.

Claudia woke from her position on the bed with such a start that both Kanuik and Jimmie jumped.

"Cancel the 911 call, Connor," Jimmie said. He braced Claudia as she sat up and moved to the edge of the bed. "What happened?" Jimmie asked.

"I saw Frank," Claudia said. She stood and balanced herself with Jimmie's help. She looked toward the light that she could still see between the two conduits.

"I think it's getting bigger," Kanuik said.

"Yes, it is definite that something is going on," Samar said. "I think you should shut down your equipment before something else happens."

"Just a minute," Jimmie said. "Are you okay?" He took a flashlight and shined it in Claudia's eyes.

Claudia waved Jimmie's hand down and nodded. "I'm fine, but I left him there."

"Definitely bigger," Kanuik said. "And I sense something on the other side now." He shifted his position to stand in front of the opening.

"Okay then," Jimmie said, stepping over to the monitors. "These are the best results I've had without trying myself. This house is a hot spot. But we may need to shut this thing down before we have a breach and something comes through."

While they spoke, Claudia made her move.

"Wait!" Samar cried out.

But she moved from the side of the bed to the portal in a swift walk and went directly into it.

Kanuik reached out for her and grabbed her hand as the rest of her body disappeared into the clear space between the coils. "Help me!" Kanuik pleaded as he started sliding into the portal.

Claudia felt cold, and a sensation of pain went through her body. She shivered and drew her arms inward and legs upward. She was lying down and couldn't see where she was, but she knew she was no longer in David's room. She closed her eyes and opened them again. Before her were long strands of grass, not green but gray. She was lying in a field. A warm hand touched her back, and another went under her shoulder.

The cold feeling overwhelmed her, and she shivered uncontrollably. Her heartbeat slowed, and she could feel life going out of her body. Then something pulled her from the ground right before she lost consciousness.

When she woke, she was in a different place and lay on long, soft grass with a warm light around her. Her vision was out of focus, and the sky above her was dark. She could make out a tree, although the trunk and leaves were gray. She couldn't tell where the warm light was coming from as she tried to sit up. "Where am I?" she whispered.

"Still stubborn, I see. Claudia, it's me." Frank turned her around so that she could see his face.

"Frank?" She took his hand as he helped her to her feet. "Where are we? Why is it so dark here?"

"I've brought you to a safe place," Frank said. "We are in their world now, the world of shadows. It's always twilight here."

"What is this place?"

Frank raised his hand to his chin. "I've thought about that many times, and I've come to the conclusion that this is the Garden of Eden, the place where humankind began," Frank said. "Sometime after humankind lost its grace in the battle between good and evil, the garden was moved."

"Moved how? Where?"

"Somewhere different where we can't see."

"You mean like those other dimensions that Jimmie speaks about?"

"Now I can tell you've been talking with him. I don't know that we can understand the infinite power behind all of this," Frank said. "Let me show you."

Frank led Claudia along a path to a stream and a waterfall. There were trees full of fruit, grass, and flowers all about. Every so often, when the light hit the plants at a certain angle, she could see the beautiful colors, but most of the time, everything was in the shade and appeared gray.

"I thought the Garden of Eden was supposed to be a paradise," Claudia said. "Maybe if the lighting were right, this would be beautiful beyond comparison. But you said we were in the world of the shadows. I don't understand."

Frank turned from the flowing water and looked toward the edge of the trees. "We are safe here, in the garden. But out there beyond, there is darkness. That is where they roam, and if you go there, they attack. It's also out there in that darkness where they somehow open portals to our world."

Claudia turned to see where the light was coming from and put her hand up in front of her eyes. It was too bright for her to keep looking.

"I don't know the source of the light," Frank said. "I can only assume. As long as we stay in the light, we are safe."

"These trees," she said, pointing, "they're fruit trees." She stepped toward one of them.

Frank put his arm out in front of her. "If this is the place I think it is, then you cannot eat the fruit. It's forbidden … 'but from the tree of the knowledge of good and evil, you shall not eat, for in the day that you eat from it you will surely die,' Genesis 2:17."

"Yes, of course," Claudia said. "I don't want to have to change my name to Eve. What have you been eating? How have you survived here?"

"It's my faith, Claudia. How much do you remember from your Sunday school classes? Man cannot live on bread alone. I have no hunger here because I am living off my faith."

"How is that possible?"

"How is any of this possible?" Frank said, gesturing to their surroundings. "How are you here talking to me but not really here? Why is it that you cannot believe with all that you've seen? The real question is how have you come here?"

"Jimmie and Connor were trying to open a portal so that we could find you."

"Connor?" Frank questioned.

"Yes," Claudia said. "After you helped him, he came to Chicago searching for us and found Mark and then Jimmie. He joined the fight against the shadows."

"It's not safe here," Frank said. "We have to get you back."

"Take me back to the place where you found me," Claudia said.

"I guess we can try to go back there, but we have to be careful and stay in the light."

"Let's go then." Claudia grabbed his hand and started back to where she remembered being.

Frank pleaded for caution, but Claudia knew that time was probably short and that Jimmie and the others might leave the house. She didn't want to ask Frank what would happen to her if she stepped out of the light, and she started to worry when the shard of light they were following grew thinner.

"What are you thinking?" Frank said, putting his hand on her shoulder.

She stopped and turned around.

"If you go into the darkness, the shadows will attack."

"Jimmie has a machine on the other side; that's how I came through. There's got to be a path back the way I came. That's what he was experimenting with. He has already perfected sending something through; he has been working on bringing people back. From the other side, the portal looked like a blue orb of light. If only we could see it."

"Okay, it sounds like the same thing that appears when the shadows are opening a doorway to the other side," Frank said. "I just don't know how they do it."

"It started in David's room."

"David's room?"

"Yes, Jimmie was doing the experiment in David Jenson's room. He thought it would be the best place since there was once a confirmed portal there. When the anomaly started, it looked like a blue bubble of liquid—you know, like when a bubble floats and reflects the images around it abnormally. How do you get through to people in their dreams?"

Frank's bottom lip disappeared, and she could tell he was considering his answer. "I get a feeling, and then a path of light appears, and I follow it. Sometimes I can hear the voice of someone calling out for help."

"That might not do us any good then," Claudia said, and she started down the path again, which was no longer soft grass, but hard, cracked dirt and rock.

When Frank didn't follow right away, she turned to beckon him forward. "Please, we've got to try." As she turned again to continue, she accidentally stepped off the path with her right leg. She felt a sharp pain in her leg as claws ripped her flesh while something else grabbed at her and pulled. She resisted, but the force was overwhelming.

Frank jumped in front of her, and swinging the wooden cane that Adnan had given him, he ordered the creatures back. He pulled Claudia into the safety of the light. Both of them fell and hit the hard ground. Claudia was breathing heavily, as was Frank. She reached down, felt the wounds, and saw rips in her pants and blood pouring from her thigh. There were gashes below her knee too.

"We need to get you to the water," Frank said. "It has the power to heal."

"What was that?" she asked.

"That was the shadows," he said. "Here they do more than attack the mind."

She stood and put her hand on Frank's face. "I can't believe you've survived in here all of this time." She stroked his cheek and ran her hand along his jaw.

He reached up and pulled her hand away from his face. "You shouldn't have come here; this place is not safe for you."

Claudia smiled, causing Frank's expression to change to one of confusion. She had spotted something while they were talking—the anomaly she was seeking. She grabbed Frank's hand and pulled him along, thrusting herself into the portal. She felt another hand reaching into the space and a voice calling to her; it was Kanuik. She grasped his hand as tight as she could and held onto Frank with the other.

"Pull! Pull!" Kanuik shouted. He, Samar, and Jimmie lined up in a chain, pulling until Claudia emerged back into David's bedroom. With the force of their pull, Claudia tumbled forward through the portal and fell to the floor, with Frank following and falling behind her.

"Close it! Connor, close it now!" Jimmie called out. A flash of sparks flew from the conduits lighting up the room. The power in the house went out.

"Is everybody okay?" Jimmie said. He flashed a small penlight around the room.

Claudia was trying to get herself upright when she heard Jimmie's voice. She turned to look behind her. "Frank!" she shouted, but the priest's eyes remained closed.

The lights flickered and came back on.

Frank's eyes opened and focused on Samar. "You," he said before his eyes rolled back and he passed out.

Claudia went to his side and felt his neck for a pulse. "He's ice-cold—get him a blanket," she said.

"Are you okay?" Samar asked Claudia as he, Jimmie, and Kanuik grabbed Frank, helped him off the floor, and laid him on the bed.

"Please don't do anything like that ever again," Kanuik scolded her.

Claudia smiled. "Sorry, but I felt him pulling on me."

Kanuik turned suddenly and looked at the portal. "Something has followed you." He reached into his vest, took out a small black leather bag, and started walking toward the coils.

"Uh, Jimmie, I think something's wrong," Connor said in a panicked voice from the other side of the room.

Jimmie ran across to his electronic monitors. "I told you to shut it down!"

"I did," Connor said. "It's not our instruments keeping it open."

Claudia turned to follow the others' gaze. There, in the place where she and Frank had just emerged, she spotted the black liquid form breaching the barrier.

"You worry about him," Kanuik said to Claudia. "I'll take care of this." He stood directly in front of the portal, reached into the bag, and pulled out several round black balls, which he flung into a semicircle before the opening. They lit on fire as they hit the wood floor. "I've contained it, Jimmie. Now is there a way to turn this thing off?"

"It is off from our side," Jimmie said, "but I've always known this was a two-way street." Jimmie rushed over to what looked like a large spotlight on a tripod and pointed it toward the thing. "I hope this hurts," he said and flicked it on. The power in the room flickered as a large pulse of blue light flashed from the object and surged forth like a lightning bolt. It struck the shadow, which pulsed violently when hit but then went almost still.

Kanuik chanted and moved forward toward the shadow. Claudia could see that it wasn't moving much after the blast. She hovered over Frank, considering that this thing that had followed them might be after him.

"No, stay back," Jimmie said, motioning to Kanuik. "This thing is not precise."

Kanuik moved to the side as Jimmie flipped the switch again, and this time the power shorted out as a large flash emanated from the device and struck the shadow again. It was enough to cause the thing to retreat, and in the light provided by Kanuik's holy fire, Claudia watched the shadow disappear and the portal close.

"Quick," Jimmie said, throwing his jacket over the balls of holy fire, "help me put these things out before we start the house on fire." He handed Claudia his flashlight as he and Connor stomped out the flames.

"You needn't worry," Kanuik said as he held one of the round balls that had ignited. "The base is treated with mineral oil that has a flash point of some 335 degrees." He winked at Jimmie as he said this. "The oil emerges when the ball hits the ground. It prevents what it lands on from catching fire. You see, we also have technology where I come from."

The group all hovered around the bed where Frank lay.

"We need to get him to a hospital," Claudia said. She pulled a pillowcase off the bed and used it to wrap the wound on her thigh.

"And how do you suggest we explain who he is and what has happened without all of us getting arrested?" Jimmie asked.

"We need to do a cleansing ritual," Kanuik said. "Those creatures followed him out; we need to make sure one of them isn't attached to him like Adnan."

"We could go to my house," Claudia said.

"Do you have the necessary items?" Kanuik asked.

"No."

"Father Uwriyer lives in Frank's old apartment," Jimmie said. "How about taking him there?"

"Yes," Kanuik agreed. "He will probably have all the salts and cleansing materials we need for the ritual."

Kanuik grabbed Frank under the arms while Samar and Jimmie each grabbed one of his legs, and the three hauled him down the steps and out the front door.

"Geez, it's almost nine. At least it's dark out now. Makes it less likely that somebody will drive by and see us," Jimmie said as they crossed the yard to the car. They loaded Frank into the back seat of the car with Kanuik. Jimmie looked around him. "We aren't all going to fit in there." He handed the keys to Claudia. "Connor and I will stay here. If you can't make it back in a few hours, we'll call a cab and meet you later."

Claudia hurried to the driver's seat while Samar went to the passenger's side. Her hands were shaking, and she had trouble getting the key into the ignition.

Samar reached over and touched her on the hand. "Are you okay to drive?"

Claudia took a deep breath and looked in the rearview mirror. As she adjusted the mirror, Kanuik's black eyes met hers, and he nodded.

"I'm fine," she said. The tires squealed as she pulled out of the driveway and headed toward Frank's old apartment. "You should have a lot in common with the man we are about to see, Samar," Claudia said.

"Is he from India?" Samar asked.

"No, Israel. But he's a history buff and keeps tabs on all the latest in the world of archeology."

"You don't think he's going to mind us coming over at this time of night?"

"No," Claudia said. "He was in the room when Frank vanished. I'm sure he'll want to know that we've managed to bring him back."

Traffic was light since it was later in the evening, and they soon reached the apartment.

"Come on," said Claudia. "It's on the second floor."

The group entered the two-story building with Samar and Kanuik carrying Frank, one of them under each of his shoulders.

Claudia went to the elevator and pressed the button. "Good thing no one is around," she said. "I think that's why he liked it here so much."

Once on the second floor, she knocked on the priest's door. As soon as it opened, Claudia pushed through, and Father Uwriyer moved back to let Kanuik and Samar in with Frank.

"Father Uwriyer, we need your help," Claudia said.

He was a fit man with intense brown eyes and a dark face framed by black hair, complete with a beard and mustache. He was about five nine, compared to Claudia's five eleven, and his eyes were wide and mouth open as the group entered. He closed the door behind them.

"Take him to the bathroom. It's in there," Claudia said, pointing. "Mark, we are going to need some towels."

Father Uwriyer nodded but didn't move right away.

"Do you remember me and Kanuik?" Claudia asked.

"Yes, Claudia, of course I do," Father Uwriyer said. "That was Frank, but how … where?"

"I'll explain everything in a moment. We need to get him in the bath, and we need some of the sea salts."

Familiar with the apartment because she had visited it when Frank lived there, Claudia went into the apartment's single bedroom, which led to the only bathroom. Kanuik had already started the water, and she put her hand down to check the temperature and adjusted the faucets.

"Here are the salts," Mark said. "What happened to him?"

"She brought him back," Kanuik said.

"How is that possible?" Mark asked. "How could he have survived there for three years?" His hands went to his head.

"Get him undressed," Claudia said.

Kanuik took a pipe out of his pocket along with some tobacco. He packed the pipe, lit it, took a puff, and breathed out the smoke, directing it toward Frank.

"This is a no-smoking building," Mark said.

"I wouldn't need to do this if you would have a cat," Kanuik protested. "But I sense no feline presence. Didn't your time with us teach you anything?" he scolded.

Mark and Kanuik started undressing Frank. When they got down to his underwear, they stopped and looked at Claudia.

Just then, Frank's eyes opened, and he blinked multiple times, trying to focus. "Hello, Mark. Hello, Kanuik. Claudia?"

"Frank?" Claudia said. She put her hand out to his cheek.

Frank struggled to stand, with Mark and Kanuik bracing him on either side.

"We have you—just relax," said Mark.

"What are you doing?" Frank asked.

"Welcome back," Kanuik said. "We need to get your senses back and cleanse you."

"All right," Claudia said, turning around. "Finish undressing him, and then give him a rag or something to cover up with and get him into the tub. Then all of you clear out. I am the only clinical doctor here, and he's a priest, so I don't want to hear any snickering."

Once the men had Frank settled in the tub, they stood. "We will be in the other room," Kanuik said. He looked around the room and down to Claudia, who was now stooped over the tub. "There is no presence of evil that I can detect. What you did was brave but rash. Next time, please tell me before you do something like that."

Claudia nodded and turned the water off as the rest of the group left the room. Kanuik closed the door.

"Do you know where you are?" Claudia asked.

"My apartment," Frank said. "What did you do that made Kanuik so upset?"

"I crossed to the world of the shadows and pulled you back with me."

"Yes," Frank said, putting his left hand to his forehead. "I remember that now. I take it we made it out."

Claudia didn't want to say anything. She was happy that Frank was here now, but a part of her wanted to scold him for what he had done in the first place.

"Kanuik was right to be upset with you—you took a big risk," Frank said.

She struggled to maintain her composure. She wanted to yell, *Me? What did you think you were doing in the first place, leaving all of us and going off by yourself?* But she simply took a deep breath. "Just relax for a moment," Claudia said. She placed her fingers on his neck again to take his pulse.

Frank reached up and grabbed her hand. "I'm fine, really."

"I'll be the judge of that," Claudia said firmly. "Just stay here for a moment until you warm up. I'm going to get you something to drink."

She stood and left the bathroom but halted in the bedroom. She could hear the rest of the group talking in the living room about what had just happened. She took a moment to recover her own thoughts. The only man she'd ever really been close to was her father, until Frank. Their close friendship and mutual chemistry, although brief, had been compounded by the intensity of the situation they were in—and then cut short by a decision he had made without telling her, a decision that had left him trapped in the world of the shadows. *Let's get him well and make sure he's okay, and then he's got some explaining to do*, she said to herself.

Claudia entered the living room to find that Jimmie had made it to the apartment.

"Well?" Jimmie's voice cracked as he spoke.

"He's conscious, and he knows us and where he is. That's a good sign. How did you get here?" She walked past Jimmie to the kitchen to get Frank something to drink.

"I took a cab," Jimmie said. "Connor stayed to clean up and make sure none of the neighbors called the police. I think he's had enough excitement for the night. Or maybe it's me who's had enough excitement with him around. Young people just make everything more intense. No offense, Father Uwriyer."

"Call me Mark. What is it you are looking for, Claudia?"

"I'm sorry," Claudia said. "Last time I was here, it was Frank's apartment. I guess I shouldn't impose. I'm looking for some hot tea for Frank."

"I'll make some," Mark said, "as long as you tell me what is going on."

"I don't know where to start," Claudia said. "It's all happened so fast."

"I didn't know you were all back together," Mark said.

"We just got back together yesterday," Claudia said. She leaned against the counter and rubbed her eyes.

"I'll make you some tea as well," Mark said. "Anyone else need anything?"

No one responded.

"Please, feel free to sit and relax."

Samar sat down on the couch, and Kanuik sat in one of two chairs across from him. A small bar will three chairs divided the kitchen from the living room, but other than a bookcase and a small table, the apartment had no other furnishings, not even a television.

Samar picked up a book from the coffee table. "*Savior*," he said, reading the title aloud. He turned it over. "The battle for the soul of humanity. Is this book any good?"

"Excellent," Mark called from the kitchen. A moment later, he walked in with a tray of cheese and crackers and set it on the coffee table. "I actually inherited that book from Frank. It was here in the apartment when I took over his parish and moved in."

"Maybe you should have been there with us tonight," Samar said as Mark headed back to the kitchen. "Speaking of that, I better call Ira before she gets too worried." He stood, reached in his pocket, and took out his cell phone, but it was completely dead. He shook it.

"That's not a good sign," Jimmie said, taking out his cell phone and shaking his head. "Every time we are around those things, a lot of electronic stuff shorts out. That's what gave me the theory that they were a form of energy in the first place."

Mark returned with two cups of tea and handed one to Claudia. She checked her phone as she sipped the tea. It was dead.

"I have a landline right over here in the kitchen," Mark said. "Here, I'll take this to Frank and make sure he has some towels," he said as headed to the bedroom with the second cup of tea.

Claudia sat down on one of the chairs at the bar. Samar called Ira and let her know they'd be home late. Then he returned to the living room and took a seat on the couch.

"Frank appears fine," Mark said, coming back into the room. "I'm going to have to call Bishop Tafoya."

"Allow me," Jimmie said, and he walked to the phone in the kitchen.

No one spoke while Jimmie was on the phone.

"Bishop Tafoya, this is Professor Barnes. You know how we had talked about trying some different experiments ... Oh, they succeeded. I would prefer to show you the results. Can you come to Father Uwriyer's apartment? I'll explain everything when you get here ... Yes, I know it's late. But you are really going to want to see this."

Jimmie hung up and returned to the couch, where he dug his hand into the tray of food. "That's the second time I've fought those things. It sure does give you an appetite."

"Tell me, Professor Barnes," Samar said. "How is it you got involved with this group?"

"Well, you see, I was a ghost hunter—you know, going out to find out the truth about the paranormal. Why, you might ask? In case you haven't noticed, I'm not the most athletic guy here."

Kanuik and Claudia chuckled.

"I read a lot growing up and happened upon this series called *The Questors' Adventures*, which was just fun and full of exciting events that inspired me. So I took after the main character in the series and started studying the paranormal. One night my buddies and I were out doing paranormal research and happened upon Adnan and Kanuik. They recruited me so that they would have some technology on their side.

The church was looking for a scientific perspective and decided it was a good idea to keep us paired together."

"Tell him what happened to your ghost hunter friends," Kanuik said. "That is a good story."

Jimmie was about to take a bite of a cracker and cheese but held off, smiling. "Well, we tried to bring them in on one of our missions, but they got too flustered and left. I haven't spoken to either one of them since."

"And you"—Samar looked to Kanuik—"how did you meet my father?"

"For hundreds of years, there has been an alliance of hunters that fight the shadows, all holy men from different religions. It is the one common theme of all religions, to fight evil. If we had not forgotten this, we would not have the wars we have. I was on a team with your father in Somalia. A warlord there was under the influence of a shadow and was killing and hurting many innocent people. Adnan tried something new; he had the ability to see the opening and the shadows. He tried to go to where they came from. This only drew more of them. He tempted one of the things to get closer, and it did. In the battle with the shadow, your father ended up killing the warlord, but the moment he did, a little part of him gave in to that evil, and it consumed him. He managed to bury it down within him, but the creature was always there, with him. It was through this relationship that he was able to seek out other shadows and was always one step ahead of them—until the end."

"In all the years we spent together," Claudia said, "I never knew this was what drove him. He handled it so well."

Kanuik reached down, took a cracker, and popped it into his mouth. After he chewed for a moment, he spoke again. "I'm sorry I never told you two this about Adnan. Frank knew about the condition because Adnan revealed it to him. He did so to convince Frank that he had to take his place and lead us."

"Well," Jimmie said, "any more revelations or secrets that we should know about?"

A knock came from the front door, and Mark went to open it. He returned to the living room with the bishop and introduced Bishop Anthony Tafoya to Samar.

"Well, I see you've got the whole group back together," Bishop Tafoya said. He removed his hat and handed it to Mark, revealing his bald head. He was a short and stocky, but not fat, man about sixty years of age. "Now why are you all here? What's all of this about?"

As if cued, Frank entered the room in a bathrobe. Bishop Tafoya went pale and stumbled to his right; only with the help of Mark did he remain standing. The silence was so great that the next sound that pierced the air was the crunching sound of Kanuik eating crackers. Everyone turned to look at him.

"What? These are good crackers," Kanuik said.

Frank didn't know what to say exactly when he met the eyes of the bishop. He was still trying to gain all of his senses, and all of the excitement had overwhelmed him. Claudia walked over to him and led him to the couch, where he sat down with his back facing the door. Bishop Tafoya came around to the front of the couch and looked at him. Mark moved some kitchen table chairs into the room, and the entire group sat in a circle around the coffee table in Mark's apartment.

"Yes, Bishop Tafoya," Kanuik said, "that is Father Frank Keller. Your warrior that you were in disbelief of has come back."

"How is this possible?" Bishop Tafoya said. He reached out, grasped Frank's hand, and shook it. "Welcome back."

"She did it," Jimmie said, pointing to Claudia. "Well, we all did it. We were experimenting with the equipment and had some anomalies. Claudia jumped into the portal, and when we pulled her out, he was with her."

"So it is possible to retrieve someone," Bishop Tafoya said.

"Speaking of that"—Jimmie shook his right index finger and pointed to Claudia—"exactly how did you know how to get back?"

"We," Claudia said, gesturing back and forth between her and Frank, "traced the path to where I had entered. Since you hadn't closed the portal on your side, we could still see the blue light. It looks like a ball of liquid light. I had spotted the same thing when I reached in from our side, so I reached in again from the other side, and Kanuik grabbed my hand and pulled us through. You know the rest."

Jimmie stood and paced with his hands on the sides of his head. "This ... this is just incredible. Balls of light ..." He stopped pacing and looked at Claudia. "All of this time in the paranormal research, we've been seeing balls of light transferring around. We always knew there was something to it. Now I know why most ghost hauntings are bad—because it's not really ghosts; it's these damn evil shadow things." Jimmie winced. "Sorry for the language there." He noticed his watch and shook it. "Man, they got not only my cell phone but my watch too." He looked at the clock on the wall. "It's getting late, and I have a lecture tomorrow."

"Yes," Kanuik said. "It is late, and we should all get some rest. If Samar would like to stay at the Kozy, he can sleep in Adnan's old room."

"That won't be necessary," Claudia said. "I've already got a guest room set up for him and his fiancée."

"Fiancée?" Kanuik said. "You must bring her by tomorrow so we can meet her." Kanuik stood. "May I suggest we adjourn until tomorrow and meet for lunch at the Kozy?"

Everyone agreed.

"We will see you tomorrow, Father Frank," Kanuik said. "Jimmie, can you drive us?"

Frank stood and shook hands with everyone but Claudia, who embraced him tightly as Kanuik, Jimmie, and Samar stepped out of the apartment.

"Don't go anywhere," Claudia said before leaving.

Frank closed the door behind her and took a seat across from Bishop Tafoya.

"I'll make some coffee," Mark said and headed to the kitchen.

"Decaf, please," Bishop Tafoya said.

"Three years ago," said Bishop Tafoya, "I didn't quite know what to believe when they told me the story of what had happened—that you went through the portal like Adnan had planned. It seemed unreal. At first, we thought you were dead."

"How did you know I wasn't?" Frank said.

"People testified," Bishop Tafoya said. "From all over the world, they came forward speaking about a man who had appeared to them in their dreams and helped. The man matched your profile, Frank. We had faith."

Frank nodded as Bishop Tafoya reached out and took his hand.

"Here you go," Mark said, handing mugs of coffee to both Bishop Tafoya and Frank. He sat down on the couch. "It's decaf."

"God has blessed you," said the bishop. "I always knew it, from the day I recruited you into this battle. It is late, and we will have more discussion about this tomorrow. But before I go, tell me—where were you?"

Frank glanced at the bishop and at Mark. He thought for a minute about how he could describe what he had seen. "It's everything we studied, but so real. I mean, all the legends about demons and about true evil—it's something I never prepared to witness. I was there in the place where good and evil exist together as opposing forces. It's hard to describe."

"I suppose it would be," Bishop Tafoya said.

"I still remember the day you brought me into your office and told me that the Jenson family had been attacked by evil forces and that evil was real, not just in people's actions, but a real energy—physical manifestations."

"Yes, that was quite a traumatic moment for us both," Bishop Tafoya said. "Frank," he said, leaning in and grabbing the priest's hand, "there are many who say we are losing the battle, and I can't say I disagree, not anymore. Can these things be stopped?"

"For the most part, I have been able to stop the shadows by cutting off the source of their existence in our world, the hosts. I can interact with them through dreams and convince them that they are in control. This is usually how I've fought these things. However, I recently interacted with a shadow who attacked me more viciously than any of them ever had. But in that attack, I found a new way to fight. I managed to grab onto it and hold it, as Adnan used to do. I dragged it into the light, and the closer I got to the source, the weaker it seemed to get, until it finally dissipated. It may have ceased to exist at that point. I can't tell. The place I've been to is so undefined compared to anything you know here."

"You said there was light where you were at?"

"I can only suppose that it may be divine light or from a divine source. It does not come from the sky, but from a direction I cannot go because the light is too blinding. When I am in the garden, the shadows are not present."

"A garden?" Mark gasped. "Sorry."

"It's okay, Mark," Frank said. "It was a beautiful garden of trees and lush green plants and flowers bathed in an unending light. Only outward and away from this light are the shadows present. I keep a post on the outskirts of the garden where there is a semicircle of rocks. When I sit and listen, I can hear those who need help calling me while in what appears to be an almost hypnotic state where they have lost sense or connection to reality. That's when the shadows influence."

"This is amazing. How can we stop these things from influencing others?"

"I'm not sure I know, but when we were at David's house before Adnan was killed, these things had the ability to warp reality and make us see things that were not there. They feed on our insecurities, our doubts. This is the premise I've used to combat them. I've tried to inspire confidence in those they attack and appeal to the compassion inside of them. Doing this, I've been able to deflect the shadows. Once the host rejects them, they don't seem to have much power and leave."

"Then our plan to send soldiers through the portal—originally to help you—is a correct way to combat them," Bishop Tafoya said.

"It might be," Frank said. "But I would not put others through what I have been through, the torment and loneliness of the place. When I held the creature that I dragged into the light, it seemed to fight back by placing thoughts into my head. It read my thoughts and used them. When I pushed back, I could feel its thoughts and learned of the plan, a vicious plan. They don't talk like we do, and they don't communicate like we do. They are not human to the touch; it's like touching electricity that bites and tears. They have a shared conscience at some level, and it was there I could hear the plan, not with my ears but through my thoughts. They are waiting for you to open the portal wider so they can attack. They see and sense patterns in behavior, and this serves them like a premonition. They know you are planning something."

"We've prepared the soldiers as best we can," Bishop Tafoya said.

"How? With swords and weapons? The battle is in the mind and in faith. These things know of your plans and that you are coming. They even know when. If these soldiers arrive at the place I was in and get caught outside of the light, the shadows will tear them to shreds. I tell you, there are many of them, more than I could fathom."

"You mean they physically attack?"

"Yes," Frank said. "In the dark areas, they are able to inflict physical pain."

Bishop Tafoya leaned back in his seat. "But you—you don't look like you've been attacked at all."

"Evil wasn't the only thing there; there was a power of light and healing. A stream flowed, and in the water, my wounds healed. After some time, I learned how to stay away from the shadows," Frank said. "The lesson was a hard one. If you send those men in without a way to control where they are, they will be vulnerable."

"We must delay our plans then," Bishop Tafoya said, "until we are certain that we can succeed. I'll call an emergency meeting tomorrow. But I'm not sure how I'm going to introduce you. I don't know whether or not you should attend just yet."

"I need to tell them," Frank said.

"Yes, I understand," Bishop Tafoya said. "But if no one has informed you, the church declared you dead two years ago. Your memorial stone is in our own church cemetery."

Mark nodded. "Seeing you running about might be too much for many to handle. They might think you a fraud," Mark said.

"Or worse," Bishop Tafoya said. "We must be cautious. You must keep a low profile until we've had time to figure out how we are going to explain this to the church." The bishop put his hand to his mouth to cover a yawn. "It's late. I should be going." He stood and headed toward the door.

Frank watched as Mark followed the bishop to the door, saw him out, and closed the door behind him.

"You can have the bed if you want," Mark said, returning to the living room.

"The couch will be fine," Frank said. "I don't know that I can sleep anyway, with all that is going on."

"Yes," Mark said, "I have a thousand more questions, as I'm sure everyone does, but I imagine you've had enough for now. Besides, I have morning mass to do."

"Do you mind if I tag along?" Frank asked.

"I'm not sure how we can do that. We held your memorial at your church. Imagine what it would be like for you to walk in after three years' absence. By the way, you look thinner, but you don't look like you've aged at all. Anyway, you should remain here tomorrow until we figure something out."

"Three years?" Frank said. "I had no way to know exactly. What has happened in the time that I was gone?"

"Let's see," Mark said. "I continued my work in taking your place at the church. The group you were with went their separate ways. Kanuik helped on the council but for the most part has been out of state. Jimmie works with the college and the church. Your nephew Connor joined our cause and bunks with Jimmie; he's also taking classes at the college. Claudia wrote a best seller and travels a lot, so we don't see her much. Bishop Tafoya is still in charge of the diocese."

Frank sat back on the couch. He felt content with the information Mark had given him.

"One more thing I should tell you," Mark said. "Your father passed away last year. I'm deeply sorry for your loss."

Frank leaned forward and closed his eyes. "Forgive me," he said. "Mark, I had no concept of time where I was."

"I'm sure your father would understand. I did his service, and he's buried at Roselawn Cemetery."

"Thank you," Frank said. "Mark, what happened to Rosie?"

Mark looked confused and shook his head.

"My cat?"

"Oh, Claudia has kept her. As far as I know, she takes that cat everywhere. She even mentions Rosie in her book bio."

"Book bio?"

Mark disappeared into the bedroom and came back with an autographed copy of Claudia's book. He showed Frank the picture of Claudia and Rosie on the back cover. "See, she loves that cat. Well, it's late. Is there anything else I can get you before I turn in?"

"No, I know my way around," Frank said.

"Yes, I guess you would since this was once your apartment. Well, good night."

"Good night." After Mark left the room, Frank looked at the book. "*Reaching Out: Time to Make a Positive Change in the World.* Great title." He opened it and started reading. Immediately, he noticed the dedication: "To Father Frank Keller, a friend and inspiration." He continued to the first chapter. It kept his mind off listening for the voices calling out for help in the darkness. He lay back on the couch, an unfamiliar texture after the soft grass he'd grown accustomed to. "Welcome back to the world, Frank," he said to himself.

CHAPTER 7
SEVEN DAYS REMAINING

Is it knowledge that helps us find the truth or makes
us face the truth?

—LPD, *The Questors' Adventures*

T he knock on the door came early for Frank, who hadn't slept a
wink but felt fine. He laid the book he was reading on the table
and went to the door. It was Claudia and Samar.

"Here," Claudia said, handing Frank hot tea in a disposable cup.
"We thought you could use some breakfast." In her other hand she
carried a pastry box.

"Thank you and good morning," Frank said. He turned to Samar.
"I'm not sure we've been properly introduced," he said, shaking Samar's
hand.

"Yes, well, you knew my father, Adnan," Samar said.

Frank turned to Claudia. "Adnan had a son?"

"It turns out Adnan had many secrets," Claudia said as she went
over to the counter that separated the kitchen from the living room and
laid out fruit and pastries.

"Yes," Samar said. "It is quite improbable that we have all found
ourselves together in this place and are meeting as though it were meant
to be—like we should be together."

"Not so unbelievable," Frank said. "I like to think that a higher
power has given us a choice to make a difference."

This drew blank stares from Claudia and Samar, who Frank
surmised were not quite ready to hear his full belief in a divine power.
He went to the counter and looked at the food. He drank the tea
Claudia had given him but did not feel hungry. Still, he picked up some
fruit and took a few bites.

"Good morning," Mark said as he entered the living room. "I thought I heard guests—and they even brought breakfast. Thank you." He helped himself to the fruit and pastries. "I have to go to the church today, and I was afraid to leave Frank alone, but I trust you two will look after him?"

"That's why we came," Claudia said. "Right, Samar?"

Samar only nodded since his mouth was full of pastry.

"Bishop Tafoya is supposed to have a meeting today on all the things we spoke about last night," Mark said. "Frank, he may need you to testify."

"I'm not going anywhere," Frank said. He noticed that his stomach ached from the few bites he had taken, and he stopped eating.

"I'll call you later," Mark said as he headed to the door.

"We will be at the Kozy," Claudia said. "The group is meeting there for lunch." Claudia sat on one of the chairs at the counter by Frank. "How are you feeling today?"

"I didn't sleep well, but I'm fine. I am very proud of you," Frank said, pointing to Claudia's book, which still lay open on the coffee table. "I read most of it last night, and it's great."

"Thank you," Claudia said, smiling. "It was your sermon that inspired most of it."

"My sermon?"

"The last one you gave before ..." Claudia stopped and put her hand to her eye to hide the tear that had formed, but not before Frank saw.

"Thank you for taking care of Rosie," Frank said.

"You're welcome," Claudia said. "She's become my best friend. We'll have to go by the house later so you can see her."

"There's somewhere else I'd like to visit before we go to the Kozy," Frank said. "Mark told me about my father."

"Yes, I'm sorry," Claudia said. "We aren't on any schedule today and can go by the cemetery. We have plenty of time, right, Samar?"

"I go where you go today," Samar said. "I am just trying to be useful. Please let me know if I can do anything."

After they finished eating, Claudia drove them to the Roselawn Cemetery.

"You coming, Samar?" Claudia asked as she parked the car.

"I think I'll just wait in the car if you don't mind," Samar said. "Walking around in a cemetery is not what I would like to do right now. Besides, I still have my friends to talk to." He waved at the two men in the car that had followed them.

"What's that all about?" Frank asked as he and Claudia exited the car and walked toward the cemetery entrance.

"It's a long story," Claudia said. "Let's just say that Samar did something that attracted attention, and he now has some admirers. Let's just hope they don't try to find out who you are."

"Right. If the church declared me dead, that might complicate my attempt to prove my identity."

"Here, wear this," Claudia said, handing him a hat.

Frank hesitated at the gate of the cemetery across from the church where he used to minister. Claudia touched his shoulder and passed in front of him. He felt odd wearing the New York Yankees cap that she had given him, but he knew that he should try to disguise his appearance. Across the road, he could see his former church, where Father Mark Uwriyer, once his pupil, now presided as priest.

Frank followed Claudia down the aisles of tombstones and monuments. He wasn't sure how he was feeling today. The time he'd been gone didn't seem to him like three years. He didn't remember thinking about his father or his sister much. In fact, it seemed that he hadn't realized the time was passing so quickly. He had kept busy fighting the shadows, meditating and sleeping, and sitting on the rock that looked over the dark landscape, waiting for the call to help and answering it as much as he could.

He noticed that Claudia had stopped a few steps in front of him. He should have known the place she was leading him to. His mother's headstone stood right on the small, grassy hill that rose a few feet higher than the path. Frank stepped forward to look at his father's headstone; it was a dual headstone shared with his mother, only now both sides had been engraved. As he read the engraving, "Beloved Husband and

Father," something caught his eye, another headstone to the left of the plot—one that hadn't been there before: his.

"We did the best we could," Claudia said. A tear formed, and she opened her small black purse and pulled out a tissue. "Your sister helped come up with the words for the engraving, but we wouldn't let her pay for anything."

She held out her hand, and Frank took it and stood by her. She clenched down on his hand tightly for a moment and then let go. "Take as long as you like," Claudia said. "I'll be back at the car."

Frank watched her walk away and then tugged at the uncomfortable ball cap. Of course, looking down at the tombstone with his name on it made him feel even more uncomfortable, and he realized the burden his sacrifice must have placed on the others.

"I came to your funeral." The young male voice that came from behind Frank surprised him. He turned to see Connor.

"Hello, Connor," Frank said. "You've really grown since the last time I saw you. I hear you are doing great things helping Jimmie. I guess we should really talk and catch up on things." Barely sixteen when Frank had last seen him, Connor was now nineteen years old and about an inch taller than Frank, and he looked very fit. His black hair and brown eyes remained the same.

"I've been training with the soldiers going through the portal for two years now," Connor said. "Much of our regimen is fitness, both physical and mental. I suppose you were happy to have your background in sport and fitness—I mean, to stand the pressures of the place you were in."

"Yes," Frank said. "It probably helped that I was in good physical condition. Tell me, how is your mother?"

"She's fine. Better than ever since I came out here, got a job, and started going to school. She was always overworried about me."

Frank stepped closer to Connor. "She cared because she loved you."

"Don't worry," Connor said. "I understand it all now. I've been told what happened at the Jenson house with David and his family. Nobody had to tell me anything. I can see how you would have been worried about me going down the same path as him."

"David Jenson was a teenager full of doubt and insecurities," Frank said. "That opened him to the influence of the shadows. They used that influence to convince him that the only way to ease his pain was to turn into a killer, and then they turned on him to destroy his soul."

"You mean they possessed him?" Connor asked.

"I don't know if that's the correct term," Frank said. "The shadows only influence. I suppose it has something to do with free will, if you believe in that. From what I've seen, if the will is weak, the host just lets the shadows take over and doesn't really exist in the here and now, but in some alternate reality. Most of the time, the person, or host, as I describe things, doesn't even know what they are doing."

"You were worried that they would influence me, so you went to fight them?"

"Yes," Frank said. "Not just for you, but for all. Bishop Tafoya is the one who told me the truth about the shadows and that they existed. However, my mentor, Adnan, taught me how to fight them. He believed that we could cross the portal and find a way to fight the things where they came from. If we could stop them there, maybe things here would get better."

"Was he right?"

"I believe I helped people in that place while I was there," Frank said.

"I think we should go," Connor said. "The others will be waiting for us. I'm sure they will be glad to see you."

"Yes, and they will undoubtedly have a lot of questions. I'm not sure how I'm going to explain what happened."

"How would you describe your time there?"

"I've simply been in a pattern of reaction in a place where time became irrelevant," Frank said.

"Right," Connor responded. "You might want to start with something else."

Frank smiled. "I'll see what I can come up with."

Connor hitched a ride to the Kozy with Claudia, Frank, and Samar. On the way, Frank listened to Connor's story about how he had graduated high school and then moved to Chicago to help Jimmie and the cause of the church. Jimmie had let him stay in an extra bedroom and even helped him find work at the college. It made Frank feel better when Connor told him that he had seen his grandfather, Frank's father, many times before he had passed away.

"I'm glad to hear he had someone visiting him," Frank said.

"I went every week," Connor said. "Claudia joined me a few times, until she started touring."

"Do I need to go pick up Mark?" Claudia asked.

"I'm happy to say he's running youth group today," said Frank. "It's a group I started. He kept it going. He may join us later."

"What about Ira?"

"She went to visit one of her college friends who lives close by," Samar said. "You should have seen the look on the government people's faces when she left and I stayed. They didn't know who to follow."

"They picked you," Claudia said as she looked in the rearview mirror.

"What's this all about?" Frank asked. "Why are they following you?"

"The men in that black SUV are government agents, I suspect," Samar said. "I stopped an attack on the plane ride over here, but I think they fear I might be a terrorist or something."

"That makes me feel better," Frank said.

"How?"

"I'm not the only one in a complicated situation."

Samar and Claudia laughed as she parked in front of the Kozy Tavern. The group exited the car. The faded blue walls and the white paint that read "Kozy Tavern" brought back memories to Frank. He hesitated at the door as Connor held it open for him. The last time he'd visited the tavern was the night before the event that had led him to a desperate path—to cross into the world of the shadows. Now he was back and worried what further decisions lay behind those doors. Connor and Samar entered, and now Claudia held the door for him. Frank smelled the familiar odors: smoke, alcohol, and Italian cooking.

"We've all felt it," Claudia said.

"What?"

"The hesitation to go back to the past. That's what you're feeling right now, whether you know it or not. The smells, sights, and sounds of the place—they are all playing on your senses and causing memories to flood back."

"What do you suggest I do?"

"Face it and come in here with me," Claudia said. "See the others and get comfortable with everyone again. Come on. Chic always makes such good food."

Frank walked forward and stopped a few steps inside the entrance as the door closed behind him. He had to let his eyes adjust to the darker interior but soon recognized the rectangular layout of the place. Across from the front door was a hallway that led to the restrooms and the door to the basement. To the right and left of this doorway were several round tables, dinner tables big enough for a family. In the middle of the room sat two billiard tables with fancy neon lights above them. To the left of the main entrance was the bar, with leather-covered stools in front of an elegant wood-framed bar and a huge glass mirror mounted behind the bar, making the place look twice as big. At the bar, he noticed a familiar face, the bartender Chic, and he walked straight to him.

Chic shook Frank's hand earnestly and smiled. The small amount of silver hair on the sides of his head beamed in the light that shone from overhead. The unlit cigar in his mouth, always in motion, stopped as he spoke. "Good to see you! Welcome back! Let me get you something to drink. Connor, give me a hand in the kitchen."

Jimmie and Kanuik were already sitting at the familiar table where the group used to meet. Both men were facing the door, and Jimmie waved to Frank. Claudia disappeared down the hall to the women's room as Frank walked to the table and took a seat opposite Jimmie. On the back of the chair next to Kanuik, he noticed a homburg hat— Adnan's hat placed there in his memory. Frank did the sign of the cross in his memory and sat down. He looked at both men again.

"What is it?" Jimmie asked.

"Something's different," Frank said. Then he noticed what was out of place. "Kanuik, you're wearing a hat!"

"Shh," Kanuik said, lifting his finger to his lips. "It's a gift from

Claudia. Besides, this is not just any hat—it's an El Presidente Stetson."
He took the hat off for a moment and spun it around so Frank could
see. "You are wearing a hat as well," he said as he returned his own to
his head. "Why?"

"Claudia," Frank said as he reached up and touched the hat. "I've
been declared dead, and she and the bishop think it would be wise for
me to keep a low profile. Where did Samar go?"

"I think he stepped outside to call his fiancée," Jimmie said.

Looking up, Frank saw Claudia exit the small hallway where the
restrooms were located and sneak up behind Kanuik. She grabbed
the hat off his head, placed it on her own, and sat down beside him,
laughing.

"I see you are making good use of the hat," Claudia said. "I bought
that thing two years ago. I didn't know it would take us so long to get
back together."

"Yes, I owe you thanks," Kanuik said.

"Oh?" She handed the hat back to Kanuik. "I thought you said
wearing hats blocked your power."

"After all of this time," Kanuik said, holding the Stetson out in
front of him, "you have finally found the one that is in flow with my
power. I think I shall be able to wear it." He placed it on his head.

Chic and Connor approached with trays of drinks and passed them
around to everyone, even placing one in the open seat where Adnan's
hat resided. Connor took a seat at the table while Chic stood with a
drink of his own and raised it. "To old friends and grand memories."

The group toasted.

"To Adnan, a great warrior." Kanuik raised his glass again.

"I am preparing some food for all of you," Chic said. "On the
house, I insist. It's great to have all of you back in my ... well, my
home." His face brightened as he said this, and Claudia stood and
hugged him.

The heavy door of the bar opened, letting in light from outside.
The group turned to see Samar entering the place with a woman. Samar
spotted the group and headed to the table as they all stood to meet his
companion.

"This is Ira," Samar said.

After introductions were made all around, everyone sat down at the table, except for Ira, who walked around the room, looking.

"This is a unique place," Ira said.

"This is the place I was telling you about," Samar said. "This is where my father lived."

She stopped at the bar in front of Chic, who was setting up glasses at the bar. "It has an old aura about it," Ira said. She ran her hand across the copper that lined the wooden bar and then came back to the table. "I sense old thoughts and patterns here that reach out to ancient history. And that man"—she pointed to Chic—"he is all part of it."

"He's the owner," Jimmie said. "And I guess you can call him ancient."

"You still haven't learned to respect your elders," Chic said as he lightly tapped Jimmie on the back of the head.

Frank caught the glance Ira gave Jimmie and considered what she had just said about Chic. Her meaning was deeper than what Jimmie might have interpreted. After Adnan passed away, they had learned that he could have been over two hundred years old, or so it seemed. Frank didn't want to guess at Chic's age. He considered for a moment that Chic had always been part of what was going on in the group, and as a bartender, he had heard many stories in his time. Although Frank was a priest and had heard years of confessions, he figured Chic probably knew more about hidden truths than he did. Chic was more than the owner; he was the man in the background making suggestions and comments and always there to support. Frank decided he would pay more attention to Chic and not take him for granted.

"You're just in time for supper," Chic said.

"Let me help you bring the food in," Claudia said, and she and Connor went with Chic into the kitchen area.

Kanuik and Jimmie shuffled positions to make room for Samar and Ira. By chance, Samar ended up at the chair where Adnan's hat was hanging. He raised the homburg hat from the back of the chair and looked around at the group. "Is someone sitting here?"

Frank, Jimmie, and Kanuik shared glances before Kanuik said, "No, that is your seat."

Samar sat down. "What should I do with this hat?"

"It belonged to your father," Frank said. "It's yours now."

Chic and Claudia returned from the kitchen first with plates and silverware, and then Connor followed with pasta, bread, and meatballs. Once the food was laid out, they were about to pray when the door opened. It was Bishop Tafoya.

"I'll get another plate," Chic said as he went to the door. "You're just in time for dinner, Arthur." Chic turned off his sign and locked the door. He headed to the kitchen while Bishop Tafoya went to the table.

"After some discussion and phone calls today, council representatives will be coming into town for a meeting tomorrow," Bishop Tafoya said as he pulled out a chair, took off his jacket and draped it over the back of the chair, and sat down.

"Tomorrow?" Jimmie said, unable to contain the anxiety in his voice. "We are cutting it closer every day. Why meet tomorrow? Now that we have proof that someone can make it back"—he nodded toward Frank—"we should delay until I perfect the method."

"Cardinal Denaro is coming," Bishop Tafoya said. "He holds the key vote because it's his sponsorship that funds all of your tests. It will just be the members or representatives who are aware of our experiment. Kanuik, I couldn't reach anyone from your delegation on such short notice."

"I'm sure they would expect me to represent them," Kanuik said. "Chief Kwanu is the one who advised me to come here in the first place."

"Yes, we met years ago," Bishop Tafoya said. "He always knows more than he is telling. So you will represent the ten tribes, and we will have only four other delegates there. But it will be up to us to present the case to them as to whether to go forward with the experiment or delay with the new information Frank has provided."

"What information?" Jimmie fumbled a meatball he was getting ready to consume. "What are you talking about?"

"Frank didn't tell you?" Bishop Tafoya said and looked to Frank.

"I haven't had time yet," Frank said.

Jimmie held the meatball on his fork and didn't move.

"There may be another reason to delay other than perfecting your retrieval system, Jimmie. The shadows know of your plan. They know you are coming and even know when."

"Well," Jimmie said, "I always suspected those damn things were intelligent. In fact, I think they've been on the other side in their little dark world, doing stuff to make my job harder. What do you think they intend to do?"

"I don't know," Frank said. "All I know is that there are more of those things than I had ever imagined."

"Until we can assess the dangers more clearly," Bishop Tafoya said, "I think it prudent to recommend we delay."

"I know Thomas won't want that," Jimmie said.

"That's why I brought Cardinal Denaro in," Bishop Tafoya said. "Thomas reports directly to him. Now"—Tafoya looked around the table where they all sat—"we need to discuss what is happening and what we are going to say. But first, let us pray."

They all bowed their heads and prayed. Chic returned with a plate for the bishop, and everyone started eating.

"I still don't understand how these things came about," Samar said. "Sorry. I know I am new to your group."

"No," Kanuik said. "Don't apologize. We need every perspective. We've all been drawn here for a reason."

"We know the history of evil," Bishop Tafoya said. "Stories tell us that evil once walked upright. Then there was a change, possibly due to a battle between the two sides."

"That is the story of the thirteenth month that Chic told me," Samar said.

"Yes. But then there was another shift," Bishop Tafoya continued. "During the time of Christ, there was still talk of demons and exorcism. But after his time, evil was no longer represented as physical manifestations but as spiritual."

"Yes," Samar said. "That is why the development of religion shifted. The battle became spiritual instead of a conflict between men, magic, and monsters, with only a few references to such evil demons being left in the world."

Frank had drifted from the conversation after Bishop Tafoya's remarks. He was trying to remember incidents where he had interacted with the shadows. Most of the time, they had ignored him as if they didn't see him, until he entered the dark where they were positioned or interfered in what they were doing; then they attacked.

"Frank," Bishop Tafoya said, breaking his concentration. "What is it you are thinking? You have been closer to these creatures than any of us. What do you know about them?"

"What you were just saying," Frank said. "I was just wondering why it was the time of Jesus that the shift happened. Through his dying for our sins, do you suppose the door to evil, the sin of it, was locked into the place where it is now? That his sacrifice had the power to seal it there and close the portal?"

"That is a powerful observation. Locked away but not destroyed," Bishop Tafoya said. "Otherwise, the shadows wouldn't exist."

"But why do they exist?" Samar said.

"Because they are energy," Jimmie said. "Energy is never truly destroyed; it just changes forms." He raised a big forkful of pasta and shoved it in his mouth. He waved his hands up and down. "Wait, just wait. I've got it." He held his finger up until he had finished chewing. "The shadows need a host to exist. They need a battery to draw energy from. But it's not just energy; it's their nature."

"Their nature," Bishop Tafoya said. "You mean like the scorpion and the frog?"

Jimmie nodded.

"Excuse me?" Samar said.

"There's a legend," Jimmie said, "about a scorpion and a frog. The scorpion needs to cross a stream, but he can't swim. So he asks a frog to help him get across. At first, the frog says no because he's worried if he gets close, the scorpion will sting him, but the scorpion promises not to, telling the frog that if he were to sting him, then they both would die. So the frog agrees to take him across the stream. Midway across the stream, the scorpion stings the frog. As he's becoming paralyzed, the frog asks him, 'Why did you do that? Now we will both die.' The scorpion simply replies, 'Because it is my nature.'"

"You think these shadows act the way they do because it's part of their nature?" Bishop Tafoya asked.

"Evil is part of us," Kanuik said. "That is what we are taught. It would not exist if we would not let the trickster in; the deceiver feeds off our power. There is a link between worlds, a spiritual link that has always been. The portal that Frank went through made that link physical."

"Can we close this link?" Bishop Tafoya asked. "Sever it to keep the evil out?"

"Maybe it cannot be closed," Jimmie said. "Only controlled."

"Many claim there is evil in this world without what you are saying," Ira said, joining the conversation, "without attributing it to demons or spirits."

"Like what kind of evil?" Jimmie asked.

"Many perceive evil in suffering brought on by natural disasters, disease, and illness. We also hunt and kill to eat, and that inflicts suffering. Are these shadows responsible for that?" Ira asked.

Bishop Tafoya raised his hand while he finished chewing to indicate his response was coming. "With the exception of hunting, which for food may be necessary but for sport is questionable, these things you speak about are brought on by that which does not have consciousness, and therefore the intent is not necessarily evil, just transformation. Nature doesn't know that thousands of people live on the coast because they like the weather and view. A hurricane would happen whether they are there or not."

"Good point," Jimmie said. "I'm going to have to invite you on campus for a lecture."

"The shadows," Frank added, "however they were created, are the shadows of the human race, a part of us. We can deny they exist, but they do whether we want them to or not. What we can deny them is the power to live in and control this world."

Frank's statement flowed across the table as everyone ate quietly.

Claudia took out her cell phone and started typing. "I'm sorry," Claudia said. "I need to write some of this down for my new book."

"As I said, you are the one who has been the closest to these things, Father Frank," Bishop Tafoya said. "If what you believe is true, then part of our battle is convincing people to be, well, better people."

"Oh boy," Jimmie groaned. "I'd rather have a sword and fight a dragon than take on such a hopeless cause."

As Frank listened to the conversation, he thought about what he'd read from Claudia's book the night before, and he realized that she had already taken on the cause of trying to enlighten people—a greater impact overall with her book's potential to reach millions than what he had been doing.

"I must be going," Bishop Tafoya said. "But first, I need to visit the men's room, if you will excuse me."

"Wow," Chic said as he sat back from the table. "I usually stand over there at the bar and only hear so much. I thought the conversations at this table were bad when Adnan was around. You people have reached a whole new level of philosophizing. It's interesting, but that's not why you are all here."

"What do you mean?" Frank asked.

"It's clear to me that you could sit here all night discussing the origins of this and that and speculate all kinds of theories. I am not a religious man—I believe in God but don't really go to church and do all the religious stuff. Regardless, it is apparent to me that you folks here are a bunch of misfits." He pointed to Frank. "A priest who didn't start out as a priest and was led there by an unexpected event in his life. Claudia, a psychiatrist who was taught that the problems with humans can be solved by therapy and drugs but clearly has been shown there is more to this world than that. Samar, who has come across the world because he was driven here by dreams and brought Ira with him, who is more than just his fiancée but has been his spiritual partner. And Jimmie, Professor Barnes, I don't even have an explanation for your presence here. You're just like a bored kid who wanted someone to play with, and this group had something exciting going on. I won't even try to explain how Kanuik, a Native American, ended up with you all, but it must be for some higher purpose than to debate nonsense."

Everyone at the table laughed at this last comment.

"Well put," Frank said. "But if we are all a bunch of misfits who were led here to this place, it must be for some purpose."

"There." Chic pointed around the table. "That's what you should be asking. Give up trying to find out the why of how this became that and ask yourself what you are here to do."

"What would you have us do?" Jimmie said.

"You think I am not aware of what is going on?" Chic said. "This war has been going on since the beginning of time. This bar and its foundation have been in service of that battle for hundreds of years. The tavern owner has been a part of this adventure, giving advice, listening to stories, giving the warriors a safe place to regroup. The war did not end just because you lost Adnan. You must put that behind you, or all is lost. Come on, Connor, help me clear the table."

"In seven days we are taking the war to them," Jimmie said, holding up his glass. "Unless, of course, Frank thinks we should shut down the tests."

"That would be a start," Frank said. "Instead of sending others through, we should try to close the portals forever and rid our world of this energy—keep these shadows locked away." He shivered when he said this.

Claudia reached over and touched his hand. "You are cold again." She took her sweater off and put it over his shoulders.

"Always," he said. "The place I've been is uncomfortably warm all of the time."

Bishop Tafoya returned to the table and retrieved his jacket from the back of the chair. "I'll see some of you tomorrow." He headed toward the door.

"You'll excuse me," Frank said to the others, and he went after Bishop Tafoya. Before Bishop Tafoya reached the door, Frank grabbed his arm.

The bishop turned and looked at Frank. "I'm sorry," he said, "did I forget something?"

"I'm going tomorrow," Frank said. "This is too important, and what better way to get them to listen than have it come straight from the source?"

"It's risky," Bishop Tafoya said. "Apart from the fact that the church declared you dead, there are other considerations."

"What considerations?" Frank asked. "You are the one who got me into all of this in the first place. I'm here to make a difference, and they need to hear what I have to say."

"Frank," Bishop Tafoya said, lightening his tone. "Many of the representatives on the council don't have the faith that you and I have. They haven't seen these things up close. Even so, the plan we've finally decided upon is about to be executed. And here you are, returning from a place we can hardly explain, a place the evil inhabits, coming back right before the attack, to tell us not to go."

"You think the shadows let me come back purposely?" Frank said.

"I think we need to consider all possibilities," Bishop Tafoya said. "As long as you are aware of the suspicion, I would be more than happy to have you with me tomorrow. You should be prepared for them to question your motives and even your story." With that, he left the bar.

Frank glanced to the table where the others were sitting and spotted Claudia watching him. He smiled, and she returned the smile as he nodded toward the door.

"I think Frank's ready to go," Claudia said.

Chic had come back to the table and was clearing the plates. She looked down at the mess and then met Chic's eyes.

"Don't worry," Chic said. "We'll clean up." He went to take Frank's plate, which was still full.

"There's something different about him," Jimmie said. "He hasn't touched a bite since he's been back. You don't go somewhere like he did and not have any side effects, not for three years. He doesn't eat, and he's looking paler than yesterday."

"It's just going to take some time for him to adjust," Claudia said.

But she knew she was guessing. She remembered what he'd said about how he'd survived in the garden without food, just by his faith. She stepped away from the table and toward the door. Chic walked with her, and they passed Frank and Bishop Tafoya, who were still talking. They stepped outside the tavern.

"Are you in love with him?" Chic asked as the two stopped right outside the door.

"Yes, but I know it cannot be," Claudia said. "But that's not what I am thinking about."

"What then?" Chic asked.

"I don't know if you get to the movies much, but in all of them lately, they always have a group of heroes standing in a circle. Must make a good profile for the movie posters. That table in there is full of heroes the world will never know. After what he's been through, Frank deserves more."

"You're absolutely right," Chic said. "But it's not about credit or being known. If you believe in the hereafter, then you know the reward that waits for them there is much better than anything here. You must also believe that you can love Frank and it's okay. What you have is a deeper love than most, a true love if that still exists. I just don't think you can expect him to go beyond the compassionate and caring part of the love you share. You better talk to him."

"There you are," Frank said, stepping outside. "I was worried you might have left."

"No, Chic and I were just enjoying some fresh air," Claudia said.

"You want me to box up your food?" Chic asked.

"No, I'm fine," Frank said.

Samar and Ira both exited the tavern.

"Frank, it was nice seeing you," Chic said. "Samar, Ira, have a good evening."

Claudia led the way to her car, and Frank got in the front seat while Samar and Ira climbed in the back seat. She drove Frank back to Mark's apartment and walked him to the door.

"Here," Claudia said, handing Frank a bag of food from Chic.

"This is your dinner that you didn't eat. Maybe there's been too much excitement still, but try to eat something, will you?"

"Good night, Claudia," Frank said and embraced her. They lingered for a moment before he turned and went up the stairs to Mark's apartment.

CHAPTER 8
SIX DAYS REMAINING

Complicity, complacency, and apathy: as long as these exist, so will evil. We overlook the bully who is beside us and laugh along if we are not the target. We won't criticize the speeder we ride with, and we protect and justify the thief if they are friend or family. Therefore, I tell you, as long as this exists, there will be no justice, and the suffering of man brought on by man will continue.

Mark drove the parish car to St. Joseph's church, the church directly connected to Bishop Tafoya's office. The neighborhood was adjacent to Frank's own parish but was even more dilapidated. Frank noticed that more houses and businesses were boarded up and more for-sale signs were posted than three years ago.

"The economy is worse than it was before you left," Mark said. "The buildings and church itself suffer even more while the politicians get richer and crime rates go up. It's been a trend for some time now. The funny thing is, the problems don't get better no matter how much money is poured into them, but the only solution that anyone has is to say that we need more money."

Frank laughed. "That's because money has never been the problem. It's human behavior and our lack of common values."

"See," Mark said, "I always liked that about you. You know how to simplify things and call them what they are."

"How about my church? How's attendance?"

Mark grinned. "Attendance in most churches is still dropping. Faith has taken a real hit in this new age. But there is an exception— your church."

"It's yours now," Frank said.

"Well, after that powerful sermon you gave and after your funeral, you became sort of a martyr to many of the youth you helped. They've kept the family tradition alive of going to church and celebrating fellowship. I've kept your message alive. It's been a powerful combination."

"That's good to hear," Frank said. "Exactly what did the church tell people about how I, well, died?"

"We made up a grand story about your missionary work and said you died overseas. I can't remember what you contracted. But we gave you a great send-off." Mark parked the car in the back parking lot where the entrance to the office was located.

"Thank you," Frank said. "Thank you for continuing my work." Frank was starting to get out of the car when he felt a hand on his left shoulder and turned back to Mark.

"Frank, what was it like where you went?"

Frank put his hand on Mark's hand. "I felt close to God in that place," he said. "I felt like I was doing his work and the work that I was intended to do."

"Wasn't it lonely?"

"I tried not to think about that and just kept doing what I felt He was telling me to do—help others. But ..." Frank paused. "I would not send anyone else to that place. I don't believe we were meant to go there."

Frank exited the car and waited for Mark, and they walked to the stone steps that led to the entrance of the large two-story building that served as the bishop's office. On the other side of the building was a grand old church. A hallway joined the two buildings. The ancient black-and-white stone structure stood solid among the crumbling ruins of other buildings that had been devastated by the collapsing economy.

Frank remembered Mark's perspective three years earlier about the state of affairs—that things were getting worse. He had said so on the same day Bishop Tafoya revealed to Frank the existence of the shadows.

"I remember the first time we met outside of this building," Frank said.

"Well, my perspective on the world hasn't changed much," Mark said.

"Hang in there, Mark," Frank said tightening his coat about him. "You know good will triumph in the end."

"Ha, ha," Mark said. "Don't forget this." He handed Frank a Yankees ball cap. "Claudia left it with me last night."

Frank took the cap and put it on.

"It is getting colder out here every day."

Frank looked up at the sky. It was cloudy with a little bit of moisture in the air, hinting of snow. He noticed that he wasn't wearing a coat and that the temperature didn't seem to bother him as much as the day before.

"I'll go in with you just in case Madeline is there," said Mark. "I'll just pretend you are with me."

Frank pulled the cap Claudia had loaned him down low as they entered the building and walked toward the bishop's office. Madeline, Bishop Tafoya's assistant, wasn't at her desk, which was good since she might have recognized Frank.

"Do you want me to go in with you?" Mark asked.

"No," Frank said. "I've got it from here. I'll catch a ride with Jimmie after and see you back at the apartment."

Finding the door open, Frank went directly into the bishop's office, where Bishop Tafoya sat at his desk. Two wooden, felt-covered, high-backed chairs sat in front of the bishop's desk, and a pulpit with a Bible on it stood to the right, where Frank had seen the bishop stand when he was preparing a sermon. The walls were full of pictures and cards sent to Tafoya from people in his diocese.

As Frank stepped through the doorway, he recalled the time he had been summoned here before, a time that flooded back to him because it had changed his entire life and the path he was on. He didn't have time to dwell on the choice he had made before Bishop Tafoya noticed him.

"Welcome," Bishop Tafoya said, rising from his desk. He walked to Frank and shook his hand. "The others are already here and in the church. I just thought I'd give you some information before we go in. You will be meeting Cardinal Denaro; he is the highest-ranking official from our church on the council. Despite help from many other faiths and religions, he holds the purse strings to our current project and is probably the one we will need to convince the most. Father Christian Thomas is his representative on-site and has been with us for the past six months. You will recognize him by the scar on his face, across his left cheek. Kanuik is representing the ten tribes, a tribal council of Native American Indians who have joined our cause. We have a bhikku from Thailand and a monk from Tibet. These will be the ones addressing us; the rest are officials sent to collect information. Are you ready?"

Frank nodded, and Bishop Tafoya escorted him down the hall and into the church. They entered from behind the altar. The main entrance was on the opposite side and faced the parking lot for the church. Chairs were arranged by the pulpit on the heightened area above the nave, and here Kanuik and Jimmie sat with some others Frank didn't know. The rest of the attendees, about twenty people dressed in a variety of robes, suits, and headdresses, sat in the pews.

Bishop Tafoya introduced Frank to the other two people seated in the chairs, Cardinal Denaro and Father Thomas. The bishop took a seat, and Frank sat down beside him. He fidgeted in the wooden chair with its red-pillowed seat and back. All eyes were on him.

It was Cardinal Denaro who spoke first, in a deep Italian accent. "This is the man who has come back to us from the world of demons, and you have something to tell us, yes?"

"As Bishop Tafoya said, I am Father Frank Keller," Frank said. "I don't know most of you. But some time ago, I followed the idea of a great leader to go where the evil comes from and face it on its own terms. I have returned to warn you that they know you are coming. I don't know how they know, but they are planning to stop you. They even know the day."

Frank's statement set off a flurry of conversations, and Bishop Tafoya held up his hands and asked for calm. Tafoya, small, short, and bald, had not a single physical character trait that suggested authority, but he had an undeniable air of nobility about him, a humble nobility that rang with genuine sincerity for all around him. That was why he was in charge, Frank thought.

"That was privileged information," Father Thomas said, glaring at Jimmie and Tafoya. "Who told you about our plans?"

"The shadows told me," Frank said calmly. This set off another flurry of murmurs.

"You can speak to them?" Cardinal Denaro asked.

"Not exactly," Frank said. "They don't speak, but when I've come into contact with them, I have been able to see their plans and hear their thoughts. I have seen the room where you are preparing the soldiers. I have seen the way the shadows attack and the outcome. Your soldiers are not prepared for the way they attack."

"You have been able to stand up to them and make a difference," Cardinal Denaro said. "Why do you think our soldiers would fail?"

"I believe I was chosen—touched by God, if you will, not by my choice, but by His. It happened during the war when I was a soldier. That experience I had gave me an unshakable faith. I'm not sure these soldiers, despite their training, are going to have the same success."

Father Thomas whispered something to Cardinal Denaro.

"Speak your mind, Father Thomas," said Cardinal Denaro. "We are all trying to make the best decision here."

"Father Frank, forgive me," Thomas said.

"No forgiveness needed," Frank said. "I agree with the cardinal. Please, say what is on your mind."

"There are witnesses here who claim you went through this portal to the world of the shadows. No doubt, you went somewhere. The question is how you survived there in their world, among them, and how it is you have come back now just when we are so close to our mission."

Frank remembered Bishop Tafoya's same point the previous night and suddenly wished he'd spent more time thinking of a response. "It is only natural that you should have doubts," Frank said. "Although I have made a difference, the battle is changing. I noticed it before, and I see it still. Religion here in our world is failing to influence and inspire compassion, good morals, and true direction. The shadows are gaining strength. I don't know that we can win in their world when it's the complicity of evil that beckons them to ours. We should focus on shutting this path they have to us instead of opening it wider to send your soldiers through."

The room was silent, and Cardinal Denaro held his hand up to his chin as his eyes scanned the floor. His voice started soft. "In the three years that you have been gone, violence has increased on a larger scale. Terrorism against innocents has to be the highest ever. And you are right that society as a whole has become even more complacent about accepting evil; many are too busy to bother unless it directly affects them. I can only see this as a gain for evil and a loss for us. You are also right about the state of the church. We have less and less influence each year. It is perhaps the failure of modern religion to embrace one true path unifying all of humanity that has brought us to this."

"Which is why we need to go in," Thomas said. "Every day we wait is another day we lose." He looked at Frank. "What would you have us do? Give up and abandon our plan?"

"I can only tell you what I've seen," Frank said. "If you go now and the shadows are waiting for you, you could lose everything you have worked for."

"Thank you, Father Frank," Cardinal Denaro said. "We will consider your advice carefully."

Frank took the cardinal's statement as a cue for him to leave. He stood and started back to Bishop Tafoya's office to wait for Jimmie and Kanuik.

Thomas escorted Frank out, closed the door to the church behind Frank, and went back to his seat. He knew he had to focus and drive the Council of World Religions to the correct decision, which was to proceed with the plan.

"Gentlemen," Cardinal Denaro said, "we have some thinking to do."

"We are ready to go in six days," Thomas protested. "We have already tolerated multiple delays, which weaken our case every time."

"Yes, very urgent matters," Cardinal Denaro said. "We are stopping all research until further notice. You are not to attempt any interaction with the creatures known as the shadows. We have let you operate with some autonomy, but we need to stop all contact for the time being."

"Why, when we are so close to an answer?" Thomas protested.

"There may be a great danger to proceeding as planned."

"The danger has always been present. That's the very nature of what we are doing. You mean you are not going through with sending the soldiers as planned?"

"Not at this time."

"I cannot believe this," Thomas said. "Surely, this source of information must be investigated. How can you be sure the shadows didn't let him return so that he could give this false testimony just in time to delay us? How do we know he's not under their control?"

Bishop Tafoya stood from his chair. "It's Father Keller—Father Frank Keller has come back to us," he said. "It's him. I knew him, and it's him. If he thinks it is dangerous for us to proceed, then I advise caution."

"Caution? We've delayed long enough," Thomas said.

"If we become rash now, we could jeopardize everything," Bishop Tafoya said.

"What Father Keller was doing seemed to be working," said one of the council members. "We've heard the testimonies from all over the world. Sending more through to do what he was doing has got to work."

"I have no doubt it was working," Thomas said, "which is why we must send more soldiers through to do battle. We are close to figuring out how to open the portal. We have the subjects to do it, and Professor Barnes thinks he can expand it enough to get the soldiers through the portal."

"Have we had any more drop out?" Bishop Tafoya asked.

"No, we are holding at about four hundred here and another five hundred on call. We will bus them in once the plan is executed."

"So we are on schedule?" Cardinal Denaro asked.

"Yes, we will be ready in six days, but now I'm wondering if we should ..."

"Yes," Cardinal Denaro said, "is there something we should be doing that we are not, an issue we should be addressing that we are not? Speak freely. That is the purpose of this meeting."

"I am concerned about Professor Barnes and his connection with Father Frank, but no more than I am concerned about members of this church council," Thomas said. "We cannot afford to delay our efforts."

"Concerned about me?" Jimmie protested. "What have I done?"

"Father Frank could be using your relationship to undermine the project," Thomas said.

"Please explain," Cardinal Denaro said.

Thomas stood from his seat and paced around the room, making eye contact with the other council members. He had always been a convincing and powerful speaker, which was why he held this position; he leaned on that expertise in this moment that he felt was crucial.

"We are about to cross a line into uncharted territory, maybe even the gates of hell. It is only natural that with such high stakes we would be nervous. But our reluctance to engage, our lack of confidence in what we are doing, could derail the entire process. We need to be firm and committed."

"The council has always been committed to the cause," one of the members said, getting nods all around. "What do you suggest?"

"We need to isolate the soldiers from this recent speculation until we can decide on the validity of Father Frank's claims. We need Professor Barnes due to his technical skills, but he must take an oath not to share any information with those outside of the project, and that includes Father Frank Keller."

"That's ridiculous," Jimmie said. "You are being ridiculous to disparage him in this way."

"Am I?" Thomas said. "Shouldn't we take every precaution to make sure we succeed? That includes Connor Dietz; he must be removed from the group."

"Father Frank's nephew?" Bishop Tafoya questioned.

"Yes. His closeness and loyalty to Professor Barnes have already caused him to question who is in charge. His relationship with his uncle may be a weakening factor. He may cause doubt in others. Our soldiers cannot face any doubt or hesitation in what they are doing."

"Very well stated, Father Thomas," Cardinal Denaro said. "This council will consider your recommendations. Now if there is anything further to be said, let it be said now. Otherwise, we should decide on the issue: do we delay or go forward with our plan?"

Frank stood in Bishop Tafoya's office on a raised step where he knew the bishop often prepared his sermons. He looked down at the podium in front of him to the passage that was open and read it aloud. "Finally, my brethren, be strong in the Lord and in the power of His might. Put on the whole armor of God, that you may be able to stand against the wiles of the devil. For we don't wrestle against flesh and blood, but against principalities, against powers, against the rulers of the darkness of this age, against spiritual hosts of wickedness in the heavenly places. Therefore, take up the whole armor of God, that you may be able to withstand in the evil day, and having done all, to stand. Ephesians 6:10–13."

"There you are," said a male voice.

Frank looked up as Father Thomas entered and closed the door behind him.

"We haven't had an opportunity to meet and talk," said the other priest.

"Father Thomas, right?" Frank said, offering his hand.

Thomas shook it briefly and took a seat behind Bishop Tafoya's desk. "Father Frank Keller, I want you to know that I've been involved in this battle for years. I heard of the workings of your little group with Adnan and that Indian holy man—"

"Kanuik," Frank interjected. He didn't want to be prejudiced in his judgment of Thomas, but the remarks from Jimmie and Bishop Tafoya the night before at the Kozy were enough to make him leery.

"Yes, that was his name," Thomas said. "While I was converting hundreds to the faith and protecting them spiritually from the evils that wait for them, you actually managed to experience this evil we fight. And you survived."

"It was a matter of faith," Frank said. "I was not born into the priesthood; it found me."

"Oh," Thomas said, raising his eyebrows. "You had a calling to serve?"

"Yes, you could say that," Frank said.

"I respect that." Thomas said. He stood, moving his hands down to his sides in fists. "I am aware of your story, all of it. The Jenson family, Bishop Tafoya bringing you into the group, and what happened to your mentor, Adnan. Let me tell you my story. Before you joined your group, it was long recognized that these creatures existed and that a combined effort of all faiths would be the best method to combat them. It is unfortunate that men cannot exist in peace and realize the true faith, but that is that. The council came together for the first time more than a decade ago, long before you knew the battle. We struggled for a path forward, for a reason and a purpose to stay together. Not an easy task"—he raised his index finger, as though pointing—"to do in such times when one of the world's religions is trying to usurp the others and in doing so has embraced killing innocents."

"I didn't know the council existed until last night," Frank said.

"Yes, I know you didn't. This council struggled to find a direction and a path and barely agreed on terms. Not an easy feat."

"You must have been grateful to be a part of something so profound."

"I was," Thomas said. "Then something came along that gave the council a single direction. It unified us when all the members revealed the truth of our battles against the shadows—however, even more when the stories of a hero, a man from the faith I represented, started appearing to people all around the world. It … it was a miracle."

"I am humbled," Frank said, nodding.

"You must understand that although what you did helped unite the council, it is fragile, always on the verge of breaking apart. Every time we change direction, it adds doubt. We had a clear direction; we were taking the battle to evil. Now you have come along and confused the plan and thrown everything into doubt."

"I'm sorry," Frank said. "I feel I was sent to warn you, and that's what I have done."

"Well, you haven't won yet," Thomas said.

"It was never my intention to win or lose," Frank said. "It was my desire to give counsel."

"I too have given counsel," Thomas said. "I have advised against any more delays, so you know. It is a matter of *my* faith!" His eyes were solid as he slapped his right hand down on Bishop Tafoya's desk.

Frank didn't respond. Through his years of service to the church, he'd had to act as a counselor many times, and he recognized when it was time to give counsel and when to listen. Thomas's passion was heightened, and Frank knew he was beyond reasoning with at this time.

"I suggest you think about what we are going to do if what you said in there stops our soldiers," said Thomas. "What do you suggest we do, Father Frank? The evil we are facing is real and, despite our faith, seems to be winning."

A knock came at the door, and Jimmie poked his head in. "Oh, sorry," he said and started to leave.

"No, Professor Barnes," Thomas said, "we are quite done." Thomas left the room.

"Sorry about that," Jimmie said. "He can be a little rough around the edges."

"No," Frank said, "he's full of passion for what he believes in."

"So was Hitler," Jimmie said.

"Jimmie!" Frank scolded.

"Sorry."

Thomas had given Frank a lot to think about. Frank knew that he had no plan for how to defeat the threat before him. Suddenly, he felt ill and bent over, holding his abdomen.

"You okay?" Jimmie rushed to him.

"Fine," Frank said. "Probably just too much stress. Don't tell Claudia."

After his conversation with Father Frank, Thomas rushed to his basement lab. He had called Mike Delgado and Kaitlyn and asked them to meet him there. He paced back and forth along the concrete floor, waiting for the two assistants. They entered together.

"Thanks for the ride," he heard Kaitlyn say as they both came down the steps.

"Mr. Delgado," Thomas interrupted, "our time has grown critical. I cannot tell you why, but we must try to separate one of the shadows from the host tonight if possible."

Mike removed his jacket and hung it on a chair close to the equipment. "Okay," he said, scratching his head. "Last time when we were using different shock frequencies on the subject, that appeared to cause more of them to appear and float around—also when you were, well, doing what you were doing to make the kid feel worthless."

"Do we know how to contain one?" Thomas asked.

"That I don't know," Mike said. "But maybe we can find the right frequency and drive the thing out of one of the subjects." Mike shook his head. "Geez, now even I'm not referring to them as people."

Thomas walked up to Mike and stood directly in front of him. "Many people with incurable diseases allow doctors to try experimental research on them so that maybe a cure can be found that will help others. These subjects are not even alive in many regards and are certainly not aware of what's going on."

"What do these things want with them then?" Mike asked.

"They desire to control," Thomas said, "to rule us. That is why we must continue. Sacrificing these few for billions is the greater good." He gave Kaitlyn the keys to the cell. "Get the boy toward the front. He's on drugs but not as bad as some of the others."

Kaitlyn went to the cell, retrieved the boy, and moved him to the chair, where she proceeded to strap him in and hook up the sensors, with Mike's help. Mike then nodded to Thomas.

"Let's proceed," Thomas said. He handed the camera to Kaitlyn and went to where the nameless teen sat. "Now where were we?" Thomas said.

As soon as Thomas's hand touched the young man, the teen growled and jumped at the priest, tearing through the straps that had held him down. The boy's flesh was torn where he had broken the straps, and blood flowed from the wounds.

Kaitlyn jumped between the teen and Thomas and tried to subdue the teen, but he turned and bit Kaitlyn on the neck, tearing out a piece of flesh before Thomas and Mike could pull him off. The boy collapsed to the floor with no fight left in him.

"Put pressure on it!" Mike yelled to Kaitlyn as he and Thomas hauled the boy back into the cell.

Kaitlyn's eyes were wide and her breathing shallow as she pressed her hand to her neck to try to stop the bleeding.

Panicking, Mike ran back to the desk and shuffled first through it and then through the cabinets, trying to find something to use as a dressing. "Do we have any bandages or anything to stop the bleeding?"

Thomas didn't respond but continued watching the boy, indifferent to Kaitlyn and intent on witnessing the behavior of the shadow. He made sure the cell door was secure and then turned around to Kaitlyn.

Kaitlyn fell to the floor as the blood pooled around her. Mike ran to her with a wad of paper towels. He pulled her to a seated position and pressed the paper towels against the wound. "It's bleeding too much," Mike said.

Thomas walked over and knelt down beside Kaitlyn. Her eyes rolled back in her head. He pulled out a handkerchief, removed Mike's hand full of blood-soaked towels, and pushed down on the wound with his own hand. Blood spurted forth. "He ruptured an artery. Either it was by chance, or he knew what he was targeting."

"We better call for help." Mike stood and pulled his cell phone out of his pocket.

"Never mind," Thomas said. He laid Kaitlyn back on the floor and stood.

Mike leaned over her and attempted CPR.

"It's too late," Thomas said. "She's lost too much blood."

Mike sat down on the floor next to the lifeless body. "What have we done?" He held Kaitlyn's head in his arms. "She was so young."

Thomas looked back to the cell that held the teens. All of them were standing, watching, including the boy who had caused the wound. Thomas knew the shadows had won this round. "Curious," he said.

"What?" Mike said.

"The location of the bite—he went for the neck. I think we may have just discovered where vampire myths originated."

"Have you no remorse?" Mike said.

Thomas turned to Mike. "Look," he said, "I will make sure she gets taken care of, but our work is secret. Kaitlyn would have wanted us to continue—to fight these things that just killed her." He held out his hand to help Mark up from the floor.

"I suppose so," Mike said. He wiped a tear from his eye, took Thomas's hand, stood, and looked down at Kaitlyn's body.

Thomas went to the chair where the suspect had been seated. He examined the straps on the chair.

"Did you find something?" Mark asked.

"I was just wondering how he could have escaped these straps. They should've been too strong for him to break."

"Maybe Kaitlyn didn't get them tight enough," Mark said.

"Or he was resourceful enough to get out," Thomas said. "Did you get any data from this event?"

Mike went back to his work screen. Raising an eyebrow, he said, "That's strange."

"What?"

"There was a spike from the boy, but also an energy reading from the cell." He pointed to where they kept the subjects.

"What he did caused the others to react?" Thomas asked.

"I don't know," Mike said. "I think I might need some help trying to understand this. We might need some help. People are dying."

Thomas wanted to push Mike and continue testing tonight, but he realized he might lose his only remaining assistant if he did. "Let's quit for the night."

"What about her?" Mike asked.

"I promise you, I'll take care of her," Thomas said. "Don't worry. She was an only child with no family and a checkered past. That's why I picked her."

"Is that why you picked me as well?" Mike asked.

Thomas knew he needed to tread more carefully with Mike. Although Mike might have fallen out of touch with his friends, and his absence might go unnoticed should he go missing, his technical skill would be harder to replace. "Of course not. Remember our goal, Mr. Delgado. There are forces at work here greater than us."

Thomas watched Mike go up the stairs before he went back to the cage, momentarily looking down at Kaitlyn's body on his way. He looked directly at the boy who had her blood on his face. "I don't know if you can hear me," he said to the shadows, "but I'll find a way to defeat you."

Jimmie gave Frank a ride to the Kozy Tavern, where they met up with Kanuik and Samar. Connor was there too, helping Chic in the kitchen. Claudia, meanwhile, had taken Ira to the grocery store because the two were planning dinner later. The men ate a late lunch while they discussed the meeting with Bishop Tafoya. The discussion was nearing its end when Frank noticed a man walk in and look purposely toward their table. Frank moved enough so that he would be obscured by one of the others sitting across from him.

"Someone just walked in who looks familiar to me," Frank said. "He keeps looking over here, but I can't place him."

The others glanced over as the man took a seat at the bar.

"That's Mike Delgado," Jimmie said. "He was one of the researchers who helped us at David's house."

"Does he come in here much?" Frank asked.

"No," Jimmie said. "I haven't seen him for years."

"It's strange that he should appear right now, don't you think?"

"I'll go see what he's up to," Jimmie said and left the table.

Frank watched the interaction that followed. It seemed to start pleasantly, with the men shaking hands. Suddenly, Mike nearly collapsed against Jimmie and started crying.

Jimmie tried to comfort him and looked to the bar, where Connor was cleaning glasses. "Connor, give him anything he wants and put it on my tab."

After Jimmie and Mike talked at the bar for a few minutes, Jimmie walked over to the table where Frank and Kanuik were sitting quietly.

"Looks like your friend's had better days," Kanuik said.

"Wasn't there another guy who helped us too?" Frank asked.

"Yes, Russ Mothner. I think he sells used cars now or something like that. Anyway, Mike has just told me quite a story about Thomas! You should all hear it."

"Bring him over then," Kanuik said.

Jimmie turned around and waved Mike to the table. Mike threw back the last of his drink and tapped the bar. Connor poured him another bourbon, and Mike picked up the glass and walked to the table.

As Mike sat down, Frank moved the drink away from him. "Let's just take a break for a moment until we've heard what you have to say," Frank said.

Mike looked around the table. "I remember you and you," he said, pointing to Kanuik and Frank, "but I don't know you." He pointed at Samar.

"I am Samar Hamish, an archeologist from India," Samar said. "You may have met my father, Adnan. I am happy to meet you."

"Mike," Jimmie said, bringing Mike back to the point of the conversation, "tell them what you said to me about what Thomas is doing."

"Well, you see …" Mike's words slurred a little, as though he had already been drinking prior to making it to the tavern. "I used to work with Jimmie, and so this Father Thomas guy, he, like, kidnaps me—no kidding, in a hood and everything—and takes me to this secret basement where he has a setup. He thought because I used to work with Jimmie that I knew more than I did. I'm pretty savvy and all, so I asked him what he wanted, and he asked for my help. Problem is, the cable job isn't really paying the bills, if you know what I mean, and he was offering good money. Plus he had the cute assistant." Mike started to cry. "Kaitlyn. That was her name. Pretty blond hair. She did aerobics or kickboxing and stuff and was just so full of energy."

"What happened?" Frank asked, putting his hand on Mike's back in an effort to comfort him.

"Thomas recruited us to work on the same project Jimmie has been working on, but in a different way. He wanted to learn how to capture the shadows and kill them."

"You know about the shadows?" Jimmie asked.

"Shhh." Mike put his index finger up to his lips. "We're not supposed to talk about it. But yes, I know about all the stuff you guys are doing."

"That's why he was taking equipment to that old warehouse building," Jimmie said. "Connor and I were leaving the church last week, and we noticed Thomas with a few other men taking some equipment somewhere. We didn't trust him, so we followed him to an old abandoned machine shop."

"Is he trying to open a portal?" Frank said.

"I don't know anything about a portal. But he's found a way to get the shadows," Mike said. "He uses teens who are addicted to drugs. He gives them drugs and keeps them locked in a cage. I guess when the kids have so many problems, the parents don't care if they are missing because no one ever comes looking for them. I mean, no one cares." He started crying again.

"Mike, stay with us," Jimmie said. "You think these kids have shadows attached to them?"

"I know they do," Mike said. "Thomas had this mirror thing that he showed me. You can see them through this mirror. I analyzed the structure, copied the materials, and made a camera lens, and now I can see them through the camera. That's why he hired me—because I can do stuff like that." Mike pretended like he was holding a camera.

"Adnan had a mirror," Frank said. "That's how I saw the shadows the first time, in this very tavern. Tell us what happened. Why are you so upset?"

Mike licked his lips and looked at his drink, which Frank still kept out of his reach.

"Just a little now," Frank said, pushing the glass toward him. Frank let him have one drink before he moved it away again.

"Thomas was unhappy last night, something about a meeting, and he was pushing me for results—you know, threatening me and stuff. However, our subject got loose, and he … he attacked Kaitlyn and killed her. She's dead now." He reached out, grabbed his glass, drank the rest of his drink, and put his head on his right arm on the table.

"Did you call the police?"

The voice that came from the table was barely audible. "He has friends who take care of all of that. He pays homeless thugs to keep watch and do stuff for him. It's not the first time someone died, but usually, it's one of the kids, not Kaitlyn."

"Mike," Jimmie said softly, "who was Kaitlyn?"

"She was our assistant," Mike said. "She was a college student that he picked up—someone who needed money."

"Do you have a safe place to go tonight?"

"I share an apartment with Russ," Mike said. "We have our separate rooms and all, and it's not like we know where the other one is all the time." He started sobbing again. "Man, how am I going to tell him about all of this stuff?"

"I don't think you should," Jimmie said. "We're going to call you a cab and get you home. And don't go back to the lab, okay?"

"Connor," Frank called, turning toward the bar, "can you please call for a cab?"

"Right away," Connor said.

"Okay," Mike said. "Jimmie?"

"What is it?"

"I really need to go to the bathroom now."

"The cab is on the way," Connor said as he approached the table. "Can I get you guys anything?"

Frank and Jimmie smiled. "Connor," Jimmie said, "would you show him where the restroom is? And don't let him fall getting there."

Connor escorted Mike away.

"Looks like Thomas didn't take the results of our meeting yesterday well," Jimmie said. "I always thought he had his own agenda. Now I have proof."

"What do we do?" Frank asked.

"I don't know," Jimmie said. "I'm not sure if this ends at Thomas or if it goes higher, so we might not be able to go to Bishop Tafoya or Cardinal Denaro. If we call the police and they start investigating, it could blow up in our faces. They may even find out about you."

"You said you followed him last week. Do know where this place is?" Frank asked.

Jimmie nodded.

"We need to get a message to Thomas to distract him, to make sure he isn't going to be there, and then go there ourselves."

"I can schedule some tests at the church," Jimmie said. "Thomas is always nosing around when I do."

"Can you do it by tomorrow?"

"Yes. What do you plan to do?" Jimmie asked.

"We are going to free those kids and shut this Thomas down," Frank said, and he looked around the table.

"I'm in," Jimmie said. "I can't stand that guy."

Kanuik nodded, and Frank knew he could count on him.

Samar had been quiet through the entire conversation and appeared deep in thought but nodded. "I think I have come here for a reason," he said. "I haven't understood what is happening to me until now. It is my time to take up the fight."

"Well, we're going to have a tough time taking you along with your bodyguards and all," Frank said. "Are those agents out there right now?"

"They are," Chic said from across the bar as he headed to the door with a tray of drinks. Chic stepped outside, and the group watched the door until he came back in with an empty tray. He brushed the cold off him and looked toward the table. "They like light beer."

"He has good ears for an older guy," Jimmie said.

"I heard that!"

"Does Claudia's house have a back door?" Frank asked.

Samar nodded.

"Then you can use it tomorrow, and we'll pick you up early in the morning."

CHAPTER 9
FIVE DAYS REMAINING

*It is impious to say that evil has its origin from God,
because naught contrary is produced by the contrary. Life
does not generate death, nor is darkness the beginning
of light, nor is disease the maker of health, but in the
changes of conditions there are transitions from one
condition to the contrary.*

—Saint Basil

After Jimmie picked up Samar and Frank, they headed to the Kozy Tavern to get Kanuik. From there, they didn't have to travel far to get to the old machine shop where Thomas had set up his experiments; it was in the same neighborhood.

"What did you tell Ira?" Frank asked Samar. They had waited for him outside the back of Claudia's house, trying to keep their plans a secret not only from the two agents who followed Samar everywhere but also from Ira and Claudia.

"I told her we were going for some male bonding and that no women were allowed," Samar said. "Are you sure we shouldn't have just told them what we are doing?"

"I'm not sure Claudia would allow me to do anything remotely dangerous right now," Frank said. "She's a tough one, but probably also the best suited to stay with Ira."

"Agreed," Samar said.

"The fewer people who know what we are doing, the better," Kanuik said. "We don't need to put them in danger. And what we are doing might stretch legal boundaries. We don't want to endanger Claudia's reputation."

"I'm not sure I want to be put in danger either," Jimmie said.

"Remind me what we are looking for," Frank said.

"Mike told me the building is not too far from the Kozy Tavern," Jimmie said. "It's one of the old machine shops that closed."

Frank nodded. "This whole part of town is full of old buildings like that," Frank said, "the exact type my father worked in before the jobs left."

"Those two men sitting over there look suspicious," Jimmie said and pulled the car up to the curb. "Like they are posted there as lookouts or something."

"You think that could be the shop there?" Frank asked. The two men they were looking at stood.

"Looks like we got their attention," Jimmie said. "Let's check it out."

Two men sitting against the wall across from them in the alley had taken notice of the car. They were dressed poorly in clothes that didn't quite fit and were starting toward the car.

"Maybe we should have asked Father Mark to come along," Frank said.

"Why?" Kanuik asked. "Anything he sees, he is obligated to report to the bishop's office."

"That's true," Frank said, "but there's something else you don't know about him. He knows hand-to-hand combat."

The men exited the car, and Kanuik came around to Frank's side. Spotting the approaching men, he said, "Now I understand what you mean. I suppose you, being a priest and all, cannot fight?"

"I'm not quite sure where I stand on all of that right now," Frank said. "I'd rather not find out."

"It's four of us," Jimmie said as he and Samar joined them.

Kanuik took the lead and crossed into the alley to confront the men before Frank and the rest could get across the road. After Kanuik said a few words, the two men disappeared down the alley in a hurry, and Kanuik turned around smiling as he gestured for the others to come.

"What did you tell them?" Frank asked as he approached.

"I told them you were from the Department of Social Services and that Jimmie was an undercover cop. You kinda look like one with your sport coat."

They shared a laugh before going to the door Mike had described to them.

"It's locked," Frank said.

Jimmie pulled out the key Mike had given him. They entered the building, and immediately to the left was a stairwell leading down.

"Smells bad," Kanuik said. "Human waste, but also something dark is down there. I definitely sense something wrong. We should have a plan."

"What do you recommend?" Frank asked.

"If we run into any people, we hold to the story I already created: we are investigators for social services, and Jimmie is a cop," Kanuik said. "We need to prepare ourselves to battle the shadows. Stay close to each other, and if you notice anyone acting strange, make sure to alert that person and the group."

"Strange how?" Samar asked.

"Like they aren't sure where we are or they get a glazed look in their eyes," Kanuik said.

"Mike said the cell holding the people is on the opposite side and to the left from where we will come out of the stairway," Jimmie said. "Looks like it's pretty dark down there as well."

"Just stay together so we can watch each other," Kanuik said, and he pulled several round mushy balls from his pocket. "You should remain behind me, Jimmie, in case I have to use these."

"What should I do?" Samar asked.

"These things have a way of getting into your mind and warping reality," Frank said. "Be careful what you trust. That's why we go together—to make sure we keep each other in the now, the current moment. If you see someone looking or acting unusual, it's okay to slap him. It may be the only way to bring him out."

"Please slap me if I start having issues," Samar said.

"I will," Frank said, grinning. "Just stay close."

The group started down the stairwell, ten steps, and emerged in a large square room that was barely lit by the light coming in from a few small windows covered with fabric.

"Anyone see a light switch?" asked Jimmie.

"Here," Kanuik said as he flipped a switch by the stairs.

The room lit up, and Frank could clearly see the equipment area, but the light in the rest of the room was not as good. It was in the darker area that he spotted a chair with straps and, further along the wall, a cell where he noticed movement but could not make out faces.

"Over there," Frank said. "That's where he's keeping them."

"Yes," Kanuik said. "I can feel the evil there. It's strong."

Frank nodded and watched as Kanuik approached the cell and threw balls of fire before him, lighting a wall of protection for them. Among the things Frank had learned from Kanuik and Adnan was that the shadows couldn't pass through the holy fire that Kanuik used.

"Make sure you stay on this side of the fire," Kanuik said. "If something goes wrong, get back up the stairs." Kanuik stepped over the fire and closer to the cell.

"What are you doing?" Frank asked.

"I'm going to see if I can help them," Kanuik said.

Jimmie went to a desk and turned on a lamp. In the light, they could see all of the equipment around the desk.

"He's got a whole setup here but no coils," Jimmie said. "So he wasn't trying to open a portal."

"I wonder what he's trying to do," Frank said.

"Mike said he was trying to find a way to kill the shadows, separate them from the host."

Frank thought about the concept for a moment and considered that Thomas was just trying to win the battle; in his own mind what he was doing was right. But he didn't want to give Thomas any credit for what he was doing, especially when it involved using unsuspecting subjects.

"This must be the camera that Mike was talking about," Jimmie said, going over to a table with multiple pieces of equipment, including a video camera that was pointed toward the chair. He managed to turn the camera on, and the light from it shot across the room. "Look." Jimmie pointed to a spot where there was still blood on the floor. "That must be where the girl he spoke about, Kaitlyn, was killed. His story checks out."

Frank crossed the room to get closer to the cell where Kanuik stood, but he did not cross the small pillars of fire that Kanuik had lit. Five lanky figures stared at him from within the cell.

"Where's our medicine?" called a male voice from the cell.

"Oh man, can you see it?" Jimmie said.

"See what?" Frank asked.

Jimmie looked away from the camera at Frank and then back to the screen. "I suppose you can't see it. Must be a camera filter or something. But you should come and look at this. I can see the shadows—black figures swarming around them."

"I see them without the camera," Frank said.

"I typically can see them if I touch one of them, but only after," Samar said as he approached the spot where Frank stood. "Also, you should know, when I have fought these things before, I usually have gone unconscious."

"Make sure you are clear of any hazards on the floor if you have to engage them," Frank said. He turned to Jimmie. "Do you have the keys to the cell?"

"No," Jimmie said. "I guess only Thomas has that key."

Kanuik went to the other side of the room and came back with a fire extinguisher. "I'd plug your ears." He swung the base of the extinguisher at the lock. Each blow made a resounding *clang* until the lock broke free. Immediately, Kanuik stepped back and threw down more balls of fire.

"Good thing this place doesn't have a fire suppression system," Jimmie said.

"I thought it did," Kanuik said and smiled. "You ready, Frank?"

Frank stepped over the fire and stood by Kanuik, prepared to do battle with the shadows.

The first two teens came out of the cage and walked toward Frank, shaking and confused.

"These two look fine," Frank said. "The shadows fled into the others." He pushed the two teens past the small fires on the floor. "Go to the stairs there and wait for us outside." He watched the two youths, one boy and one girl, hurry to the stairway, and then he turned back to the cell. "Looks like they are going to make us go in there and get them," Frank said. "I wish I had my cane. Get ready, Samar. I'm going to grab one and send him your way."

While Kanuik started chanting, Frank grabbed one of the male teens and pulled him. He moved him toward Samar, feeling the cold grip of the shadow on him the entire time. Once he had cleared the fire on the floor, he let Samar take him, and then he went back in where the last two, a boy and a girl, were huddled together.

Frank reached out, touched the boy, and immediately found himself transported to another place. He was in a subway tunnel, off the main route in a maintenance access tunnel. He spotted the girl and boy sitting around a small fire. Near the fire was an old mattress, and a bunch of clothing and food items were scattered around. He knew this must be a representation of where they had lived before Thomas got hold of them.

The girl was the first to notice Frank, and she pointed at him. "This is our home—get out," she said. Her face was dirty, her blond hair stringy and unkempt, and her hands black from the fire and the pieces of paper she was feeding it.

The boy, sitting with his feet on the ground and knees up, had his hands tucked under his legs as he rocked back and forth. "It's so cold," he said.

"I know, honey," the girl said. "I've got a fire going. What you need is some soup." She started fumbling around the mess that surrounded them.

"What is your name?" Frank asked.

She stopped what she was doing, picked up the remains of what used to be an umbrella, and headed toward Frank in a defensive posture. He put his hands up to show her he meant no harm.

"What are you doing here? We ain't got no money, no food," the girl said. "Why are you here?"

"I am Father Frank Keller," Frank said. "I am from St. Joseph's church. Do you know of it?"

The girl's eyes went to the ground and then back to Frank. "You think I ain't never been to church?"

"No," Frank said, "I'm sure you've been many times, and that's why I'm here. They miss you there. They sent me to make sure you are okay."

"Ava," the girl said. "My name is Ava."

"Ava, will you allow me to come over there and pray with you?" Frank stepped forward, but the moment he did, the boy stopped rocking and turned to him. Frank could see the black swirls around him, coming in and out of his body, and he knew the shadows had taken notice of his interference.

"He's a liar," the boy said. "Don't go near him."

Frank reached out and grabbed Ava's hand before she could step away. He closed his eyes, started praying, pulled her close, and hugged her. He felt the shadow claw at him, but it had no power and fled. Then a flash of heat rushed right by his head, and he opened his eyes to find himself back in the basement with the girl, who was sobbing. Kanuik took hold of Frank and pulled him and the girl out of the cell and across the fire. The boy was still in the cell, but he was now standing, kicking the sides and slamming the door back and forth.

"Samar?" Frank said. With the girl free, Frank was hoping the boy was the last victim, but he didn't know how Samar had fared with the other boy.

"I am fine," Samar said. He took the girl from Frank and escorted her and the boy who was already with him to the stairs. "Jimmie and I are going to wait with them in the alley."

"The fire is only going to last another few minutes at most," Kanuik said. "If you're going to do something, do it now."

Without hesitation, Frank went to the cell and grabbed the boy. The boy tried to attack him, but Frank overpowered the weak youth and held him. He started praying and whispering in his ear. "Ava has gone to a new place," he said. "I am Frank, Frank Keller, your friend."

"Where is our home?" the boy said frantically. "You took us from our home."

"No," Frank said, "I have come to take you home, away from harm." He felt the darkness trying to attack his mind, but he was able to block it out, and its power started to fade. For a moment, he spotted a blue anomaly in the back of the cell. He hoped the shadow had fled.

"Ava is waiting upstairs there," Frank said, pointing. "Open your eyes and see the truth. What is your name?"

The boy stopped fighting him. "Kyle. I'm Kyle."

Frank slowly released his grip on him. "Kyle, how about we go see the sun and get some food?" Frank sensed that the evil had fled. He knew his theory would be tested if he could get the youth across Kanuik's holy fire.

They stepped across the barrier without incident, and the boy, Kyle, and Kanuik walked to the alley, where the other teens were sitting against the wall. Kyle sat down by Ava.

Jimmie and Kanuik went back downstairs, leaving Frank and Samar in the alley. When they emerged again, Jimmie shut the door to the building, came back to the group, and motioned the others a few steps away from the teens. "I think we disabled most of the equipment and rendered the cell unusable." Lowering his voice to a whisper, he continued, "I also called the cops. I told them I was a college professor and one of my students tipped me off about some teens doing drugs who were in trouble. They are on the way and bringing someone from the rehab center to take them into custody."

"Great," Frank said. "What else should we do?"

Jimmie handed Frank the camera and a key. "Here's my extra car key. Put the camera in the car for me, leave the key under the floor mat, and get out of here. I don't want the you-know-who asking a bunch of questions and needing IDs and stuff. You're supposed to be dead, and for all we know, Samar is on the watch list for terrorists, and then we'll all be headed downtown, trying to explain why we are here."

"We'll meet you back at the Kozy," Frank said. "What we've done so far will stop Thomas now, but we may have to confront him."

With Kanuik and Samar following right behind him, Frank went back to Jimmie's car and put the camera inside. He left the key under the floor mat as Jimmie had instructed and then pulled out the baseball cap and put it on tight before he locked and closed the doors. "Looks like it's the bus for us," he said to Kanuik and Samar.

The three headed to the nearest bus stop. "I'm going back to the apartment to get cleaned up," said Frank, "and then I'll meet you down at the Kozy."

Frank left on the first bus that was going toward Mark's apartment while Samar and Kanuik waited for a different one that would stop closer to the Kozy Tavern.

Back at Mark's apartment, Frank showered and shaved. It was midday, and Mark was just returning from morning mass and business at the church when Frank exited the bathroom.

"Oh, you're still here," Mark said. "That's good. I thought you'd be off with the group already. I hope you had some time to get some sleep. I was about to make some coffee if you want some."

"Sounds good," Frank said. He sat down on a stool at the kitchen counter while Mark prepared the coffee.

"What's next?" Mark asked a few minutes later, handing him a cup of hot coffee.

Frank didn't want to keep information from Mark, but he wasn't sure if he should tell him what the group had been doing. He wasn't sure Mark would keep it from Bishop Tafoya. Since Mark thought he had remained in the apartment all morning, Frank decided this would be a good alibi should something come up.

"I don't know what's next," Frank said. "I guess we wait to see what Cardinal Denaro decides."

"No, I mean what's next for you?" Mark said. "Regardless of what the council decides to do, you have to figure out what Father Frank Keller needs to do."

Frank stared forward, considering Mark's words. "I haven't given it much thought. I've been so caught up in what's going on, everything else seems secondary."

"I'd offer you your parish back, but I'm not sure how we would pull that off. You didn't happen to have a twin brother? We could pass you off that way."

Frank laughed. "No, just a sister."

"Besides," Mark said, "if we go displaying you around as a priest who came back from the dead, our true meaning is kind of lost, don't you think?"

"Remember, Jesus was persecuted and executed," Frank said. "There was an actual body and an actual resurrection. I never really died, and there was no body that was buried and came back."

"Yet here you are, and you've returned looking exactly as you did three years ago."

Frank bit down on his lip, trying to piece together what was going on. He needed to figure out his purpose, why he'd been brought back. He knew something was wrong—he hadn't really slept since he'd come back, and he wasn't hungry. He wondered how long it would be before someone noticed he was different. It was as though his body, no longer bound by physical limitations, was physically *dead*.

"If the decision is to send the soldiers through the portal, I'll go with them as a guide," Frank said.

Mark, about to take a drink of coffee, stopped and put his cup down. "I don't know if that's going to go over too well with your friends."

"No, I suppose not," Frank said. "Speaking of them, I'm heading back to the Kozy to meet with them and have lunch if you want to go."

On the way to the Kozy Tavern with Mark, Frank thought more about what he was going to do next. It was clear to Frank that he had been allowed to exist in the world of the shadows only through divine intervention. That same force was guiding him now. He felt he needed to learn more about the shadows—why and how they existed. If he could understand the origins of the creatures, maybe he could find a way to defeat them.

When the two men got to the Kozy Tavern, Jimmie's car was out front. They entered to find Jimmie at the bar.

"Hey, good to see you," Jimmie said, shaking hands with Mark. "Why don't we go sit at our table?"

"Everything go all right back there?" Frank asked, whispering as the three headed to the table.

"You haven't told him?" Jimmie said.

"No," Frank responded.

"Nothing I couldn't handle," Jimmie said. "Back in my

ghost-hunting days and in my days running around with Adnan, I had a few chance encounters with the local law enforcement."

"Oh," Frank said with a smile.

"Enough times that some of them know me by my first name," he laughed.

Frank noticed as they sat down that the three of them were the only ones in the bar.

"Yep," Jimmie said, "the place is its usual hub of activity today."

"Where's Chic?"

"Chic went to take Kanuik some towels. He wanted to clean up after, you know, last night and all. I'm sorry—where are my manners?" Jimmie went behind the bar and poured Mark and Frank each a cup of coffee. He hurried back around, watching the opening to the hallway. "Did you know that underneath this place is a set of tunnels with several bedrooms, a bathroom with shower, and a laundry room? It's like a whole underground world down there."

"I've seen some of it," Frank said. "We went to the room Adnan was living in but never any farther." He looked at the walls of the tavern around him and at some of the woodwork he'd previously overlooked. "Kind of makes you wonder how old this place really is."

"Anyone for pizza?" Claudia called as she walked in the tavern door with Ira and Samar in tow. All three of them carried pizza boxes.

"Oh, I see how it is," Chic said, emerging from the hallway, his cigar firmly in his mouth and his eyes narrow. "I step away for a minute, and everyone just helps themselves to the drinks and brings their own food."

Claudia led Ira and Samar to the table where Frank and Mark sat and put her box down. "Oh, come on, Chic. We can't expect you to feed us every day. I thought I'd give you a break today. Come and join us."

"Humph!" Chic shrugged. "Since you all have decided to take over, I might as well." He took a seat at the table as Claudia handed him a paper plate. "But after this, I'm back in charge."

Everyone grabbed a piece of pizza while Jimmie filled a cup of coffee for Chic and brought it to the table. They all stood around the table and held hands.

"Should we wait for Kanuik?" Claudia asked.

"I think he's going to be a few more minutes," Chic said. "Besides, if we don't eat before he gets here, we might have to give him a whole pizza."

"Really?" Frank said. "I didn't think he ate that much."

"You should see how he eats when you are not around," Chic said. "I think it would be appropriate for you to say the blessing, Frank. It's because of you we've all gotten together."

"Please," Frank said, "bow your heads and pray. Dear Lord, we ask that you bless us and watch over us today and every day and look out for those who haven't found you. Let this food nourish us and strengthen us in our service to you and each other. Amen."

"Amen," the others said in unison.

They all had just sat down to eat when the door to the tavern suddenly opened. Two men dressed in black suits entered.

Samar sighed. "It's the agents. They probably found out I ditched them this morning. Don't do anything. I'll take care of this."

Frank sank down in his chair. He had removed his hat for grace and suddenly hoped no questions would be asked about his identity.

The two black-clad men headed toward the table as Samar headed toward them. Samar started his apology for sneaking out the back door but was cut off by the shorter of the two men.

"Mr. Samar Hamish," the agent said, sticking out his hand, "I am sorry for any inconvenience we may have caused you and your fiancée. We were just doing our jobs."

Samar shook the agent's hand. "This means I am not under arrest?"

"Of course not," the agent said. "Your background check came back clean. We confirmed you're from India and really an archeologist. We are also big fans of Ms. Walden there"—he gestured toward Claudia—"and understand from what she's told us that she is consulting you for more ideas on her next book. Please, excuse this interruption and go back to your dinner. We just wanted you to know we won't be around to give you any more rides. We've been assigned a new mission."

"Why don't you have some pizza before you go?" Samar offered, and the two men sat down at a small table as Claudia served them pizza and Jimmie brought them club sodas.

Claudia returned to the table and apparently noticed that Frank's plate was empty. She selected a large piece and set it in front of him. She kept her eyes on him, as though waiting for him to eat. He didn't know what to do at first, but then Samar cleared his throat, and Frank noticed that Claudia, Ira, and Samar had nothing to drink. He stood so suddenly that he startled Jimmie, who'd taken a seat next to him.

"Sorry," Frank said. "What do you three want to drink? I can get it." His plan worked, and by the time he returned to the table, Kanuik had emerged from the basement and sat down where Frank had been sitting and was eating the slice of pizza. Frank borrowed a chair from another table and sat slightly back between Mark and Samar, across from Claudia. He listened to the conversation in progress. The group was currently focused on Claudia as she answered questions about all her book signing and television appearances.

"What's the hardest part?" Chic asked.

"The traveling is not so bad," Claudia said. "My agent usually finds me a great place to stay, and the bookstore managers are exceptional. I guess the one thing I struggle with in the interviews, and from the publisher, is the demand for a follow-up."

"Tell me about this new book you are working on. Is it the same type as your first?" Frank asked.

"Yes," Claudia stated. "I'm still searching for the title, though."

The group recommended several titles, none to Claudia's liking.

Chic had to go back to his tavern duties because it was now evening and several patrons had entered. By the time the group finished talking, it was past dinnertime. The agents had left the bar, and Frank noticed that Ira, though smiling and laughing a lot, had not said much.

"Ira, how are you enjoying your stay?" Frank asked, attempting to draw her into the conversation.

"I am so happy," Ira said. "I've been able to visit a friend from college and go to one of my father's outlets. However, I am just glad Samar has finally found his place. He has been looking for some time."

"My place?" Samar said, leaning away from Ira.

"Yes," Ira said. "For so many years you have been confused, going to school studying this and that and chasing and digging up fossils."

"Relics," Samar said, "ancient relics."

"Of course." Ira waved her hand, rattling the several wooden bracelets of different colors that adorned her wrist. "My point is, since you found out who your father is and more about this gift you have, you are focused and at peace. You even slept last night without tossing and turning."

"Yes, that is so," Samar said. "But we cannot remain here indefinitely."

"What can you go back to now?" Ira said. "These people are your family, and they need you."

"What about our stuff, the apartment?"

"I'll arrange to go back and move our stuff here."

"I have space in my garage, and you can stay with me until you find a place," Claudia said.

"Then it's settled," Ira said.

The conversation silenced the table. Frank knew the statements made by Ira and Samar had implications for the other people around the table. They were where they needed to be to support each other, and each person around the table was smiling and laughing, probably more than any of them had for some time. He felt the warm atmosphere surround him, and it was good, but how long would it last?

Ira stood. "I am ready to go back to the house."

"Anyone else need a ride?" Claudia asked.

"I think I'm ready to go home too," Mark said. "Frank?"

"I think I'll stay awhile if you don't mind," Frank said.

"I can give you a ride," Claudia said to Mark. "It's not that far."

Mark handed Frank the keys to his car and headed toward the door with Claudia and Ira.

"I'll be there in a moment," Samar said. He leaned in to the center of the table. "It was a most electrifying experience to work with you two this morning. I just wanted you to know."

"I think it's good that you are thinking about staying," Frank said. "We could use the help."

"Ira may have to go back," Samar said. "But I would like to stay and be of service."

"You can stay in the room where your father lived if you need to," Kanuik said. "I'm sure Chic won't mind a bit."

"That's very kind of you," Samar said. He pushed his chair back and stood to leave. Ira, Claudia, and Mark were still waiting for him at the door. "I just wanted to tell you that."

Once Samar was gone, Kanuik turned to Frank. "There is more we need to talk about from this morning before you go home, Father Frank," he said.

"Yes," Frank said. "What do we do about Thomas?"

"He's well connected in the church," Jimmie said. "Even if you tell Bishop Tafoya, I'm not sure there is much we can do. We left no evidence that we were the ones who sabotaged his lab. I say we leave it at that."

"You don't think he'll try again?" Frank asked.

"Not right away," Jimmie said. "I think he will wait to see what happens with our plan to send soldiers through before he makes a move. Besides, it will take him some time to get more equipment and find a place. We can keep an eye on him for now."

"I think I will still try to find a way to tell Bishop Tafoya what is happening," Frank said.

The front door of the tavern opened. Frank followed Kanuik's gaze and spotted Connor Dietz walking toward the table.

"Where've you been all day?" Frank said.

"At the rec center, where I was supposed to be, just like you, Jimmie." Connor sat down in the chair Ira had vacated. "Thomas was not pleased that you told everyone we were doing tests today and no one else showed up."

"Ahhh." Jimmie lowered his head. "I forgot to go there after our diversion worked."

"What rec center?" Frank asked.

"The rec center is where we are setting up to go through the portal," Connor said.

"I thought you were using the basement of the church?" Frank said.

"That's just for experimenting," Connor said. "We can't get everyone down there, so we had to find some place bigger."

"Jimmie, just how many soldiers are you getting ready to send through?" Frank asked.

"About seven hundred and twenty," Jimmie said. "We had more at one time, but some of them have quit due to all of the delays. Did Bishop Tafoya attend?"

"Yes, he gave instructions for everyone to be ready," Connor said. He picked through the boxes still on the table and found a slice of pizza to eat.

"Did he tell you what the council has decided?" Frank asked.

"I don't think he knows yet," Jimmie said. "I think he would come down here and tell us if a final decision had been made. He's just sticking to the original timeline in case. That's four days away, for those of you wondering."

"We are ready," Connor said.

"Yet we are still not sure if we can bring any of you back," Jimmie said.

"I'm going," Frank said. "If they decide to send you, I'm going."

"But you haven't been through the training," Connor said.

"He just spent the last three years kicking the crap out of those things," Jimmie said. "He might be the only one truly qualified to go. Besides, after what I witnessed this morning, I'm not sure your training is going to be enough."

"What happened this morning?" Connor asked. Just then, Chic came by and started clearing the plates and boxes.

"Connor," Kanuik said, "it would be most helpful to us if you would help Chic. As the youngest at our table, it falls to you."

Connor shoved the rest of the slice of pizza he was eating into his mouth. "Here, wet me halp you," he said with his mouth full.

After he was gone, Frank asked, "Why did you want him to leave?"

"Because he wasn't there this morning," Kanuik said. "He's young, and just as he's giving us information about all of the events of his day at the church that he probably isn't supposed to share, he might carelessly tell of what we have been doing, and Bishop Tafoya would find out.

Please, give me a moment." Kanuik reached in his pocket and pulled out his pipe. He took out a small bag of leaves and packed them down in it. "Do you mind?"

Frank shook his head, as did Jimmie, as Kanuik lit the pipe.

"The shadows, as you refer to them, don't have the technology we've developed. However, they are wise and old; they adapt and fight in the mind. They use the material things against us, our vanity against us."

"Exactly what we should be discussing," Jimmie said. "We need to know how to fight them before we send these soldiers through."

"That's not what Father Frank is thinking," Kanuik said.

"Sorry," Frank said, sitting up in his chair. "What do you mean?"

"How did you know how to fight those things this morning?" Kanuik said. "You were greater this morning than Adnan ever was." He puffed his pipe and blew smoke above the table. "From ancient times, the warriors against the shadows have been chosen, not by men but by a higher calling. Adnan, Father Frank, Samar, and I were recruited not by choice but by events that led us to the war."

"Yes," Jimmie agreed. "What does that mean?"

Frank answered, "It means the soldiers you are about to send through the portal weren't chosen. They weren't led to the cause like we were. Unless we figure out how to help, we might just be marching them to their death, or worse, we might be turning them into weapons for the enemy. Remember what it was like when you were attacked by the shadows at David's house?"

"I've never forgotten," Jimmie said. "But what if you're wrong and Thomas is right? What if we keep delaying and the shadows only get stronger and things get worse?"

"It won't matter much who is right or wrong," Frank said, "not if the council is set on sending them through in four days."

"What do we do then?" Jimmie asked.

"If we can determine the origins of the shadows," Frank said, "figure out how to stop them from coming through the portals, we might have a chance."

"We need to consult the council," Kanuik said.

"I don't think the council is going to listen to us," Frank said.

"Not that council," Kanuik said. "The tribal council. Kwanu and Alo, two of the chiefs, often talk about the spirit world. At times, they enter it to fight the tricksters. Perhaps it is they we need to speak with."

"We don't have that kind of time," Jimmie said. "We are going in four days!"

"It would only take a day to fly there. One day to meet and one day to travel back," Kanuik said. "I would be back before your deadline."

"*We* would be back before that time," Frank said. "I'm going with you!"

"Then we go tomorrow," Kanuik said.

"Wait, I'm not sure I'm ready for all of this," Jimmie said.

"You have to remain here and prepare just in case," Frank said. "Keep an eye on the rest while we go."

Jimmie shook his head.

"Anything we can do now to get information would help," Frank said. "I don't see another choice."

"You will have to tell Claudia this time," Jimmie said. "Let me know if you need a ride to the airport. I have classes all morning, but I can get an assistant to cover if needed." Jimmie got his jacket and put it on.

"I'll get us there and back," Kanuik said. "We will see you on the third day."

Frank and Jimmie exchanged glances.

"What?" Kanuik said. "Did I say something wrong?"

"No, it's just that, well, that's what Jesus told the disciples," Jimmie said. "That he would see them on the third day."

"Oh, well, he and I are not from the same time," Kanuik said. He patted Frank on the shoulder as he left the table. "Come downstairs with me before you go."

"Be careful," Jimmie said.

"Why are you worried?" Frank asked.

"Because you've never flown with Kanuik."

"I don't know what you mean. Is he scared of flying?"

"No, but you may be after you're done."

After Jimmie left, Chic locked the door and went to the bar, where he started cleaning glasses and wiping down the stools. Frank watched for a moment and then went downstairs to find Kanuik in the hallway by Adnan's room.

"You sure you can get me on a plane?"

"Not a problem," Kanuik said. "Just be ready by seven. We will have to get permission to speak with the tribal council, but I think they will make an exception on your behalf since you have been to the other side and back; they will welcome you. We have to go through a ritual. We will start now since our time is short. First, you have to fast for the next day, which you should have no problem with since you are not eating."

"Yes, well, don't tell Claudia," Frank said.

"Why do you not eat?"

"When I was in the spirit world, there was no need for sustenance. I never hungered as long as I believed in my faith. I think my system is just trying to get used to processing food again. I can drink a little, but food upsets my stomach. Now what is this all about? Why did you want me to come down here?"

"We have to start the purification ritual tonight to be within tribal law. Are you afraid of death?"

"No," Frank said. "I've already experienced it. With my faith, I believe in a hereafter. Why are you asking me about this?"

"I just don't want to be flying with you if you are afraid."

"Oh."

"Stand still," Kanuik said, and he went into Adnan's room. He came back with a leather pouch and a long pipe, which was lit and producing smoke. Frank recognized the fragrance as cedar. Kanuik put the pouch on the floor. With the pipe, he walked around Frank and let the smoke float around his body. Then he changed the ingredients in the pipe—Frank now smelled sage—and repeated the ritual.

"It's a wonder with all the pipes and holy fire that you don't set off more smoke alarms," Frank tried to joke.

"This entire basement area is made from stone, very fireproof," Kanuik said. "Now sit."

Frank sat down, and Kanuik removed several items from the

leather pouch. "The smoke was for cleansing and to wash away any negativity. These items represent the elements of our world. The shell represents water. The unlit herbs and ashes represent the earth. The lit herb represents fire. And the smoke represents the air." He set out a long eagle's feather and lit the herbs over a small tea-light candle. He put the herbs down on a tray and used the feather to direct the smoke toward Frank. After he was done, he sat in silence.

Frank prayed. He didn't want to disrespect Kanuik's religion or ceremony, and he didn't see that it was harming anything because Kanuik wasn't asking Frank to pledge himself to his beliefs or do anything unsafe. In fact, to Frank, the ritual seemed very pure. He considered what he'd heard about the Council of World Religions that had come together. Although he was already prejudiced against Thomas and some of his actions, the council might be a good thing— combining forces of all faiths to battle evil.

Frank noticed Kanuik had stopped and was just looking at him. "Sorry. I was in deep thought. Are we done?"

"No," Kanuik said. "Now we have to smoke peyote and travel to the spirit world." He stood and extended a hand to help Frank stand. The he laughed a deep laugh. "You should have seen your face, priest. I was just kidding."

"You got me," Frank said. "You sure that going down to the tribal council will help?"

Kanuik nodded. "They have information that can help. Come on, I'll let you out."

Frank walked back to Mark's apartment and enjoyed the time alone. The experience reminded him of his former life, when he went freely about the town, and it was late enough that he didn't have to worry about disguising himself for fear someone would recognize him. As he wandered down the road, which was void of traffic at this time of night, he thought about the journey he was about to undertake.

Frank felt it was time for him to find new solutions and go for any options. Although he was able to battle the shadows in the realm where they existed, he was not able to completely stop them, and that was his ultimate goal. At the same time, he considered the possibility that the reason he was so willing to go with Kanuik was that he needed a break; he was running away from a situation unfolding before him that he couldn't handle.

"No," Frank said aloud as his breath materialized and took form in the cold night. "I was committed in what I did before and saw it through knowing the danger. I am committed now to this because I know it is what I must do."

He listened to the quiet night around him. The click of flashing streetlights was the only sound. In no hurry, he walked slowly back to the apartment. Once there, he found that the door was unlocked and Mark had already gone to bed. Frank lay on the couch and started a litany of prayers that he had done when in the realm of the shadows. It was something that centered him and gave him foundation.

CHAPTER 10
FOUR DAYS REMAINING

The world will not be destroyed by those who do evil,
but by those who watch them without doing anything.

—Albert Einstein

Frank didn't sleep during the night. Although Mark had offered him the bedroom when he first arrived, he had accepted the couch instead, knowing he wouldn't sleep but not knowing why. He found himself up early and quietly packing the few clothes he had left. He wasn't sure when he was going to call Claudia and tell her that he was leaving with Kanuik or how Kanuik was going to get the two of them to the airport. He wasn't sure how he was going to manage getting on a flight since he was legally dead. "Legally dead," he said to himself. His apartment was no longer his, nor was his church. Life had gone on without him.

A light knock came at the door. Frank opened it and was stunned to see Claudia.

"Good morning," Claudia said, coming into the apartment. "Surprised to see me? How did you think you two were getting to the airport this morning? Did you think I'd let you go without saying goodbye?"

Frank had spent half his night considering what he was going to say when he called her, but no words came to him, and all he could muster was "Uh, I was going to call you."

"You don't have to now," Claudia said. "Kanuik told me he is taking you to see the elders in his tribe, something he thinks will help." The tension in her face and the hands on her hips let Frank know she was upset.

"We are only going to be gone a few days," Frank said. "We are going to visit the Council of Ten, the Native American tribal council. Kanuik thinks they have some knowledge that can help us."

"And you can't just call and ask them?" Claudia said.

"We are going to one of the plateaus where they live. I don't even know if they have cell phones there or even electricity. Outsiders are usually not allowed. It's important we gain any information we can."

"I guess we should be going then," Claudia stated.

Frank grabbed her before she could pass by him. "Look, you're the one who said emotions rule over reason in tense situations. We've all enjoyed being back together lately. It's been good food, drinks, and company at the Kozy Tavern. Samar's likeness to Adnan even adds elements that make me not miss Adnan so much, or at least I don't dwell on the fact that he's gone."

"Is that what you think I'm doing? Dwelling on this?" Claudia asked.

Frank took both of her hands, looked in her deep blue eyes, and could see the tears forming. "What are we doing, Claudia? I've been to and come back from a place not of this world. I was declared dead, yet here I stand. I am not fragile or going to break if I go on this trip. Your worry for me is not needed."

"But I like worrying about you," Claudia said.

The two embraced.

"I just don't like the idea of you leaving when you just came back to us."

"I'm not sure I can explain it all," Frank said. "It seems everything has been so confusing since we met. All I can tell you is that I need to see this through now."

Claudia released him and backed away. "Leave it to me to fall in love with a man who's a priest and who needs to go out and fight evil." She took some tissues out of her purse. "I'm fine," she said as Frank came closer. "It's good to get it out. I've been dealing with this for years. I just wish it could be different."

Frank didn't want to say anything to make matters worse or upset Claudia, but he felt the same. If not for his calling to a higher duty, he would have been happy to go with her and leave everything behind.

"Kanuik's probably wondering where we are," Claudia said. "We better get going."

After picking Kanuik up at the Kozy, the three headed toward the airport. The trip took nearly an hour, but conversation was nonexistent. As they neared the airport, Frank noticed that they were heading not for the main hub but toward a smaller, off-line set of hangars. They had to stop at a check-in point, where Kanuik exited the car and showed an ID and signed them in. After that, it was a short drive to an airfield with dozens of small planes adjacent to the main airport.

"Here you are," Claudia said. "If you can manage, give me a call me when you are starting back, and I'll come and pick you up."

Frank exited and got his bags out of the trunk, after which Kanuik retrieved his own bags and closed the trunk, and Claudia drove away.

Kanuik led him to a small four-seater plane, opened the door, and put his stuff inside. He untied the tie-downs, took off a few covers, and stored them in a compartment on the plane. "You can get in on that side," Kanuik said, pointing, and proceeded to get in the pilot's side.

"Kanuik, you can fly this thing?" Frank said as he opened the passenger's door and entered the aircraft. Suddenly, he remembered Jimmie's warning about flying with Kanuik.

"Of course," Kanuik said. "Been doing it for years."

"I didn't think you even had a driver's license."

"You don't need one on the reservation," Kanuik said. "But these"—he pointed to the controls—"are the only way to get where we need to go fast."

"Claudia knows you can fly a plane?"

"Of course," Kanuik said. "We even met up once when she was touring, and I flew her to her next stop."

"How can you afford this?"

"I can't, but the tribes own many casinos and have money," Kanuik said. "And the plane is a Comanche." He laughed and handed Frank some headphones.

Frank buckled in, and Kanuik started the engine.

"Tower, this is Comanche 41," Kanuik said, "requesting clearance for takeoff ... Roger, Tower. You have a fine day."

Frank gripped his seat as they rolled down the small runway and lifted off. He soon found that Kanuik had no fear of heights, which he demonstrated by climbing immediately and leveling off at ten thousand feet.

"Are you sure we should be this high in such a small plane?" Frank asked.

"The big jets go much higher," Kanuik said. "The wind is calmer at this altitude and will make for good time and conserve fuel. You haven't flown much, have you?"

"Only a few times when I was in the military," Frank said.

"Well, sit back and take a nap if you want to. We'll be in the air for four hours."

It was early morning when Samar heard Claudia drive away from the house. He got out of bed while Ira was still sleeping and headed into the kitchen. Claudia had left them a note that breakfast was in the refrigerator and that she would return after taking Kanuik and Frank to the airport. Samar opened the refrigerator, pulled out a plate of fruit and croissants, and set the plate on the coffee table in the living room. Claudia had shown him how to work the gas fireplace, and he turned the knob to watch the hypnotic flames, which he found soothing.

It was a brisk November morning, and he had already decided that sitting in front of the fireplace was one of his favorite things to do. He chose a piece of pineapple and was putting it in his mouth when Ira came into the room. Still wrapped in a blanket, she sat beside him.

"It's too cold here all of the time," Ira said. "The fireplace is lovely. We should just sit here all day."

"Do you want some?" Samar said, pointing to the tray of food in front of him. "I'll get you a fork."

"No, not yet. I just want to enjoy the morning. With your friends taking a trip today, I was hoping we could spend some time together. I've decided to head back tomorrow."

Samar stopped eating. "That soon?"

"It will give me time to arrange packing up our apartment so we can be out by the end of the month. That way we won't have to pay another month of rent."

"I should go and help," Samar said.

"No. I can take care of it. You have found your place here. The next few days are critical. You don't need any distractions."

"But I'll miss you," Samar said.

"It won't be long. I'll have your stuff sent to you and move the rest back to my father's house."

"What will you do after that?" Samar asked.

"I'll go home to my family for a while. We will remain in touch. Perhaps within a month or two, you will have things sorted out, and then we will decide what is next for us."

Samar moved closer and put his arms around Ira. After helping the group fight the shadows the morning before, something he still hadn't revealed to Ira, he knew he'd found the place he was needed and people who understood his gift. "I am sorry things are this way, but they need my help."

"I understand," Ira said.

"But I don't want to say goodbye to you either," Samar said.

"You see," Ira said, "this is why I am here for you—because you cannot decide. This is just temporary. Now that you have found your place, I can find mine." She smiled at him and added, "With you, of course!" They embraced. "You did not think I would leave you all alone here. I'll be back by Christmas, and we will celebrate and decide if we are living here or somewhere else. I'm sure the friend you've made, Jimmie Barnes, can help get you a job at the college if you ask him."

Samar released his embrace and started eating again. "I'll see if they will allow me to stay at the Kozy Tavern where my father lived. I can help out around there as well."

"See, things will work out, I'm sure," Ira said. She stood up from the couch. "I'm going to take a shower so when Claudia comes back, we can go out for a while and do something fun."

Samar looked into the flames of the gas fireplace as he continued eating his breakfast. He enjoyed the quiet that he suspected would not last long.

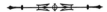

"Sorry about that landing," Kanuik said. "These planes have been known to have issues with landings. The tribal council got me the plane so I can get around and meet with all the tribes, and I'm not used to having a passenger—it throws the weight balance off."

The two had landed on a worn but paved small airfield with only one runway and a few small buildings and had just stepped out of the plane. Two men came out of the center building, entered a white van, and headed out to meet them.

"Get your things," Kanuik said. "These men will drive us to the mesa, where we will wait to be escorted into the village. I did not inform the elders that I would be coming, so it may take some time to get approval for an audience."

"Will they still see us?"

"I think they will see us after I tell them who you are," Kanuik said.

"You make it sound like I am some type of celebrity."

"Don't discredit yourself, Father Frank. You may still be trying to piece things together, but when you joined our team, Adnan knew there was a reason for you to come to us. He selected you because of your power, and he was not wrong. Every religion, including ours, has been struggling to gain an upper hand in the battle against evil in a world that seems to have its eyes shut to what is going on. You found a way to enter their world and battle them."

"Tell me your impression—what do you think is going on in the world? Why are things getting worse?"

"I don't know," Kanuik said. "We have turned away too far from our respect for life and replaced it with desire for material things. That is my thought, but it is something to ask the tribal council."

The few bags they had brought were out of the plane, and Kanuik reached in to get one last item, his hat. He put it on and started walking toward the coming van. Frank started to get his ball cap but threw it back in the plane at the last minute, knowing that it wasn't necessary here; no one knew who he was.

The two men exited the van and loaded the visitors' bags in the back. Frank took his seat in the back. Kanuik introduced himself to the pair and mentioned something about the eagle and owl. After a brief stop at a one-pump gas station, they were on their way to what was known as the first mesa. The drive took longer than Frank expected. Kanuik kept his eyes closed, and Frank thought he was either napping or meditating. Frank prayed for guidance but found his mind drifting. He was wondering what the rest of the group was doing today.

Jimmie parked his car several blocks away and walked to where Connor was keeping an eye on the building Thomas had used for his experiments. The two had set up in an abandoned building across the street from the warehouse, and although they couldn't see the side door exactly, they could see who was entering and exiting the alley.

Jimmie entered the abandoned building on the opposite side through a doorway with a broken lock. He carefully dodged piles of scrap wood and metal on the floor as he walked to the window where Connor had pulled some wood pallets and set up a makeshift chair. Connor was sitting on the pallets with earphones on and binoculars in hand, looking through the window.

"Sorry," Jimmie said. "Thomas called me, and I had to make up an excuse for why I didn't show up the other day and why I wouldn't have time today. I told him I had to go in and do some lectures this morning. I've been having my teaching assistant fill in enough lately."

Connor didn't respond, and Jimmie wondered if he even knew Jimmie was there. He touched him on the shoulder, trying not to surprise him too much. Connor didn't flinch.

"Anything happen?"

"He's in there now," Connor said.

"For a minute there, I didn't think you could hear me. Why didn't you call me?"

"Oh," Connor said, removing the headphones connected to his cell phone. "The batteries ran out a half hour ago. That's why I didn't call you. Guess I was listening to music too much."

"No problem," Jimmie said. "Is there anyone with him?"

"No, just Father Thomas," Connor said. "But he's been in and out a few times. The first time he entered, he was in there a good ten minutes and then came out in a hurry, looking around. Now he appears to be removing stuff to cover his tracks."

"That's good," Jimmie said. "I'm still not sure how we are going to tell Bishop Tafoya about all of this, especially now with Kanuik and Frank gone. Let's hope he doesn't start asking us questions."

"Look," Connor said.

Jimmie grabbed the binoculars from Connor and pointed them toward the alley. A van, the same van that they had seen Thomas use before, pulled into the alley. Two men got out and helped Thomas load items into the vehicle. The men also took cleaning supplies inside with them.

"Looks like he's trying to erase any evidence that could connect the tests to him," Connor said. "Hopefully, this convinces him to stop."

"Guys like that don't stop," Jimmie said. "I just hope my friend Mike took my advice and got out of town. But they're not going to be able to salvage much. I made sure of that. It will take him a while to find a new place and get new equipment."

"We should call the police," Connor said. "They'd have to try to explain what they are doing. That might get rid of Thomas."

"Or it might lead them to us," Jimmie said. "If the Council of World Religions shuts the project down, Thomas will be gone soon enough."

"You think they will shut it down? What happens then? I came out here to fight these things and make a difference."

"You have," Jimmie said. "Even if we don't go through with our plan, that won't mean this thing has ended. Long before we discovered the portals and began attempting to use them, there were teams battling the shadows. Your uncle, Father Frank, was part of one of these teams. From what I see going on at the Kozy, the team is back together."

"You think they'd let me join them?" Connor asked.

Jimmie couldn't help but like the young man, who often reminded him of himself. He was curious and well-mannered and a hard worker. "I think they'd be stupid if they didn't let you join," Jimmie said. "Come on. You've been here all morning. Let's go get something to eat." Connor put the binoculars away and followed Jimmie to the door.

"I'm always amazed that you have so much equipment," Connor said. "It's like you're a caped crusader or something like that."

"Well, I used to be a ghost hunter," Jimmie said. "Who knows? Maybe it's time to get back into it if I could get a partner."

"What happened to your other partners again?" Connor asked.

"They got scared and gave it up."

"Oh."

Frank and Kanuik arrived at the top of the mesa in the middle of the afternoon and parked in a lot with several other vans.

"I'm glad we don't have to worry about cold weather here. Where in Arizona are we exactly?" asked Frank.

"Northeast Arizona," Kanuik said.

"Those people up there don't look too happy." Frank pointed to a group of what looked to him to be tourists. The two walked to the edge of the parking lot, where a heated discussion was taking place.

Kanuik confirmed Frank's impression with his next statement. "They are tourists," Kanuik said. "They travel here to see the ancient culture but need a guide. They can't go into the village without one."

"You're my guide, right?" Frank said.

"Yes," Kanuik said. "But that's not the issue here. Something else is wrong. There is some other reason that they won't let these people in. Follow me."

The two tried to go around the group but were stopped by two men dressed similarly in park ranger shirts. They looked like they were either guides or guards for the village. Frank didn't understand all the words they were saying because they spoke in a different language, but he clearly understood when they said "no."

Frank felt that his limited knowledge of Native American tribes would be a detriment to him now. Whatever the men were saying, he had no way to communicate with them. He was sure that Kanuik, who towered over the shorter men at six feet seven inches and was now engaging them, was not from the same tribe. However, he heard Kanuik speak in the same tongue as the men, and again he understood only a few words—"owl," "eagle," "wolf," and "holy man" were among the words he could make out.

The men looked at Frank, and the one who had done the most talking and was apparently the leader of the group smiled. "Father Frank, you can follow me," he said in perfect English.

Kanuik and Frank moved forward with the one guide while the others continued to talk with the aggravated tourists. The man led them to a small adobe house, where they entered. The room was small, and both Kanuik and Frank had to duck due to the low roof. The room held a small bed with a cot beside it and two chairs.

"Our lodging for the night," Frank said.

"This will be fine," Kanuik said to the guide. "Please let us know when Alo will see us."

A few other people came in and brought Frank and Kanuik food while they waited. Frank managed to drink some coffee they brought but gave his plate of food to Kanuik.

"Welcome," an elderly man said as he came through the door.

Kanuik immediately stood, but the man protested.

"No, sit, sit. I understand you have had a long journey." Wise eyes looked out from a short, stout frame. The man had long white hair and was dressed in leather with a single band around his forehead. "This is the man who has traveled to the other side," he said as he offered his hand to Frank and shook it many times. "I look forward to our discussion tomorrow."

"Frank, this is Chief Alo. He was my guide for many years and like a father to me," Kanuik said.

"I have some questions for you," Frank said. "Would you like to sit down?" He moved from his chair and offered it to Alo, but the chief remained standing.

"We will have plenty of time to talk," Alo said. "You two should rest now. There is a ceremony tonight, and you are welcome to watch. I'll make sure they know you are coming."

"Chief Alo," Frank said, "I don't mean to be rude, but we are short on time. You see—" Frank didn't get to finish his statement.

"Yes, yes, I know that time is short. We are all feeling it here; there is a great disturbance around us. The owl has come, and the coyote is not far from our door. I think they have followed you, and we are making sure they cannot find you or harm our village. Rest and prepare yourself." With that, Alo left the room.

"I hope I wasn't rude," Frank said.

"You will take the bed," Kanuik said.

"I don't need it," Frank said. "I haven't been sleeping."

"Try, if you can. As Alo said, you need to rest and prepare yourself. You must understand, the people here don't have the sense of time and hurry that we do. We are lucky to get an audience with the elders tomorrow."

Frank lay back on the bed and stared at the roof; it looked ancient to him, and he was suddenly taken in by the peace and simplicity of the place. He turned on his side and faced Kanuik. "I heard you at the airport and outside speaking of the eagle and the owl."

"Yes," Kanuik said. He had finished eating and moved to another chair, which to Frank's surprise was a rocking chair. He sat back in the chair and started rocking. "Kwanu, the elder chief we will meet tomorrow, is the Eagle, and the Owl is you."

"Oh," Frank said. "I also heard mention of the coyote. Is that you?"

"No, I am Kanuik. Sometimes I have been called the Raven. The coyote is the evil spirit, the trickster, the shadows we are fighting. Many warriors in the camp tonight have fought against this evil. They felt the presence of the coyote and came to protect the villages."

"The shadows? Gathering here?" Frank asked.

"Yes. However, don't worry. They will be performing a protection ceremony tonight. You should come with me and watch. These ceremonies have been closed to outsiders for hundreds of years." Kanuik closed his eyes and seemed content to keep rocking.

"Do you want the bed?"

"No," Kanuik said. "I enjoy the rocking … it's soothing."

Frank couldn't steady his mind. "So I am the Owl. What does that mean?"

"The owl represents change and one who can see what others cannot," Kanuik said.

"At least it's a good name. I like owls." Frank felt quite content.

"I should tell you, the owl is also a sign of death coming."

After Kanuik's comment, Frank didn't feel like talking anymore.

Claudia felt uplifted as she entered the Kozy Tavern with Samar and Ira. After spending much of the day doing little more than sitting around the house, the group had decided to have a send-off for Ira, who was heading home with plans to return once she'd settled her affairs. But that wasn't what had Claudia feeling good. Although Frank was out of town, for the first time in years, she felt a belonging with the people around her. The white painted word "Kozy" on the outside wall described perfectly how she felt at this moment.

Connor sat at the bar, and Chic stood behind it in his normal place. Connor turned to greet the group and then went to the kitchen and started hauling out dishes to set the table.

"I didn't even have to ask this time," Chic said.

"Where's Jimmie?" Claudia asked as Connor passed her with a set of plates.

"I suppose you mean because we are always together, I must know where he is?" Connor snapped.

Claudia didn't reply but watched from the bar as he set the table.

He slowly returned with his head down. "Sorry," Connor said. "I always get teased about my young age, and I try to not let it get to me, but then sometimes I just let my immaturity show."

"That's a very mature thing to say," Claudia said. "But what is really bothering you?"

"Jimmie had a meeting with Bishop Tafoya today, and then he said he'd come here. That's all I know."

"Is that what's bothering you?"

"I'll get these," Chic said, picking up the rest of the silverware and taking it to Ira and Samar at the table, leaving Connor and Claudia to speak.

"I traveled all the way out here to be part of this plan," Connor said. "Now that I've finally gotten to know the man who inspired me to this cause, my uncle, he's the very one putting my participation at risk."

"I don't follow," Claudia said.

"The people involved in the project think Frank is … infected somehow. And because I'm related, they are treating me the same way. Like, they don't trust me just because I'm his nephew."

"Trust issues," Claudia said, clasping her hands together. "It is one of our greatest weaknesses that we cannot learn how to trust and give others the benefit of the doubt." She put her hands on Connor's hands. "You and I don't know each other that well, but I trust Frank more than I do any member of that religious council. And I'm sure that whatever plan he and Kanuik come back with, they will include you in it."

The smile Connor returned told her she had chosen her words well. "Thank you," he said. "I'll get the food. If Jimmie's late, we'll just eat without him."

Just as Connor left for the kitchen, the front door opened, and Jimmie entered the Kozy Tavern. A cheerful person, Jimmie normally had a way to find humor and liven the mood. But as he approached Claudia, his eyes lacked their normal cheer and went past her to the kitchen, where Connor had just gone.

"They are going tomorrow," Jimmie said, removing his jacket and setting it on a barstool, "a day early. Before Frank and Kanuik return."

Claudia didn't know how to respond to Jimmie's revelation and stood silent.

"I'm sorry," Jimmie said. "I don't know why I told you that other than I needed to tell someone. Please, don't tell Connor anything. They aren't going to let him go."

"What are you going to tell him?" Claudia asked.

"I'll think of something," Jimmie said. He stepped behind the bar, poured himself a beer, and took a drink. "The truth is, I'm glad he's not going to be there tomorrow. If anything Frank warned us about is true, maybe it's better."

"Why are they doing this?"

"They think there's something wrong with Father Frank. They think that even if he doesn't know it, he is somehow signaling those shadows, or they are somehow using him."

"You don't think that, do you?"

"I don't know what I think," Jimmie said, finishing the beer and pouring another. "Frank isn't the same since we brought him back. You know that. He doesn't eat, doesn't sleep. But I don't think there's a single bit of him that could be evil."

"Frank and Kanuik think they are coming back a day ahead of your plan," Claudia said. "What are we going to tell them?"

"I don't know," Jimmie said. "I'm hoping they find something that can still help us and that it's not too late. Otherwise, Frank's credibility won't be worth much."

Connor emerged from the kitchen with plates of food and smiled as he went past Claudia and Jimmie. "I cooked this myself," he said.

"I guess we should go eat," Jimmie said. "It's supposed to be a send-off celebration, right? Then let's start celebrating."

The group sat down at their usual table as Chic and Connor brought plenty of raviolis and garlic bread to the table. Chic said the blessing, and everyone else started to eat. Chic raised his fork to eat as well, but some customers came in and kept him occupied.

"I can put you up at my place for a while if you need a place to stay," Jimmie said to Samar.

"I am going to move out of Claudia's house and into my father's room downstairs here at the tavern," Samar said. He reached out and squeezed Ira's hand. "Ira will go back to Israel and send me my things."

"Oh," Jimmie said, looking at Ira, "you aren't coming back yourself?"

"Not right away," Ira said. "I am returning to India to visit my family first."

"Your father will be happy to see you, I'm sure," Samar said. "He has been accusing me of stealing you away for the last year."

"I am sure when he finds out that we are planning to go even farther away and live in the US, he will be ready to come here himself and talk to you," Ira said.

Samar's face went blank, and the group laughed.

"It's okay, Samar," Jimmie said as he handed Samar some garlic bread. "You're just going to have to do the honorable thing and ask her father politely for this lovely lady's hand in marriage." He broke out laughing as Samar took a big bite of the bread.

"No more drinks for that one," Chic said, pointing to Jimmie as he joined in the merriment, and the group continued eating.

When everyone was done, Ira said, "That was a wonderful meal. You are truly a great chef."

"Chic, you are a great bartender, a great cook, a handsome man, and so polite. How is it no woman has snatched you up?" Claudia asked.

Chic pushed back from the table and patted his belly with both hands. "Oh, I wouldn't say none of them have," Chic said. "I've been married three times and widowed three times. I just figured I'd had enough." He stood. "Connor, Jimmie, help me clear the table please."

Connor and Jimmie stood and started clearing the table.

"We should get going," Samar said, pushing his chair back from the table. Claudia watched as he walked to the bar and visited with Chic. She felt a tug on her shoulder and turned to find Ira's hand on it.

"I wanted to thank you so much for allowing us to stay with you," Ira said. "You and I are a lot alike—we are both in love with men who have been touched somehow by something we cannot fully understand."

"I don't think Frank feels like we are together," Claudia said.

"He knows you care," Ira said. "That is why I must tell you: Frank will feel the need to do something that he is called to do, and there is no way you can turn him from his path. You can only do what you are supposed to do."

"What is that?" Claudia asked.

Ira grabbed her purse and pulled out her copy of Claudia's book. "Support him as you do others. You inspire others. That is your gift."

"Thank you," Claudia said.

"I bet we'll be seeing a lot of each other when I return," Ira said. "I feel like I've known you for a long time, although we met only recently."

Frank and Kanuik returned to the modest house after hours of watching ceremonial dancing. Frank wasn't sure he could decipher all of what he'd seen, but he recognized a lot of it as metaphorically pointing to the battles between the tricksters—as the people here referred to the shadows—and the good spirits.

"No outsiders are let in during days of ceremony, to keep them sacred. What you have seen, you must not tell," Kanuik said.

"I wouldn't know how to describe it anyway," Frank said. "It's like I could feel the mood while they were dancing. It was captivating." He looked around the room. "You want the bed or the cot?"

"I'll sleep in this chair tonight," Kanuik said, and he sat comfortably back into the rocking chair. "I find it suits me."

Frank went to the bed and then looked up at the single light hanging in the room. He wasn't sure if he wanted to turn it off since it was his only guide to the unfamiliar surroundings.

"You are lucky we have that light," Kanuik said. "The rest of the village lives like old times. They don't have electricity. Some believe that technology is evil. What is your thought on this?"

Frank sat on the edge of the bed and removed his shoes. He had always liked Kanuik for his honesty and strength. He was a straightforward character, and Frank never had to worry about him. He also didn't impose his ways or beliefs on anyone, but Frank knew Kanuik had a solid foundation of beliefs, perhaps even more solid than his own.

"I've always believed that evil exists in the world because humankind lets it exist," Frank said. "Technology has allowed us to have light and dispel the myth of darkness being more than it is. It has allowed us to feed more people and improve many areas of our world, from medicine to education, which has led to a higher quality of life for many. No, technology is not to blame. Just like guns, bombs, drugs, and alcohol are not to blame. Human behavior has always been the cause of our condition."

"Human behavior?" Kanuik asked.

"Yes," Frank said. "Our inability to trust, to believe, to have faith. Our willingness to give in to temptations. Our selfish motivations that can outweigh our sense that we belong to something greater. In essence, our lack of discipline and self-control. All religions try to set guidelines for behaviors because without them, we have no common values and are led only by our self-interest. That's what I believe anyway. I have been thinking on these things recently because I'm putting these thoughts down in some writings to share with Claudia for her next book."

"I think your response was highly analytical," Kanuik said. "And I never use that word. I think you and Dr. Walden have been talking more than I realized, and her technical terms are rubbing off on you."

Frank laughed. "Yes, perhaps we have. So tomorrow we will meet the chiefs?"

"The chief that you may know from your history does not exist so much today. Councils govern most tribes. The elders you will meet are sometimes called 'Chief,' but it is more of a title used for the head medicine man or religious leader of the tribe. In our culture, our religion and medicine are considered together and not separate."

"I understand," Frank said.

"The spiritual, mental, and physical health are all combined." Kanuik held his hands apart and then joined them together. "You cannot have one without the other."

"Our faith professes the same," Frank said. "I'm just not sure our followers understand that message."

Kanuik closed his eyes and continued rocking. Frank knew he wouldn't be able to sleep but didn't want to keep Kanuik up all night, so he lay back on the bed and stared at the ceiling. He heard many sounds during the evening, including people walking by, chanting and singing, and even what sounded like someone walking on the roof of the small building. He glanced at Kanuik often, and though his eyes remained shut, the chair remained rocking.

Frank started collecting his thoughts about what he wanted to ask the elders he would meet. He wanted to know if they had information on where the shadows originated and if there was a way to stop their influence. He was hoping that maybe they knew how to destroy the shadows—not just combat them, but destroy them.

His vision went blurry from having his eyes open so long. He tried to blink but suddenly found himself back in the world of the shadows, sitting on his rock and looking out at the landscape. Behind the set of stones, the garden was lush and full of grass and trees, and water flowed. Out in front of him, the ground was hard and rocky, and the trees, though there were many, were barren of leaves; the branches reached out, wanting, but there was nothing to give them.

It was here on this rock where Frank had concentrated and heard voices reaching out to him. He closed his eyes to see if anyone was calling for help but heard nothing. An eerie feeling overtook him, and he shivered. Opening his eyes, he immediately spotted a large, dark form at the edge of the trees. It was not like the other shadows. It seemed to consist of a more solid mass and had a firmer shape. It started moving toward him, and Frank, feeling the danger, tried to move and find his wooden cane. That's when he realized he couldn't move from the stone. Never had the shadows come into the garden or passed the barrier of stones unless he had dragged one there, yet this thing seemed to have no fear of him or the garden as it approached.

Frank tried to stand but found he was not able to control his legs. He felt like he was stuck between dreaming and reality and not yet able to control his muscles. Fear started to well up inside of him, and he didn't understand it. He had always been led by his faith—where was it now, and why was he afraid? The entity was halfway across the clearing now, and Frank struggled to gain control. Suddenly, he heard a loud screeching sound and looked up. A huge eagle had come from behind him and barely cleared his head, its large talons clearly open. The bird was visibly in hunting mode and went directly at the dark form and dived at its head. The form dodged the eagle, which pulled up and then came around for another pass. This was enough to cause the thing to turn around and head away from where Frank sat.

He watched the eagle fly along the edge of the trees where the dark form had gone. Frank could no longer see the dark form, but the eagle remained circling for some time before it swooped down over him and disappeared behind him.

CHAPTER 11
THREE DAYS REMAINING

Instead of cursing the darkness, light a candle.

—Benjamin Franklin

"You ready, priest?" was the next thing Frank heard. He opened his eyes to find he was indeed in the small room with Kanuik.

"I just had the strangest vision," Frank said. He noticed that Kanuik was dressed quite differently than normal; he looked like he'd come straight out of a history book with his decorative shirt, pants, and moccasins. His normal boots were at the base of the rocking chair.

"Good. You did it without having to do any drugs," Kanuik said. "We are becoming more alike every day."

"Why are you dressed like that?"

"These are my ceremonial clothes," Kanuik said. "But don't worry, you don't need to change. They brought us some food this morning, but I don't suppose you want any?"

"Then they have agreed to see us on such short notice?" Frank asked, avoiding the question about eating.

"They were expecting you," Kanuik said. "That was what all the ceremony was about yesterday. They are curious to meet you because of your supernatural nature. I think that's how I should translate it."

Kanuik headed outside, and Frank followed. It was colder than Frank had expected, and he held his arms in tight as they walked.

"How do we greet them?" Frank asked. "Do I shake hands, bow?"

"Definitely don't reach out to them," Kanuik said. "Once they offer you a seat, sit comfortably and listen. At times, they may take a while to respond to what you have said. The elders like to think about things and choose careful words before they respond. Be patient."

"Sit and be patient," Frank said. He noticed that many of the villagers had lined the path they were walking to see him and Kanuik. It made him nervous.

Kanuik stopped and turned to Frank. "Just be yourself," he said. "If they ask you a question, answer truthfully. Now come on. Let's get this done so we can get back to our friends."

After walking for fifty feet or so through a village that to Frank looked like it had stood still as time passed, they came to a roofed kiva. Outside of the kiva Frank counted thirteen men—one adjacent to every opening. Each held a long pipe emitting smoke. These men too were dressed in colorful, ceremonial dress. He tugged down on his shirt to straighten it and put his hand across his collar.

Kanuik led him to one of the entrances, and the man standing before it chanted and danced around both of them, with the smoke from the pipe encircling them. Frank recognized this as a cleansing ritual like the one Kanuik had performed on him the night before. After this, they stepped through the doorway, went down four steps, and entered a round room about twenty feet in diameter. Two fires were lit in pits in the middle of the room. Large blankets were placed on a dirt floor on opposite sides of the fire pits. Kanuik proceeded to the middle of the room and remained standing. Frank moved forward next to him, glad it was warm inside the kiva. His eyes adjusted to the lighting, and he could see five gray-haired men standing in a row opposite them, facing where he and Kanuik had entered. Three of them wore headdresses, while the other two wore simple bands around their heads. The latter two were not quite as fanciful as the others in the way they were dressed. All of the men appeared to be older than Frank, and all of them were shorter than he.

"Please, be seated," said one of the men wearing just a band around his head, in good English.

Kanuik sat down, and Frank sat down to the right of him, where the blanket lay.

"Kwanu, this is Father Frank Keller," Kanuik said. "He is a fellow warrior, and we have fought together. I ask that you listen to him and give him your counsel."

"Father Frank, we are pleased to meet with you," said Kwanu. "I understand you have some questions you would like to ask. We will also have questions for you. I'll speak to you in your tongue as much as possible."

Kwanu continued by introducing the other members who stood before Frank. Frank heard many names that he knew he would have trouble remembering. He tried to remain patient through the introductions, as Kanuik had counseled him. He remembered the name of the elder beside Kwanu, who also wore just a headband and whom he'd met the night before, Chief Alo. Frank's attention was brought back to the present when Kwanu stopped talking.

"I have seen you sitting on your rock. You are surprised, I see. But we"—he motioned around the room—"have been traveling between worlds for a thousand years. We don't do so in the form you take, but in our spirit form."

Frank thought about the vision he'd had the night before. "Are you the eagle?" he asked.

"You learn quickly," Kwanu said. "Yes, I am the eagle you have seen."

"Then what happened to me last night was indeed not a dream but a vision?"

"Yes," Kwanu said. "The evil you fight has been here for all time. It is one and many, created by the wrong deeds of men."

"Do you know why they are gaining strength?" Frank asked.

"We have lost our young people, and that is where we are losing the battle with the ones who deceive. Our youth are impressionable, like children. There is too much confusion and mistrust among them. Lacking true faith, lacking direction and purpose, they latch on to emotional and passionate causes that give them meaning, but in doing so, they abandon faith and reason. They believe in what they can see and feel. And whatever does not fit what they want to believe in, they deny."

"The shadows exploit the weakness of insecurity," Frank said.

His comment caused some side discussion from the men sitting in front of him.

"Did I say something wrong?"

"No," Alo said. "Understand, we represent multiple tribes but not all tribes. Out of the many languages between us, there are many names for what you call 'shadows.' How were you able to exist among them for so long?"

Frank thought for a moment before responding. He wasn't sure how to tell them about the portal Jimmie had created and how he had stepped through it. Plus, he didn't really know how he had survived in their world. The answer he'd given Mark and Bishop Tafoya was that he had done so through faith. Kanuik's advice to be honest and be himself came back to him.

"The group that I was with"—he motioned to Kanuik—"has a way to open a doorway, a portal to the world where the shadows come from. I managed to step through. When I did, I couldn't get back. The world I went to had a place where the shadows couldn't go, a safe place. As long as I stayed in this place, a warm place full of light, I could survive."

"What did you see while you were there?" Alo asked. "Please tell us."

Frank proceeded to tell the group what he remembered about the trees, the grass, and the light that came from one side of the place, the source of which he couldn't discover. He told them about the battles he had fought and how the water had healed him when he bathed in it. After he was done, there was a great silence. He looked to Kanuik, who nodded his approval of Frank's description.

"Do any of the tribes know where the shadows come from?" Frank asked.

"The shadows are from men," said one of the elders who wore a headdress. "They are sin, as you call it, that we created. They have walked with our spirits from the first time we committed sin."

"Is there a way to defeat them, to kill them?" Frank asked.

Again, there was a lot of side conversation.

Then Alo spoke. "Your messiah tried to abolish this sin by sacrificing himself. He closed the doorway to sin and opened one to a new place, your heaven, a place where those who believe can travel without the shadows. He stopped the shadows, as you refer to them, for some time. And for years after, there was a new awakening, and men became more spiritual—but not without committing further acts of evil that drew the tricksters back into this world." Alo looked to the other members of the tribal council.

Kwanu nodded and took up the next part of the conversation. "There are many prophecies of an awakening for humankind where we acknowledge and respect the gift of life," he said. "The pale prophet walked among the ancients, and many are wondering if you, a man who can walk between worlds, are the returning prophet. You have come to us seeking knowledge, but it is we who seek knowledge from one who can walk through and come back from the spirit world."

Frank concentrated on the words said to him: *Sacrifice. Awakening.* "Claudia!" he exclaimed aloud. He suddenly felt he had the answer he had been seeking.

"What is it?" Kanuik asked.

Frank leaned over to speak to Kanuik. "Claudia is the key. The movement she started through her book is a new awakening. Her message is reaching more than I have ever reached. I must help her by closing the door, and then her message will spread. We need to ask them if there is a way to close the door and then head back as soon as we can."

"What door are you speaking about?" Kwanu asked.

"He speaks of the veil between worlds, the shadow world and ours," Kanuik said. "Can it be closed?"

There was much quiet discussion between the tribal council members before they became silent. "We don't know," Kwanu said.

"Chief Kwanu," Kanuik said, "we thank you for your time and counsel. We have found great wisdom in your words. If you have no more questions, we have a long journey ahead of us."

"Yes, a deadline," Kwanu stated.

The elders stood, and Kanuik and Frank did the same. Without any handshakes, four of the men left, including Kwanu. Only Alo remained.

"Chief Alo was my guide who trained me," Kanuik said.

Not sure what to do, Frank put out his hand, which Alo grasped. He didn't shake Frank's hand but felt it, as though he didn't believe Frank was real.

"I can see you are fading, priest," Alo said. "You must decide which world you are going to remain in, or you won't be able to be whole in either."

"What do you mean?"

"You have a calling to serve, and you haven't decided which path to take," Alo said. "You still exist between both worlds. There will soon come a time when you must choose which one you belong in."

Frank turned to Kanuik, who shrugged his shoulders and then said, "I won't tell Claudia," which made Frank smile.

After a few more questions from Alo, Frank and Kanuik said a polite thank-you and left the kiva, going back to the small room where they had spent the night. Kanuik arranged a van to take them back to the plane, but by the time the van arrived at the small landing strip, evening was approaching.

"It is too late for us to go back today," Kanuik said. "I am tired, and it's dangerous to fly at night. These men have a few cots, and we can stay here at the airfield tonight and leave at first light. That will put us back in Chicago between ten and twelve."

"That should work fine," Frank said.

Kanuik and Frank were led to a small one-room shack next to the main office. They entered to see two chairs and a small table inside, as well as two cots folded up against the rear wall. One of the airport attendants entered and looked around the floor as though performing an inspection. He said something to Kanuik that Frank couldn't understand.

"What is it?" Frank asked.

"He said sometimes they get snakes in here, but it appears clear," Kanuik said, smiling.

"Oh, that makes it at least a four-star lodging," Frank said. "Do you think they have some paper and pens so I can do some writing?"

Kanuik turned and talked to the men, and in a few minutes, Frank's request was granted. The men also brought them some food, and Frank tried to eat, but the first bite that went into his stomach caused him severe pain.

Kanuik ate and watched him write. "You are really going to write her another sermon so she can use it in her book?"

"Yes," Frank said. "If you call it a sermon. Maybe we can even get the church to help her spread her message; they can make it a sermon for every church. If we get the positive message going, maybe we really can start a new awakening."

"First we've got to stop the current plan," Kanuik said. He finished eating and went over to the wall, grabbed one of the cots, and began assembling it. "You want me to put one up for you?"

"No," Frank said.

Kanuik lay down on the cot. "We can leave as soon as the sun comes up."

"Do you need me to turn the light out?" Frank asked.

"No, I am fine," Kanuik said. "I was just wondering … when you described to the elders the place you went to, what did you think when you couldn't find a way back to us?"

"I just did what came naturally and started helping people. I remember the room David was in and what I did to tempt him. I remember grabbing the shadows and jumping into the portal and asking Jimmie to close it."

Kanuik was up on his side, intently listening, and Frank knew by the look on his face that he would have to tell him more.

He put down his pen and turned to talk. "I remember battling those things as it got darker and darker. I called out to my Lord for help. Next thing I knew, I was on the hard ground, in their world. I could see the light, and my instinct was to run to it."

"How did you know that would save you?" Kanuik asked.

"I wasn't born into the priesthood, as you remember," Frank said. "In fact, there were many events in my past that turned me away from belief in any gods whatsoever. My mother was my first influence leading me to my faith. She was just so sure that Jesus was the savior. She herself was just a blessing to everyone she met."

"So you went into the priesthood for your mother?"

"In a way, I suppose," Frank said. "I just wish it had happened sooner. She wanted me to be a priest when I graduated, but I chose the path of a soldier and went into the army."

"And that's when the event happened that Adnan has spoken about, when you were touched by the Supreme Being."

"Yes," Frank said. "I couldn't explain it. Those missiles were falling, and I closed my eyes and prayed, and the next thing I knew, they were gone. Even some of my friends at the time knew I'd had something to do with it. I had a habit at the time of confronting difficult situations and coming out unscathed."

"What did you think about while you were in the land of the shadows to keep your wits about you?"

"I thought about my church, the group, and yes, I thought about Claudia."

"She took it the hardest out of all of us," Kanuik said. "She went to see your father every week until he passed away. Even with her work on her book, she never missed a visit."

"We have a lot in common from our childhoods," Frank stated.

"I think it is much more than that," Kanuik said and rolled on his back.

"What happened to the officer who was investigating the Jenson murders? Detective Jennings?" Frank asked. "I thought he seemed interested in her."

"He tried, but Claudia couldn't commit to him. I think he got promoted and went to New York or something like that."

"That's too bad." Frank started writing in the journal. "You sure you don't want me to turn out this light?"

Kanuik didn't respond, so Frank kept writing. In the back of his mind, the idea had occurred to him that since he couldn't go back to his church and had been declared legally dead, he could start a new life if he wanted to. He could decide to leave the priesthood and fight the shadows with the rest of the group like Samar and Kanuik were doing and maybe even be with Claudia.

He looked at the pen that he held in the air. "We're not going to get much done if I keep getting distracted, now are we? Let's focus on one issue at a time." He started writing again.

CHAPTER 12
TWO DAYS REMAINING

*It is during our darkest moments that we must focus
to see the light.*

—Aristotle

"That landing was a little better," Frank complimented Kanuik as the plane touched down. "Looks like Claudia is already here waiting for us." He could see the light blue AMC Ambassador on the other side of the fence and Claudia leaning up against the car.

Kanuik parked the plane and started putting on the covers and securing the tie-downs while Frank unloaded the bags. As the two headed toward the car, the concerned look on Claudia's face let Frank know something was wrong.

"I thought you'd be happy we made it back safely," Frank said as they approached Claudia.

"I'm sorry," Claudia said. "It's great to see you both, but something is terribly wrong. Jimmie came to the Kozy last night and was very upset. He said that they were going through with the plan, and they weren't waiting for you."

"What did he say?" Frank asked.

"He just said they weren't ready in his opinion, and there were still too many questions, but they were going anyway."

"Did Bishop Tafoya come?"

"No, just Jimmie."

Kanuik put the bags in the car trunk and closed it. The three of them stood together outside of the car.

"Bishop Tafoya told me he would let me know when a decision was made," said Frank. "I didn't tell him about our trip because we were coming back today. I'm surprised he didn't try to find me at the Kozy."

"Maybe Mark told him," Claudia said.

"Why don't we just take things one at a time? Drop me off at the apartment, and then we will all meet later at the Kozy and find out what is going on."

"No, you don't understand," Claudia said. "I can't get hold of them, any of them. Jimmie won't answer his phone, and even the school is looking for him. Mark is not at the apartment or at the church, and Bishop Tafoya isn't answering his phone. Not even Madeline will pick up."

"Is Samar with them?" Frank asked.

"No," Claudia said. "He is at the tavern with Chic. Ira has gone back to Israel to move out of their apartment. He didn't think it was appropriate to remain at my house anymore, so he moved in at the tavern."

"Let's go to Bishop Tafoya's office, now," Frank said, and he got in on the passenger's side. Kanuik got in behind Claudia, who started the powerful V-8 engine and headed down the road.

"They weren't supposed to execute the plan until tomorrow," Frank said. "Maybe they're just at the site getting ready, and no one is allowed any communication since it's supposed to be a secret."

"You don't suppose ..." Kanuik didn't finish.

"Suppose what?" Frank asked.

"You told them that the shadows knew of the plan and when they were going. What if they moved up the timeline because they found out you were gone?" Kanuik said.

"That would make sense after what Jimmie told me," Claudia said.

"What did he tell you?" Frank asked.

"He told me that they weren't going to let Connor go because of your relationship. They think you were influenced by the shadows."

"God help us!" Frank said. He looked to the sky and noticed clouds closing in. It would be a cold day.

When they reached the bishop's office, they didn't see Jimmie's car or many other vehicles in the lot either.

"I'll go in and see if he's there," Frank said. "Stay in the car. If no one is here, we will go down to the recreation center."

"Your hat?" Claudia said.

"I don't think that matters at the moment," Frank said. "I'll be right back."

"I'll go with you," Kanuik said.

As the pair neared the front door, Kanuik put his hand out to Frank. "I sense something wrong; there is evil here that I have never sensed before."

"I feel it too," Frank said. "It's something from the other side. Let's make sure we stay together. If the shadows are here, they might try to separate us." When they reached the front door, the first thing they noticed was that the door had been compromised; someone had forced it open from the outside.

"Are you sure Claudia is safe in the car, or should we send her home?" Kanuik asked.

"There's only one way in and out of this place. She's safe as long as we don't let anything or anyone get by us," Frank said.

They entered cautiously, and Frank noticed that Kanuik had already reached into his pocket and pulled out the round objects he threw down to emit holy fire. Madeline was not at the reception desk. They listened but heard no sounds coming from the rest of the building.

"It appears no one is here," Kanuik said.

"I still want to check Tafoya's office," Frank said. "And perhaps even the church."

They went directly to Bishop Tafoya's office. Blood along the hallway floor confirmed Frank's suspicion that something was terribly wrong. He entered the bishop's office to find Father Thomas sitting at Bishop Tafoya's desk. He was slouched back with his arms wide on the armrests, staring forward. He held a cross in his right hand and had blood on his neck and shirt. Frank approached slowly and waved his hand in front of the priest's face, but Thomas seemed to pay him no attention.

Kanuik stepped into the room.

"Don't throw those things," Frank warned, pointing to Kanuik's hands. "There's carpet in here. It might soak up the oil and negate the effect."

"You are wise to think of such a thing," Kanuik said as he put the objects away.

"Just watch him," Frank said, pointing toward Father Thomas. "I don't see any of the shadows, but if he makes any sudden moves, we might have to take him down."

Frank walked forward until he was a few feet away from the desk. He grabbed one of the high-backed red felt chairs to keep between him and Thomas until he could assess his state of mind. "Father Thomas, it's Frank Keller. Can you hear me? Father Thomas, what happened here?"

Thomas slowly closed and then opened his eyes. His long stare went past Frank to something that wasn't there. Frank took a chance and stepped closer, right into Thomas's gaze. This time he tapped his hand on the desk. The noise seemed to have the needed effect because Thomas shook his head and noticed Frank.

"Father Thomas, do you know where you are?"

"Father Frank?" Thomas said.

"Yes, it's Father Frank Keller. What has happened? Where is Bishop Tafoya?"

Thomas sat up in the chair, causing Frank to take a step back and Kanuik to move forward alongside him. As Thomas moved, he turned his neck enough for Frank to see that he was bleeding from the right side of his head.

"They're dead, most of them," Thomas finally managed to say. He pointed to Frank. "You were right. They were waiting for us. I barely made it out of there."

"Out of where?" Frank raised his voice slightly and moved closer to Thomas. He was getting desperate for information. "What happened? They weren't supposed to go for another day."

"Oh," Thomas said. His eyes moved slowly to Frank. "You warned us, but some of us didn't trust you. So they decided to go anyway and went today. I'm partly to blame for that. They believed me, and I didn't trust you."

"He's in shock," Frank said.

Thomas waved the metal cross in his hand at Frank. "Are you one of them?" His eyes focused for a moment, then looked beyond Frank. "I suppose not. Those things got in our minds, and men went crazy." Thomas started crying. "You were right. We failed. I failed."

"My God, what is going on here?" Mark came into the room, surprising Kanuik and Frank. He immediately ran to Thomas. "What are you doing?"

"Mark, be careful," Frank said. "We just got here and don't know his condition."

"Well, he's bleeding, and judging by the amount of blood in the hall and around him here, he's going to be dead of we don't get him help."

Frank grabbed a cover from Bishop Tafoya's Bible stand and handed it to Mark. "Use this and put pressure on the wound. Will you stay here with him and make sure he doesn't leave? He's already caused enough trouble."

"Yes, but where are you going?"

"We'll go get help. Just remain here. I'll contact you later."

Frank and Kanuik hurried out of the office and exited the building. When they reached the car, Frank had Claudia call an ambulance to Bishop Tafoya's office.

"Where to now?" Claudia asked.

"We need to go to the rec center," Frank said. "But first, let's go by the Kozy. We're going to need Samar."

The drive to the Kozy Tavern was quiet. Frank was reflecting on yesterday's meeting with the elders that had inspired his writings, which he'd hoped Claudia could use in her work so that her work in turn would lead to a new awakening. He wasn't prepared for a direct confrontation with the shadows. He needed time to think of a plan. It was late afternoon by the time they got to the Kozy. The air was cold, and the clouds had moved in, indicating snow was about to fall.

Frank entered first and found Connor and Samar both at the bar. They turned and seemed surprised to see him.

"Welcome back," Samar said, unaware of what was going on.

Frank walked up to his nephew. "Connor, what happened with the plan?"

"I haven't heard anything," Connor said. "Jimmie told me last night that he had to go in today and do some adjustments. He mentioned that the church didn't want me along with him because I'm your nephew, and they're worried that something is imprinted on you. Can you believe that?" He shook his head. "They think the shadows know we're coming because I know you, and they somehow can read it through me." Connor looked past Frank as Kanuik and Claudia approached. "I see you brought everyone else with you," he said. "Should we get a table?"

Frank, Claudia, and Kanuik remained standing.

"Welcome back," Chic said from the bar. "Why don't you all take a seat and I'll fix something?" Then he set down the glass that he was cleaning. "What's wrong?"

"They tried to send the soldiers through today," Frank said. "It failed just like I warned them."

"Damn them!" Connor said. He grabbed his coat off the barstool, as did Samar. "I take it we're going to the rec center to find out what's going on?"

"Yes. Claudia, you stay here with Chic," Frank said.

"I'm not staying here," Claudia said, shaking her head. "You might need someone with medical experience. Besides, I'm not letting any of you drive my car."

The group headed out to Claudia's car. Frank sat in the passenger's seat while Kanuik, Samar, and Connor got in the back.

"Do you know where the center is?" Connor asked Claudia.

"Yes, it's at the riverbank, right?" Claudia said.

"That's right," Connor said. "They picked it because it's in an even more remote part of town than this area. No one goes there anymore."

"What kind of weapons were you supposed to take into the portal with you, Connor?" Frank asked. "What will we be facing?"

"Most of the stuff we had was holy water, crosses, Bibles, food and water supplies, and stuff like that," Connor said. "We didn't really have weapons because the shadows were not physical. A few of the soldiers had swords, though."

"That doesn't sound too bad," Frank said.

"I forgot," Connor said. "Everyone had a knife, a six-inch blade with a saw on the back and a top that came open and had matches, compass—you know, survival stuff."

"Great," Frank said.

"Why are you worried about the knives?" Connor asked.

"The shadows have a way of warping reality," Frank said. "They may have turned those men on each other and could use them against us. You should expect them to try to get into your head and find whatever doubts and insecurities you have and use them against you."

"Like what?" Connor asked.

"Well, for instance," Frank said, "Jimmie told you that the church was suspect of my motives because I came from where the shadows are, and they think I might be tainted, and that's how the shadows know of their plans. You have to have some doubts yourself, right?"

"I guess I've considered it," Connor said.

"Then you should expect that if you come into contact with one of the shadows, they might use this against you and try to turn you against me. They won't attack directly, but through these insecurities." Frank turned to look at Samar. "Samar, you can have no doubts about your part in this. You must be clear on why you are here."

"I am clear," Samar said. "This is the clearest I have been in a long time."

Frank nodded at his conviction. He had done what he could to prepare Connor and Samar and knew he didn't have to worry about Kanuik. As he faced forward, Claudia spoke, as though knowing his concern would now turn to her.

"Don't worry about me," Claudia said. "I can stay in the car until you need me. I don't need to go rushing in."

Claudia pulled into the crumbling parking lot of the rec center. Once a solid place for multiple churches to hold events, the old brick building stood faded and worn like the parking lot.

"The buses are here," Connor said. "That door over there is where we should go; it leads to the gymnasium. That's where they'll be."

"Not all of them," Frank said, pointing. Several men wearing khakis and backpacks were stumbling around the parking lot. A few were on the ground by the bus. Claudia pulled the car up by one of the buses, and Frank could see there were men inside the bus as well.

"Don't get too close," Frank warned, "not until we can tell what state those men are in."

As soon as Frank exited the car, he could hear men calling for help and one yelling out commands.

"Get the wounded on the bus!" shouted an older man wearing a black beret, with silver hair visible above his ears. He recognized Connor as the group approached. "Mr. Dietz, you should get out of here as soon as you can."

Connor started moving toward the man, but Frank grabbed him.

"Wait," Frank said. "There are shadows all over the place. Can you see them, Samar?"

"Yes," Samar said.

Another soldier stumbled out of the rec center door, and Kanuik ran to the entrance, where he immediately deployed his holy fire in a semicircle around the doorway.

"What's he doing?" Connor asked.

"The shadows have infected some of the soldiers. Every one of them who leaves this place is a threat unless we make sure they are clean." He pointed. "Kanuik is setting up a barrier. The shadows cannot cross the holy fire, but it won't last for long."

"I'll start with them," Samar said and went to the men by the bus. He started touching them, and Frank could see the shadows reacting.

"What's his name?" Frank asked, pointing to the man who appeared to be in charge.

"Sergeant Lee," Connor said. "He was once a first sergeant in the army, so we all call him that."

Still holding Connor's arm, Frank tugged him along as he approached the sergeant. He could tell that although the sergeant was in distress and wounded, he was not infected with a shadow.

"Sergeant Lee," Frank said, "how many men have come out of there? Did any of them leave this place?"

The sergeant turned to look at Frank with stern brown eyes. "You're with the church?"

Frank nodded.

"This damn thing's a mess. We got wounded on the bus and in there." Sergeant Lee pointed to the center. "But there's something wrong with the men—they started attacking each other."

"I know," Frank said. "We are here to help." He put his left hand on Sergeant Lee's shoulder to try to get him to focus more. "Did any of the men leave the facility?"

"Most are still inside," Lee said. "A couple wandered off that way." He waved his hand to the left. "But no one has left this area."

"Good," Frank said.

"I've contained the door," Kanuik said as he walked up to Frank. "But there may be other exits."

"We need to get these men medical attention," Sergeant Lee said.

"If we call the police or ambulances in, we will just be giving the creatures more hosts," Frank said. "How long will the fire hold?"

"I have enough to last about an hour," Kanuik said. "I'd have to go back to the tavern to get more."

"Connor, take Claudia back to the Kozy. Chic will know how to protect her."

Connor shook his head. "No, I trained to fight these things."

"I know," Frank said, "but Claudia did not. The plain fact is that I need Kanuik and Samar to fight the shadows, and I need Jimmie for what he knows about the equipment. Get Claudia to safety and get back as soon as you can." He turned to Kanuik. "Can you tell him where you keep your supplies so he can bring more back?"

Connor turned away with his head down. Kanuik followed him to the car to give him directions.

"Sergeant Lee," Frank said, "can you drive this bus?"

"Yes."

"Okay then. Samar there"—he pointed—"and I are going to make sure that your men who are out here are clean. Then I want you to take them to the Kozy Tavern downtown. There's someone there who can help them."

"What about the rest inside?"

"We will take care of them," Frank said, and he moved to where Samar was battling the shadows. Although Samar had to make contact with a host, Frank could see the shadows without making this contact. He watched the shadows exit the man Samar was helping and flee back to the rec center.

"I've gotten all the ones that were on or around the bus," Samar said. "Now I fear there are more inside, and I don't know if I can keep going."

"Don't worry," Frank said. "Kanuik," he called, "the shadows are fleeing back to the center. You're going to have to open a way for them to get in and then close the door behind them."

"I'll make a path," Kanuik said and headed toward the door.

"We need to get those men over there." Frank pointed to an area between the bus and the rec center where five men were sitting on the pavement. "Sergeant, help me."

"What are you going to do?" Samar said.

"I am going to use the power I have been given to send these things back to where they came from," Frank said. He went to the men and looked at the black figures surrounding them. "Lord, protect me and guide me," he said. Reaching out to the first man, Frank didn't touch the man but grabbed the dark form around him. He wasn't sure it would work, but he felt the cold, cutting edge of the creature and concentrated until he latched on. Then he did this four more times until he had all of them bundled up in his arms. Frank could feel the weight of the evil on him as he headed to the rec center. "These men are clean," he called out. "Get them on the bus!"

You left your father to die, said a voice in Frank's head.

Then he saw a vision of his father lying on his bed at the Sacred Hills nursing home, looking up at him. "Why did you leave me?"

Frank ignored the hallucination and shook his head clear as he kept moving toward the rec center entrance. Kanuik was by the door. He had opened a gap in the holy fire and put more down, making a path.

Frank needed to get the shadows on the other side and close them in. The next one attacked him, this time by going after his faith. It showed him pictures of his childhood and his mother dying. It showed him how he had been unhappy with God and crying because his mother was gone.

"Too late for that," Frank said. "I have been saved, and all that hate is gone." The vision disappeared.

He was only a few steps away from the entrance when the next attack came. This one stopped him. It was a vision of him and Claudia in what used to be his bedroom, when he had just come back. He was wearing only a towel because he'd just gotten out of the bath, and she was helping him put a robe on. His eyes moved to her long hair, soft as it brushed against him. Her smile and her eyes made him feel good, and he recognized the desire rising inside of him. A voice spoke to him. *You are a man of the cloth; you are not supposed to harbor such needs. You want her. It's not right. Forget the vow.* Claudia brushed up against him, and the light scent of her rose-hip perfume wafted over him.

"Frank, wake *up!*" Kanuik's voice pierced Frank's vision, and he continued his march down the path.

Kanuik opened the door to the center, and Frank released the shadows, who fled from him down the hallway. He turned to see Kanuik throwing more fireballs to encircle the doorway again. Frank carefully stepped back over them.

"That was very impressive," Kanuik said.

"Thank you for helping me," Frank said.

Behind them in the parking lot, Samar and Sergeant Lee had loaded all the survivors, about fifteen in all, on the bus. After Samar exited the bus, Frank watched it pull away.

Once Samar had joined them, Kanuik asked, "What now, priest?"

"That big bus probably held about fifty people," Frank said. "With the ones the sergeant said got away and the ones he just took, there are probably thirty or more left, and that includes Bishop Tafoya and Jimmie. We are going to need Jimmie's help to shut this thing down."

"He's probably in there," Kanuik said.

"There's too many of them," Samar said. "I can't do it."

"You haven't passed out yet," Frank said as he bent over for a moment to catch his own breath. He noticed his strength had been tested.

"You cannot keep up this pace," Kanuik said.

"We need to go in there," Frank said. "We need to shut the project down."

Kanuik pulled out a cell phone, which was something Frank had never witnessed before; he hadn't known Kanuik owned one. He was on the phone for just a minute and spoke in his native Cherokee language, which Frank couldn't understand.

"What was that about?" Frank asked.

"Calling in reinforcements," Kanuik said. "They should be here within the hour."

"We can't wait that long," Frank said. "We go in as a tight group and stay together. "We go until we find Jimmie and Tafoya, and we don't engage any of the others who are infected."

"We have to wait," Kanuik said. "You should know from your military background that if we go in there now, weak and outnumbered, we won't make it out."

Frank started heading toward the center, but Kanuik stepped in front of him. "No, Frank. We just got you back. What would Claudia think if I let you go in there? Trust me, we will go as soon as we have this contained."

"They better get here fast," Frank said. "Jimmie's in there!"

"I know," Kanuik said. "Look around. If it's this bad out here, then it may be too late for those in there. It's clear the portal's open. We need to figure out how to contain the evil to just this place until we can close it."

"I'll wait, but not for long," Frank said.

After twenty minutes, a car pulled up, and several men got out, all of them with features similar to Kanuik. One of the men gave Kanuik a bag. Kanuik opened it and pulled out several necklaces, more balls of holy fire, and some feathers. The men nodded to Frank and went by him. They started spreading ash around the doorway, and then two of them went to the other side of the building.

"These men will guard the doors to make sure the evil is contained," Kanuik said. "They have brought these to help protect us." He handed one necklace to Frank and one to Samar.

Samar put his on, but Frank declined.

"This is all I need," Frank said, brushing his collar and the cross that hung around his neck. He knew his faith had brought him this far, and he would depend on it now.

"It's your choice," Kanuik said. "Lead the way."

Frank opened the door, and a foul-smelling rush of air went past him. The lights in the hallway were out, but enough light streamed in through the windows for them to find their way. Samar hesitated for a moment.

"Samar, are you okay?" Frank asked. "We need to move fast and get this done. The longer we're in here, the more dangerous it gets."

"I smell something burnt," Samar said.

"I smell it too," Kanuik said. "It smells electrical mainly, but possibly some flesh."

At the end of the long, empty hallway, two large double doors led to the gymnasium. The doors were closed as Frank approached them, and he and Kanuik looked through the small square windows. What they beheld was more than Frank was ready to see. Most of the soldiers were either lying on the floor or sitting up against the walls. The huge coils were in the middle of the room, but they looked like they'd been burned. Immediately inside and left of the doorway stood a few tables and equipment. Much of the equipment was still smoking.

"There," Frank said, "that area by the equipment—that's where we will probably find Jimmie." He started to open the door, but Kanuik held him back.

"Tell me what you see in there before we go," Kanuik said.

Frank stepped away from the windows. "There are more shadows than men in that room. Some of them are roaming without form, but every soldier in there is being attacked. There isn't even one of them who knows where he is or what is going on right now. We can't trust any of them. I suspect Jimmie is by the equipment to the left of the room. That is where we will go."

"What then?" Kanuik asked.

"I'll get Jimmie if he is being attacked. Once he has been released, Samar, you will help him out of the building. Kanuik, you will use your fire to keep those things away from us."

"I'll make a pattern to protect our exit," Kanuik said as opened his leather bag and filled both of his palms with balls of fire. "Remember, they cannot cross the holy fire, but once you cross to their side, you are not protected."

"Understood," Frank said.

"Are you sure my father did all of this?" Samar said.

"No," Kanuik said. "He never had to face anything this big."

"How fortunate for me that I am here with you today," Samar said. "Let us go and teach these things a lesson."

Frank and Kanuik smiled. Frank closed his eyes and prayed and then said, "Let's go."

Kanuik slung the fire out to both sides as they entered, making a path to the equipment tables. Frank watched, but the shadows seemed unconcerned about them.

"Take your time," Frank said as they stepped in deeper. "They haven't noticed us yet and will probably ignore us until we interfere."

Blue flames two feet high and white smoke billowed from the floor where Kanuik had thrown down the holy fire. "I'm nearly out," Kanuik said.

"That's okay," Frank said. "I see Jimmie on the ground a few feet in front of us. He looks unconscious."

"What's that over there?" Samar pointed.

Frank looked toward the coils and saw a group of soldiers clearly under the influence of the shadows. They were carrying someone and hoisting him up to one of the coils. Frank stopped moving to watch. It was Bishop Tafoya, and he was still alive.

"Frank!" Kanuik's voice was harsh. "Get Jimmie!"

Frank moved forward to where Jimmie lay on the floor. He expected a battle from the shadows attacking Jimmie, but as he touched Jimmie, the professor's eyes opened. "Frank?"

"Jimmie, are you able to stand?" Frank said. He helped Jimmie to his feet.

"Oh my God!" Jimmie exclaimed as he looked around the room.

"Yes, that's about the size of it," Frank said. Samar had approached, and they steadied Jimmie between the two of them. Frank noticed a good bump on Jimmie's forehead. "Take it easy. It looks like you've had a fall. It injured you, but the fact that you were unconscious may have kept them from attacking you."

"They were waiting for us," Jimmie said. "Just like you said they would be."

Frank noticed movement from both walls; the soldiers were starting to close in on them.

"Yes, well, we can talk about it once we get out of here," Frank said. "I think they've noticed us!"

The creatures swirled in shapeless black forms at the outskirts of the fire. Frank could see forward to a place where Kanuik had left too much space between individual fires, and the shadows were probing it and starting to enter.

"Kanuik, in front of us, there!" Frank pointed.

Kanuik reached into his pocket and pulled out a bag of powder. He filled his hand with it and put it up to his mouth. "Cover your eyes," Kanuik said.

With one arm under Jimmie's shoulder and the other holding his arm, Frank shut his eyes as tight as he could. The flash and heat made it feel like his skin was burning. When he opened his eyes, the path was clear, and Kanuik was pulling on them to go forward to the door.

They had made it past the point where the shadows were coming through when Frank remembered something. "We have to go back for Bishop Tafoya! Here," Frank said to Kanuik. "Take him and get out of here."

"No, there are too many, and we are not prepared. You need to come out with us now!" Kanuik said.

"I'll be right there. I'm going to get Bishop Tafoya."

Kanuik, Jimmie, and Samar made it to the hallway. Frank looked back to the room, which was now full of smoke. The soldiers, numbering about sixty or so, were all standing now but no longer coming toward the door where Frank stood. Instead, they had turned their attention to the middle of the room, where Frank had seen a small group carrying the bishop. Aware that the fire was getting lower and would give him less protection, Frank tried to stay on the one side until he could see what the shadows were doing. He could see a group of men around one of the coils, which stood about eight feet tall. When they moved away from it, Frank witnessed what they had done.

There, suspended from the coil, with electrical cords tying him to it, was Bishop Tafoya. Frank moved forward to the breech in the path and looked toward the bishop, who briefly glanced at him. The men had moved to the side, as though clearing a path for Frank to go to him. He closed his eyes, summoned his courage, and stepped forward, but he didn't get far. He felt the tearing at his flesh, and the dark, cold sensations overwhelmed him. He kept his place and held firm. When he opened his eyes, he looked between the coils. The shadows held onto him; they weren't attacking anymore but making sure he stayed in place. He could see through the doorway to a dimly lit and foggy place. He glanced down, and his view was from aboveground overlooking the place where he had been: the garden. There, at the edge of the garden, he could see the forms lurking and shifting back and forth. The opening grew wider, and he saw farther, to where an army, thousands of shadows, was waiting on the other side. The message was clear although unspoken: *If you want your bishop back, open the door and bring us more hosts.*

Frank didn't have the chance to take another step forward. A large flash and surge of heat surrounded him, and something stronger than him pulled him from behind and dragged him out of the room.

"Not today, priest," Frank heard Kanuik say. He dragged Frank down the hallway and outside into the fading sunlight, where both men collapsed. "That was a trap, and you know it," said Kanuik.

"We must do something," Frank said, the vision still fresh in his mind. "If they find a way to open that portal, we're done for."

Connor ran up to them. "Jimmie's asking for you."

"Oh, hi, Connor," Frank said. "Glad you made it back."

Connor helped Frank and Kanuik to their feet. Frank went with Connor to the car while Kanuik went to speak to the men who had come to help him.

Jimmie sat in the back seat of the car, facing Frank, with his legs out of the vehicle. He was feeling the large knot on his forehead as Frank approached the car. "Hi, Jimmie," Frank said, not sure what to tell him but sure that he was hurting.

"I'm sorry," Jimmie said. "I should have refused. I should have told them no."

"Damn right," Connor said.

Frank gave his nephew a cross look and shook his head, causing Connor to go to the other side of the car. He got in the driver's side and sat down.

"You did what you thought you had to do," Frank said. "I did that myself once. It just happened to work out. Jimmie"—Frank placed his hands on Jimmie's shoulders and looked directly into his eyes—"I need to know if the portal is closed. Can those things open it?"

"No," Jimmie said. "I closed it good. I shot a beam of energy at that thing that should've blown the top right off the rec center. But it didn't. It went straight into the portal and fried a bunch of those damn things."

"Then you burned up the coils?" Frank asked.

"No, I didn't do that," Jimmie said. "Remember how I told you that the shadows are made of energy?"

Frank nodded.

"Well, the force of the beam I sent through caused a reaction when it hit them; that's what caused the coils to burn. Boy, I'd love to see what it looks like on the other side because they got the worst of it."

"How did you end up on the floor?"

Frank followed Jimmie's stare to the doors of the rec center. His eyes went blank, and then he looked down. His next words were full of hate.

"Thomas," Jimmie said. "When the shadows attacked and the soldiers started turning, he ran out and locked the door. We were all stuck in there with them. I was trying to find something to open the door, and I fell."

"Well, that might have been the best clumsy thing you've ever done," Frank said. "Mark is watching Thomas until we have time to neutralize him."

"What are you going to do to him?"

"If he weren't already wounded, I'd kill him. Right now, I don't know if he's in any condition to cause us trouble." He noticed Kanuik coming toward them.

"Do you know where Bishop Tafoya is?" Jimmie asked.

"He's still in there, and the shadows have him," Frank said.

"He's still alive?" Jimmie said.

Frank nodded.

"Then we have to go back," Jimmie said. He started to move, but Frank grabbed his arm.

"The shadows are too strong," Frank said. "We aren't prepared for this!"

"Then what do we do now?" Jimmie asked.

"I don't know," Frank said.

"We need to go back to the tavern and regroup," Kanuik said. "My friends will keep the shadows contained here."

"Leave?" Frank said. They were all tired, but Frank couldn't see leaving the rec center.

"In our state, someone is going to do something careless. We weren't prepared for this," Kanuik said.

"Okay," Frank conceded. "Let's go."

Samar and Kanuik got in the back seat with Jimmie, and Frank got in the front passenger's side. "Take us to the Kozy," Frank ordered Connor.

When they arrived at the tavern, they found the bus from the rec center parked outside. The Kozy's Closed sign was up, and the doors were locked. After they knocked, Chic let them in.

Frank entered last, looking up and down the street before he crossed the threshold; he had an uneasy feeling that they wouldn't be safe for long.

"You look like hell," Chic said. "Come over to the bar, all of you." He put some ice in a towel and handed it to Jimmie.

"Thanks," Jimmie said, lifting the ice to the bump on his forehead. "Ouch."

"How are things here?" Frank asked as he sat down with Connor, Jimmie, Kanuik, and Samar. Claudia and Sergeant Lee were moving from table to table, where the rest of the soldiers they had evacuated were sitting.

"Considering what a mess this all is, I think we're doing fine," Chic said. He handed each of them a drink. "Are there any more coming?"

"No," Frank said.

Chic raised his eyebrows.

"At the current moment, the rest are contained in the rec center, which has been overrun by shadows from a dark realm beyond our world," Jimmie said. He slammed back the drink Chic had placed in front of him. "Whoa. Give me another."

"What did you give him?" Frank asked.

"Whiskey," Chic said. "He looks like he needs it. You do too, but since I haven't seen you eat anything for days, I'm worried it might make you sick."

"We need to get those things out of there," Kanuik said. "How do we send them back?"

"We will have to entice them back," Frank said. "Give them a reason to give up their hosts."

"But if we open the portal, won't more come through?" Kanuik said.

"They don't seem to be able to get through," Frank said. "Not without more hosts."

"The coils are what keep the portal opened," Jimmie said. "I shut them off!"

"But you could still see through it," Kanuik said, nodding at Frank.

"Yes," Frank said. "It may have something to do with my condition and the residual effects from being there—I am my own host."

"You think they cannot remain here without a host?" Kanuik said.

"I think that is what they are trying to do. Become whole again. But they can't, not yet," Frank said. "They need more to come through. I've watched them combine when there are enough of them; merge into a more powerful force. They are using the men in there as hosts, maybe even hostages, until they can open the portal again."

"We need to open the portal to send them back somehow that we don't know yet, but by opening it, we may allow more to come through?" Kanuik said.

"Yes," Frank said. "That's out dilemma. But I think I have a way to lure them back, if we can get the portal opened."

"It doesn't matter now," Jimmie said. "All the equipment is destroyed. I can't do anything. The electrical pulse fried all the circuits on the transmitters."

"Then we need another way to open a portal," Connor said.

"There is another way," Frank said.

"How? Do you know another way?" Connor asked.

Jimmie and Frank locked eyes.

"It's okay," Frank said. "I'll take this. The night that we went to see David in the psychiatric ward, I remembered something Adnan had told me—the main goal of the shadows was the ruination of a person. I used this concept to trick them. When the portal opened near David, Jimmie kept the shadows at bay and also kept the portal open for me to go through."

"But how? How did you trick them?"

"By pushing David to the brink. Adnan had said the shadows swarm around a suicide. I pushed David, and when he attempted suicide, I stopped him, but not before the shadows had swarmed and opened the portal wide enough for me to get through."

Sensing a presence behind him, Frank turned and saw that Claudia had walked up behind him. He wasn't sure how much she had overheard. He stood to face her.

Claudia backed away from Frank. "I can't believe you would do something like that to that boy."

Frank stepped forward, but Claudia continued to retreat.

"Just … just give me some space," she said and headed to the restrooms.

The front door started to open, catching Frank's attention.

"I must've forgotten to lock it," Chic said. He headed toward the door but didn't get there before Thomas stumbled in, accompanied by Mark.

"There you are," Thomas said to Frank. His wound was freshly bandaged, but his clothes were still bloody. "You knew what would happen, didn't you?" He stepped closer to Frank.

Mark stood between the two to keep them separated.

"You're in league with them, aren't you?" said Thomas.

Thomas didn't get to say another word. Jimmie ran over from the bar and hit him with a right cross, knocking Thomas to the ground, fully unconscious.

"Damn it, damn it!" Jimmie shouted, hopping around in a circle. "I think I broke my hand!"

"Hey!" Chic yelled as he approached the group. "There's no fighting allowed in here."

"Sorry, Frank," Mark said. "He insisted we come to see you."

"It's okay, Mark," Frank said. "It's better you're both here. We need to keep anyone else from learning what is going on until we figure out how to handle this."

"Handle what?" Mark asked.

"Oh, nothing," Jimmie said. "We just opened a portal to hell is all." Jimmie continued to hold his hand.

"Don't mind him," Chic said. "He's just upset. Come on, Jimmie. Let's get you some more ice." Chic led Jimmie to the bar and sat him down.

"Here, help me," Kanuik said, and he and Mark lifted Thomas off the floor and set him on one of the pool tables.

Claudia ran over to check on Thomas. When Frank approached, she turned away from him, so he went back and sat at the bar, where Chic was putting ice on Jimmie's hand.

"What now?" Sergeant Lee asked as he approached the bar where Jimmie and Frank were sitting.

"I think I'm going to go crazy if one more person asks me that," Frank whispered.

Chic heard him and gave Frank a stern look. "You are the teacher here," Chic said. "There is no Adnan. It's up to you."

Frank went back to the table and sat down. He took a drink of the tea Chic had put in front of him earlier. It was still warm and felt good as it went down. He could taste the sweet honey and then felt the undeniable burn of the small amount of whiskey Chic had snuck in the drink. He closed his eyes, wiped his lips, turned to Sergeant Lee, and stood.

Frank spoke loud enough for the entire room to hear him. "If any of these men are able to get out of here, have them go home. The project is over." He turned to look at the men. "You are all in danger now because these things will seek you out now that they know your weaknesses and how to use them against you. Leave from here. Get as far away as you can and don't come back."

When Frank turned back to the bar, the disapproving look was still on Chic's face. "Not what you expected?" Frank asked.

"I think you better clean up a little before your next speech," Chic said and pointed to the restrooms.

Mark approached Frank as Chic turned away and went into the kitchen. "Do you need anything from me?"

"No, Mark," Frank said. "I have enough help here. I need you to go home and write your sermon and prepare for Sunday's mass. You must keep getting through to people, especially the youth. It's the best thing you can do right now to help."

"You sure?" Mark asked.

"If we need you, I'll send someone. I promise," Frank said.

"I'll come by tomorrow afternoon and check on you," Mark said and then left.

Frank headed to the men's room and washed his face and hands. He looked in the mirror and noticed the rips in his shirt for the first time. He remembered that back in the rec center the shadows had attacked him. He lifted his shirt to see the scratch marks on his torso. None of them were too deep, and the blood had already clotted over the few that had penetrated his skin. Here there was no blessed stream to fix his wounds. He let the cold water run in the sink and put his head under it. He used the air dryer to dry his hair and then tucked in his shirt, combed his hair, and fixed his attire the best he could.

When Frank walked back into the bar's main room, all was quiet. The soldiers had left, and the rest of the group was scattered. Jimmie, Connor, and Chic were at the bar. Claudia was with Thomas, who was awake, at a table across the room from the bar, and Kanuik and Samar were at the table where the group normally sat.

The situation reminded Frank of when they had failed before and lost Adnan; the group had been downtrodden and not sure what to do next. Frank wasn't sure he knew what to do next this time either. He went to the table and sat down with Kanuik and Samar. Kanuik was smoking, but the scent was one Frank couldn't place.

"This is a smoke for focus," Kanuik explained. "I usually smoke for power or cleansing. This is the first time I've smoked this."

Chic brought some bread over to the table. Frank took the bread and very ceremoniously said a prayer, broke the bread, and ate it, leading Kanuik to raise his eyebrows. The bread was still warm and tasted good to Frank, and for once, eating didn't upset his stomach.

Thomas came to the table with his hands out. "Please, may I sit with you?"

Frank nodded. "Please, sit down."

Thomas took a seat opposite Frank. "Today was the first day I actually came into contact with those …"

"We call them shadows," Kanuik said. "Evil spirits, deceivers, tricksters—they are known by all of these names."

"What do they want?" Thomas asked.

"I can feel them," Frank said. "When I come into contact with them, I can sense their thoughts. They desire and feed on weakness and doubt, not fear, as many have believed. They don't desire death as much as torment and confusion—suffering. They are the opposite of truth. They exist to lie, to make us lie. They are the ever-present dark alternative to what we strive to make light. Creation made them possible. Free will caused them to exist, but that same free will allows us to follow the darkness or turn from it. It is a decision. Just as these entities want destruction, we must teach the way to defeat them: constructive thoughts and respect of life. If we deny them hosts, they will fade."

"Fade," Thomas said. "Is it that simple?"

"No," Kanuik said. "Simple would be taking a spear and killing them, but that is not the fight that we are in. Instead, what Father Frank is suggesting is that we have to convince people to be good and treat each other with respect; in order to love and have faith in each other, we must replace hate and contempt."

"The awakening," Frank said.

Kanuik nodded.

"What happened to Bishop Tafoya?" Thomas asked.

"He is still in there with them," Frank said. "We couldn't reach him."

"We have to go back!" Thomas started to get up from his chair, but Chic appeared behind him and put a hand on his shoulder to keep him seated.

"None of you are going anywhere tonight," Chic said, and he started unloading drinks in front of them. "Night has always been the realm of the shadows. You just got your butts kicked today, and if you go back out there without preparation, I won't see any of you back here again. There's a shower downstairs and plenty of room for you to stay here."

The men fell silent as Chic left the table. Frank looked at the clock. It was only nine, but it seemed much later.

"Bishop Tafoya is alive but captive," Frank said. "His faith has surely kept them from influencing him, but they are keeping him as a hostage. They want us to open the portal."

"Then we need to open it and let them go back to where they came from," Thomas said.

"That's not their plan," Frank said. "They have amassed an army on the other side that is waiting to come through."

"So how do we beat them?" Thomas asked.

"Jimmie, Connor," Frank called out, "would you please come here?"

Connor and Jimmie came over to the table but went to Frank's side, away from Thomas, and remained standing. Frank watched the uneasy glances pass between Jimmie and Thomas. Claudia, meanwhile, went to the bar and sat down across from Chic, who was cleaning glasses.

"Jimmie, do you still have the camera Mike made?" Frank asked.

"It's in my car," Jimmie said.

"Would you please get it?"

Chic let Jimmie out and then back in with the camera they had confiscated while raiding Thomas's hideout.

"All truth is on the table tonight," Frank said. "If we are to succeed tomorrow, the first thing we need to agree on is that our mistrust of each other has to end tonight."

Frank noticed Thomas looking at the camera Jimmie held, as if he recognized it.

"Yes," Frank said, "we are the ones who raided your lab and set your subjects free. If I had my way, I would shove you in that place with the shadows. But it's not up to me." Frank knew that he himself had done something extreme in the quest to fight the shadows. He knew it was not for him to pass judgment. "I'm going to give you a chance to redeem yourself, but you need to do exactly what I say."

Thomas nodded.

"You know how this thing works?" Frank asked.

"Yes," Thomas stated. "I have seen the dark forms through it."

"Jimmie," Frank ordered, "give the camera to Thomas so he can use it to look at me."

Jimmie put the camera on the table and slid it partway across the surface. Thomas had to stand to reach it. Once he had the camera, he turned it on and looked at Frank through the lens and then at the others.

"You can see that there is no evil here in this place," Frank said.

"I'll take that back," Jimmie said, grabbing the camera from Thomas.

"I have a plan to free Bishop Tafoya," Frank said. He proceeded to explain his plan to the group. He reminded Kanuik of how he had been able to grab the shadows and hold on to them. He would do this, he said, while the others freed the bishop.

"That might get Bishop Tafoya free, but how do we send those things back to where they came from and free the others?" Jimmie asked.

"You said the coils were fried, but does the gun you used to blast that blue electric pulse still work?"

"Yes," Jimmie said. "It's what burned up everything else."

Frank's voice was light but carried across the table as he continued with his instructions. They were going to open the portal just enough for him to drag the shadows back through and leave them on the other side. But someone would have to be willing to hold onto him and retrieve him like Claudia did when he first came back.

"Your plan calls for me to protect your escape and then drive the remaining shadows into the portal," Kanuik said. "That means I can't be close enough to pull you back when you reach through."

"I'm sorry, but I'm not getting anywhere near those things," Jimmie said. "I can rig some equipment to help you if, once you open the portal, more start coming through."

"I'll do it," Connor said.

Frank didn't answer but simply looked at Thomas.

"You want me to do it?" Thomas said. "That's the only reason I am sitting at this table, isn't it?"

"Yes," Frank said. "There are only three of us here who can fight these things: Kanuik, Samar, and myself. While I appreciate your willingness, Connor, I have something else I need you to do. Besides, it will take a man of faith to do what I am going to ask."

"I'm not sure you have the right man," Jimmie said.

"I am sure," Frank said. Although Jimmie understandably didn't trust Thomas, Frank knew that Thomas was a man of conviction who would follow through. "Jimmie," Frank said, "please take Connor and do your best to rig up one of those things to send a blast through and close the portal after it opens. We need it ready first thing in the morning."

"Come on, Connor," Jimmie said. "We'll be back by six." The two left the tavern.

"Your plan didn't include me," Samar said. "I can help. What do you need me to do?"

"I can only hold so many of the shadows," Frank said. "Once we open the portal and I drag them through, I am counting on the rest to follow. If any remain, it will be your job to free those men. Kanuik will drive them to me."

"Why would they follow you?" Kanuik asked.

"Because of what I am going to offer them," Frank said.

Kanuik didn't respond to Frank's statement. He stood from his chair. "Come on, Samar. Let's get some rest. We are going to need it." Samar and Kanuik went downstairs, leaving only Frank and Thomas at the table.

"I panicked and ran out of the room today," Thomas said. "Why are you so sure I'll be able to help you tomorrow?"

"Redemption," Frank said. "I know about Kaitlyn, the assistant."

Thomas's hollow eyes grew wide.

"You have been responsible for two deaths that I know about. You are partly responsible for the mess we are in because you wouldn't trust me and pushed the council forward. I am giving you a chance to redeem yourself, but it will cost you."

"Pray for me, Father Keller," Thomas said to Frank.

"I already have," Frank said.

Thomas sat back in his chair. He looked around the Kozy Tavern and then back to Frank. "This is a strange place you have chosen to meet."

"It has a special history," Frank said. "My father used to come here when I was a kid. He worked in this neighborhood—car part manufacturing."

Thomas took the last drink from the glass in front of him and put it down on the table slowly, purposefully. He closed his eyes and sighed. He leaned forward, put his elbows on the table, and gestured with both hands as he spoke. "I tried to find out the truth about you, Father Frank, the truth about the shadows. Cardinal Denaro put me in charge because I am a believer in the cause. I know that evil does exist and that we must do everything in our power to stop it."

"I have no doubt about your conviction, Father Thomas," Frank said. He didn't want to get into an argument with Thomas or tell him he had gone too far and needed to see a psychiatrist. Frank needed him and his sense of over-conviction. "In fact, I am counting on it."

"What do you need me to do?"

Frank spent the next twenty minutes filling Thomas in on the role he would need to play. After Frank was sure his instructions were clear, he went to the bar, where Claudia patiently waited.

"It's getting late," Frank said, sitting down on the stool beside her. "Aren't you going home soon?"

"I wanted to talk to you before tomorrow," Claudia said. "Besides, I brought your bag in from the car."

"Good," Frank said, and he lifted the bag onto the bar and opened it. He pulled out the notebook he had been writing in the night before.

"I know you are going to tell me to stay back and that you don't need my help," Claudia said.

"Actually," Frank said, "I was going to ask if you could be here early tomorrow and if you would mind sticking around in the rec center parking lot in case we need someone with your skills—you know, medical assistance?"

"Oh," Claudia said.

"I just wanted to give you something first." Frank handed her the notebook. "It's something I wrote with you in mind. I hope it gives you inspiration for your new book."

Claudia opened the notebook and read the title aloud: "'What You Do Matters, by Frank Keller.' No Father Frank Keller? Is this a sermon?"

"That's just me, the man. But the words were inspired by my faith."

Claudia leaned in and kissed Frank on the cheek. "Thank you. Chic, will you let me out?"

Chic escorted Claudia to the door, let her out, and locked the door behind her. Frank glanced over to see that Thomas had pulled up another chair to put his feet on and was sleeping soundly.

"Time to call it a night, I think," Chic said, returning to the bar.

"You think we should do anything with him?" Frank gestured to Thomas.

"It stays pretty warm in here all night, but I'll get him a blanket just in case. What can I get you?"

"Do you have any paper?"

CHAPTER 13
LAST DAY

We accept sorrow in our lives and build our beliefs around it. We say that it is inflicted so that we may learn from it, grow from it. We say that sorrow is necessary in order to find God. I say, on the contrary, there is sorrow because man is cruel to man.

Frank stirred from his sleep. He had felt tired and weary from the day before, so he had put his head down on the bar. He noticed someone standing by him and turned to see Kanuik there, dressed but drying his hair with a towel.

"You finally got some sleep," Kanuik said. "I noticed last night that you ate some bread as well."

Frank nodded.

"How did it make you feel?"

"Human," Frank said. "Where's Thomas?" Frank stood from the barstool and stretched his arms above his head.

"He's down in the shower," Kanuik said.

"Good, he needed one."

"You sure you can trust him?"

"I think I can count on him to do what he thinks is right, and that's exactly what I've asked him to do."

Samar entered from the hallway at the same time that the front door opened. Chic came in with several bags of groceries, and the others helped him take the food to the kitchen. Soon, eggs and bacon were frying, and the group was assembling for breakfast. Jimmie and Connor arrived, and now they were only waiting for Claudia.

While the others were waiting at the table and Connor was back in the kitchen helping, Chic walked to the bar, where Frank sat watching the door.

"Do you think Mark will stop by?" Chic asked. "We could set another place."

"I don't know," Frank said. "He said he might come by and check on us, but I don't know when he'll do that."

"You don't want him along with you today?" said Chic.

"No," Frank said. "I was kind of hoping to keep him out of this today. I think we need to be aware of the severity of our situation and recognize that some of us might not make it back. I need someone to keep running my congregation and be successful."

"Anything you need from me?" Chic asked.

"Why?"

"Regardless of how things go, you aren't planning on coming back. I could tell by the way you talked to Claudia last night," Chic said.

Frank shook his head. "If there was another way … Please give this to Samar later." Frank handed Chic an envelope. "And this one to Claudia. It's a note asking her to share with Mark what I wrote in the notebook I gave her. I'm hoping he will use it in one of his sermons. I would give it to her myself, but then she might get suspicious."

"You think they can make a difference?" Chic said.

"Yes," Frank said. "If Claudia writes her book and the church spreads the same themes, the message is bound to hit a large audience. Perhaps then we would see a change."

Chic picked up a napkin, removed the cigar from his mouth, rolled it up in the napkin, and threw it in the trash. "Are you going to tell them?"

"If I were to tell them"—Frank glanced to the table and back to Chic—"our plan would fail. What I do today will buy the world some time to right itself."

"And you think it will?" Chic asked.

"I don't know. The evil has already made inroads in one of the world's predominant religions and infected followers to strike out and kill innocent people in the name of that religion. The religion I believe in is losing followers, and people are worshipping material possessions more than life itself."

"We may have already lost," Chic said.

"Still, I can't give up hope," Frank said. "What are you going to do after this is over?"

Chic looked back to the kitchen. "That Connor kid, he's been helping out a lot around here, and he's pretty good at it. Plus, he already knows about the real battle. I think it's time for me to do the same thing that Adnan did—find someone to take over. Not right away maybe, but in a few years. He and Jimmie are like family. Maybe I can get them to branch out."

"I think that's a fine idea," Frank said.

Chic put out his hand, and he and Frank shook hands.

"Thank you," Frank said, "for all that you've done. Take care of everyone."

The front door opened, and Claudia stepped inside. She waved to the group at the table and to Frank and Chic.

"Your Closed sign is still up," Claudia said as she headed to the table.

"Good," Chic said. "I think it will remain there today with all that is going on. Plus, I don't intend to make it a habit to be open this early and serve breakfast. Now that everyone's here ..." Chic turned toward the kitchen. "Connor," he called out, "let's serve breakfast."

Frank joined Claudia, Samar, Jimmie, and Kanuik at the table while Chic and Connor put out eggs, bacon, waffles, and toast. The group stood together.

"I think Father Frank should say a blessing for us all," Chic said.

The words had barely left Chic's mouth when Thomas came out of the hallway. He stopped just inside of the main room.

Frank knew that Thomas had one of the hardest tasks today. "Please, Father Thomas," he said, "join us for breakfast."

The group joined hands and bowed their heads.

"Dear Lord," Frank prayed, "I ask that you watch over everyone today and send us strength to accomplish the task you have set before us. Help us through our trials and show us your great power. We have come together in fellowship to serve, and although we might not understand the why of what happens, give us the faith to believe in each other and give support in these trying times. Amen."

There wasn't much conversation during breakfast. Everyone seemed to be deep in thought, contemplating what lay before them. Frank looked around at the group. Kanuik wore his usual jeans, along with a brown shirt and a jean vest with pockets. Jimmie was dressed like a professor in his dress shirt and brown sport coat. Connor wore khaki pants and a loose-fitting black shirt. Frank and Thomas were both dressed in the uniform for their order: black pants and shirt and white collar. Claudia wore a long-sleeve blue cashmere sweater that made her blue eyes glow against her pale cheeks and long, flowing hair. *Not exactly dressed for battle*, Frank thought. Other than Thomas, who was deservedly out of place, Frank couldn't help but think how unlikely it was that this group of people who had found each other could be so content with each other's company.

"We should get to it," Thomas said. "Every moment we stay here, Bishop Tafoya remains in that place."

"He's right," Frank said. "We will need to take two cars."

"I'll drive mine," Jimmie said, "since no one else has a car but Claudia."

The group exited the Kozy Tavern to an overcast November day. Frank, Samar, and Thomas went with Claudia while the rest of the group went with Jimmie.

When they pulled up to the rec center, the men Kanuik had called the day before immediately greeted them. They reported that all had been quiet during the night.

Claudia got out of the car and gave Frank a small hug. He embraced her for a longer one.

"I've always thought about another place and time," Frank said, "where things could be different, and you and I wouldn't be in such confusing roles, and we could be together."

"I think I would enjoy that," Claudia said. "We can keep dreaming that one day it may come to be … Be careful in there."

Snow started to fall as Frank headed to the entrance. Jimmie had pulled his car up close to the door, and he and Connor were unloading equipment. Jimmie turned as Frank walked up to him.

"This is what I salvaged. If you can get me to the coils, I can get them enough power with this device"—he held up a small electrical box—"to open the portal. But it might not work for long."

"All I'll need is a moment," Frank said. "What's that thing for?" Frank pointed to a large piece of equipment that Jimmie was carrying. It resembled a rifle, although what powered it was a set of batteries.

"This will release energy that I hope will keep more of them from coming through. It will be good for a few bursts before it shorts out." Jimmie lifted it and put a makeshift sling around his shoulders to carry it. "It's probably a huge fire hazard, but I figure with Kanuik throwing all his holy fire down, we will probably just end up burning this entire building to the ground already. That might be the best thing to do anyway."

"Let's just make sure all of you are out of it before we do," Frank said. "Is everybody ready?"

By this point, everyone had gathered together outside the door. Kanuik, Samar, Thomas, Jimmie, and Kanuik all nodded. Connor stared at the entrance.

"Connor, remember not to make contact with any of the soldiers in there. Your job is to get Bishop Tafoya down when we tell you it's clear and drag him out as fast as possible."

Everyone headed to the door, but Frank reached out and held Thomas back. "Remember what I told you," Frank said. "The others won't understand, so you must be ready to act."

"Don't worry," Thomas said. "I understand that I am the Pharisee in this group and what I must do. They already hate me, so I haven't a thing to lose."

Frank looked into Thomas's black eyes and sensed something more than a man staring back at him. He started to wonder if he was wrong in what he was about to do. He shook the doubt from his head and turned toward the entrance with Thomas.

They entered the brick building and proceeded slowly down the empty hallway, which still smelled of electrical fire, with the added scent of Kanuik's holy fire. The doors to the gymnasium were closed. Frank was the last to make it to the doors, where Kanuik and the others had already taken a look into the room beyond.

"What do you see?" Frank asked.

No one spoke as they backed away to make room for him.

He stepped forward and looked through the windows. The shadow-infected soldiers were lined up on both sides of the room, leaving a clear path to the coils, where Bishop Tafoya was suspended by electrical cables wrapped around his arms. He wasn't moving, and Frank prayed they were not too late.

"Looks like they've been expecting us. At least we won't have to clear them out of the way," Kanuik said. "Why are they letting us have him?"

"Somehow they know what's about to happen," Frank said. "Or at least part of it—a trade for the one they want more. Remember your roles."

They opened the doors, stepped into the path that had been cleared for them, and slowly walked to the coils. Frank stood between the two burned-out devices. Wires and cords stuck out of them, and they smelled like burnt insulation.

The only one tall enough for the task, Kanuik reached above his head and helped get Bishop Tafoya down while Samar and Connor grabbed hold and lowered him.

"He's still alive," Kanuik said. "But he is weak. We must hurry and get him out of here."

Frank noticed that the path to the double doors was no longer clear; the men positioned by the doors had moved in.

"Thomas, come stand beside me," Frank said. "Jimmie, you're up."

Jimmie went to the coil to his right, attached the small device to it, turned a button, and backed away. A small spark emerged from the box and then bounced to the other coil, connecting the two with a thin line of electricity. In a moment, a blue orb appeared between the coils, and Frank knew the plan was working. The portal was small but visible enough to get the soldiers' attention. Connor and Samar hurried along the path with Bishop Tafoya. The portal started getting bigger, and wind moved about the room as the doorway to another dimension was opened. The lights in the building flickered on, allowing Frank to see the soldiers more clearly as they moved closer to the opening, unnerving him. The men's faces were blank of any expression, and their eyes were rolled back, exposing only whites of their eyes.

"Jimmie, I thought you said the power was out in the building," Frank yelled, trying to make sure he was heard over the low roar of the wind that continued to increase. Ruptured electrical cords added to the noise, throwing sparks in a flash-like effect that made it hard to see.

"It is," Jimmie called back. "Whatever is causing the power is coming from there." He pointed to the ever-growing opening. "It shouldn't be getting that wide from what I've done. It's coming from the other side."

"As I expected," Frank said. He knew that the darkness inside of Thomas was drawing them. "Get ready, Jimmie. Those things on the other side are going to try to get through. If they come before I get the ones on this side across, you must send that pulse of energy through to keep them back."

"Tell me when," Jimmie said, adjusting the harness that hung around his body and pointing the device at the portal. Sweat poured from his forehead as he gripped the trigger switch.

Kanuik filled his hands with balls of holy fire and nodded to Frank.

"Clear the way!" Frank said, and he and Kanuik moved toward the double doors with Samar and Connor, who continued hauling Bishop Tafoya. Frank reached out and latched on to the shadows of the few men blocking the way, allowing Samar and Connor to exit down the hall. Kanuik stood at the doorway.

Frank turned and headed back to the portal. He stopped about ten feet away and watched as it grew slowly at first. Then a black form emerged through it and seemed to somehow increase the size. He looked back to make sure Samar and Connor had cleared the hallway with the bishop.

"Now, Jimmie!" Frank called above the noise, and he moved forward and flung the shadows he held toward the portal.

Jimmie pushed the button on the device hanging around his chest, and an electric arc surged forward into the portal. It was not a straight line, and the sides of the arc hit Frank and Thomas, who were both shocked and thrown away from the portal and to the floor. Jimmie, too, was shocked, and he threw the smoldering device down as he looked at his burned hands. Frank watched the opening and no longer could see any shadows coming through. The plan had worked so far.

"Kanuik, get him out of here!" Frank yelled, pointing to Jimmie, as he stood and went to help Thomas back to his feet.

Kanuik threw balls of holy fire at the end of the path to keep a way to the double doors open. After he and Jimmie exited, Kanuik looked back through the window. Frank nodded to him.

"We're up," Frank said. "Go to the coils and wait for me."

"Is it closed?" Thomas yelled, looking toward the coils.

"No," Frank said. "Jimmie just stunned them. We've got to close it now. We're going to send these things back to where they came from and seal it shut."

Thomas stepped to the coils as the soldiers from both sides of the room closed in. Frank reached out to the soldier closest to him, found the cold form, and grabbed on. He did this to as many soldiers as he could reach on his way to Thomas, worried that he couldn't contain them all. Each one he grabbed slowed his pace and increased the hate he felt coming at him. *The feeling's mutual,* he thought as he struggled to keep his senses focused on the current moment. The shadows attacked him with visions again, but he was getting good at blocking the attacks. He stumbled twice, and both times Thomas tried to help him. "No!" Frank shouted. "Stay where you are and don't let any of these things touch you."

Frank was only a few steps away from his destination. He could see through the portal to the gray, barren landscape. The shadows on the other side were regathering and heading toward him.

When he finally made it to the portal, he concentrated and reached out to the shadows. He made his plan clear: *any of you that remain on this side when I close this thing are going to be trapped here.* He sensed the shadows he held leave him and go to the other side. The others in the room started releasing their hosts and going through the portal as well. As they did, the men they had been holding fell to the ground.

Frank felt the burden lifting from him as more of the shadows he'd grabbed left his grip and fled to the other side. He kept watch to see if every soldier the shadows influenced had been released. The last few shadows didn't let go of him, though, as he had expected. They clung to him for they had reached inside his mind and read his intention—to close the portal forever and lock them on the other side.

The men waking up around the room were all confused. Some yelled out for help, while others tried to make sense of what was going on around them. Kanuik appeared in the gym's doorway and called out to them, motioning for them to get out of the building.

"Thomas, get ready," Frank said.

Thomas took the cross Frank had given him from around his neck. He pushed in on the sides, and the blade revealed itself.

Frank stood in front of the portal. Looking forward, he did not see the other side of the room behind the coils but gazed through a blurred, hazy opening to the place where he had spent the previous few years. The shadows were gathering and piling on each other, making a mass that reached toward the opening. As more piled together, the dark mass got closer to the opening. Frank placed a hand on each side, grabbing at the coils' burnt wires to get a grip and hold on. He was blocking the portal as he looked across to the other side. There were thousands of the dark forms in front of him, all coming toward him. He waited until they were close enough for him to feel them.

"Now, Thomas! Now!" he shouted.

Thomas hesitated. He moved the sharp edge of the knife toward Frank.

"This is the only way!" Frank said. "Hurry—I can't hold them any longer!"

Thomas raised the blade high and stabbed it deep into Frank's back three times.

Frank tightened his grip and remained standing as blood ran to the floor. The wind reversed direction and rushed from the room into the portal, sucking the air completely out. Thomas coughed and fell to the ground, struggling to breathe.

"This is the sacrifice I give to you," Frank said, and he raised his hands before falling to his knees. He felt energy enter his body, and it felt glorious.

Kanuik stood in the gymnasium's doorway, bracing himself against the pull of the vacuum. Blinded by a flash, he raised a hand to cover his eyes. A large crash and twist of metal sounded as the equipment still in the room bounced off the coils and flew into the portal. Another flash followed, and Kanuik thought he could see two men in the portal; one was Frank, and he thought the other one resembled Adnan, but he couldn't be sure. The light flashed one last time, and then the room went totally dark. The building shook, and light fixtures and debris fell to the floor. Kanuik held his hands over his head to protect himself from the falling debris. Finally, it was silent.

Kanuik slowly reached into his pocket, found two round balls, and threw them to the floor in front of him. The fire activated, and he looked around the room. Other than Thomas lying near where the coils used to be, the entire room was empty. The windows, floor, and walls were coated with a black, sooty ash that created a slick surface. He moved carefully to Thomas and helped him to his feet.

"What have I done?" Thomas said, still holding the bloody knife. "Oh, how foul I am—look what I have done. Forgive me!" He turned the knife toward himself, but Kanuik intervened and grabbed his hand.

"You did what you were told," Kanuik said as he shook the knife out of Thomas's hand and onto the floor. "You did what was needed. Frank misled the shadows to make them think he was going to give himself to them. Instead, his sacrifice, the release of his life's energy, became the force needed to seal the opening again."

"As one did before him," Thomas said.

"The others may not understand what you did."

"But you do?" Thomas asked.

"Yes, I understand," Kanuik said. "And I'll protect you, but you must repent."

"I will," Thomas said. "After what I've seen, how can I not?" He started to collapse, and Kanuik reached out to keep him from falling to the floor.

Kanuik put his shoulder under Thomas's to support him and walked with him out of the gym to the front of the building. Out a window, Kanuik could see Connor and Samar scrambling to the cars as the sky turned ominously black and hail began to fall. The deafening sound of the storm filled the hallway, and glass shattered on the side where the hail hit hardest. After three minutes, the hail ceased, and the light returned. Samar and Jimmie ran to the doorway and helped Kanuik get Thomas to the car.

Sergeant Lee had returned with the bus, and the remaining soldiers were loaded. He waved to Kanuik and the others as he entered the bus and closed the door. The engine roared as the bus pulled out of the parking lot, crushing hail with its tires as it went.

"Where's Bishop Tafoya?" Kanuik asked as Jimmie and Samar headed away from him, taking Thomas to Claudia's car.

"He's in the car," Jimmie called back over his shoulder. "He's talking and coherent. We saved him."

Kanuik looked across the snow- and ice-filled parking lot to Claudia's car. She spotted him and exited the vehicle. He saw the concern on her face change to dread as she scanned the lot and hurried toward him. Kanuik moved to intercept her as she headed to the rec center door.

"He's gone," Kanuik said as he prevented Claudia from entering the building. "He's gone."

"We can get him—there's still time!" Claudia sobbed and fought against Kanuik but made no progress against the nearly seven-foot-tall man. "Jimmie!" she shouted. "Jimmie!"

Jimmie and Samar came running, but Kanuik shook his head as they approached. "It's over," he said. "The portal is closed, and the shadows are gone. Father Frank is gone."

Kanuik stayed back and spoke to the friends he'd called on to help him. Jimmie, meanwhile, took Claudia, Bishop Tafoya, and Thomas in Claudia's car. He was to take Bishop Tafoya and Thomas to the church and then meet the rest of the group at the Kozy Tavern.

Connor was in the driver's seat of Jimmie's car with Samar seated next to him as Kanuik got in the back.

"What were you telling those men?" Connor asked, pointing to the three men still in front of the rec center.

"These men are in the construction field," Kanuik said. "The one there in front is a building inspector. I asked him if he could make sure the building is condemned and torn down. He said with the damage it shouldn't be a problem."

"What caused the explosion?" Connor asked.

"I believe it was a power that we cannot understand," Kanuik said. "But it was on our side and due to Frank's sacrifice. Take us to the Kozy Tavern, Connor."

As they drove to the Kozy, snow started falling so heavily that the streets became nearly impossible to drive on. When the three men entered the tavern, the Kozy was void of other customers, its Closed sign still visible. Jimmie and Claudia had not yet arrived.

Kanuik relayed the events to Chic to prepare him. Then he went to the table, removed his hat, hung it on the chair where Frank normally sat, and took his seat. Samar joined him while Connor remained with Chic, helping him at the bar and in the kitchen.

Jimmie and Claudia arrived shortly and came to the table. Claudia's eyes were red and her face pale. Chic was there in an instant with drinks for everyone, and Connor brought out some bread.

Kanuik searched for something to say, but he couldn't think of anything that would sound right. The group remained silent, not interacting beyond a few glances. Before Frank, Adnan had been the leader and coordinated events. Then it had been Frank. When Frank had left the previous time, they had all gone their separate ways. Kanuik knew that if that happened this time, they would never get back together because it would be too painful.

Chic finally broke the silence. "I have been told what happened," he said. "I know you are all feeling bad right now, but this is war, and in a war, there're going to be casualties. It's always been that way."

Kanuik noticed that everyone kept their eyes fixed on the middle of the table as Chic spoke.

"Frank knew what he was doing, and you've got to trust that what he did was for a reason. He left me a note to give to you, Claudia. He wanted you to use his writing in your new book. And he wanted you to share the message with Mark."

Claudia took the envelope Chic handed her.

"Samar," Chic said, handing Samar another envelope. "He left this for you. He's bought all of you some time, time to make a difference. So mourn tonight if you must, but then it's time to move on."

Chic left the group and went back to the bar, where he started making drinks.

After another long period of silence, Kanuik finally spoke. "I think I will no longer report to the Council of World Religions but will remain here," Kanuik said.

"I have talked to Ira, and she is planning to come back here for the new year," Samar said. "She wants to stay here. Professor Barnes, I was hoping you could help me find a job at the university. Maybe Ira and I could find a place to live here, and I could help the group."

"Call me Jimmie," Jimmie said. "I would be more than happy to help you find a job, as long as I still have one."

Samar opened the envelope from Frank, took out a letter, and unfolded it.

"What does it say?" Jimmie asked.

"He gives his thanks for my help," Samar said. "Then he gives me a list. He says, 'If you're going to join the team, here are a few items you will need: (1) wind chimes, (2) alarm clocks, (3) watch alarm, (4) batteries, (5) flashlights, (6) long underwear, (7) a heavy coat, (8) bath salts, (9) a cat. Don't skip the cat!'"

"Yes, it's important you don't skip the cat," Kanuik said. "They have a way of sensing the shadows. From old times, they have been worshipped as gods because of this. It is important that you stay. You won't only help the group; you will be its leader."

After a few moments of silence, Kanuik spoke again. "And you, Claudia, will you finish your book?"

"Yes," she said. "I'll finish my book, and I promise not to be gone so long when I tour. My car is ruined from the hail damage, so I might need a few rides."

"My plane is ready, wherever you need to go," Kanuik said.

Chic returned to the table with a platter full of shot glasses and started passing them around. Each glass held hot tea with honey. "A toast," Chic said, raising his glass. "To Adnan and to Frank."

The group toasted.

"Then it's settled," Kanuik said, and he reached out to grasp Claudia's hand. The rest of the group followed until everyone was holding hands around the table. "We stay in touch this time."

"Did we win today?" Connor asked.

"Yes," Kanuik said, "for the moment. Who will say the blessing?"

CHAPTER 14
DAY ONE

Many people seem to think it foolish, even superstitious, to believe that the world could still change for the better. And it is true that in winter it is sometimes so bitingly cold that one is tempted to say, "What do I care if there is a summer; its warmth is no help to me now." Yes, evil often seems to surpass good. Then, in spite of us, and without our permission, there comes at last an end to the bitter frosts. One morning the wind turns, and there is a thaw. And so I must still have hope.

—Vincent van Gogh

Claudia took her seat next to Samar and Kanuik and then looked back at the entrance to the church. "Jimmie's late as usual, I see," she said.

Samar and Kanuik smiled back but didn't say anything.

"It's okay to talk now," Claudia said. "Just don't talk once the mass starts."

The organ started playing, and they all stood together as Mark came down the aisle in a procession and took his place at the front of the mass. He gave the opening prayer and smiled at Claudia and the others. A small shuffle came from the back of the church, and Claudia turned to see Jimmie, Connor, and Chic coming up the aisle. They took seats beside her.

"You're late," Claudia said.

"I had to wait for him." Jimmie pointed toward Chic, who for the first time Claudia could remember was wearing a full suit—and no apron. "He's had me and Connor busy down at the Kozy. Now that we're partners and offering some new stuff, the place is really taking off."

The entire group turned their attention to the front as Father Uwriyer began the sermon.

"Today's message comes from a beloved friend to all of us, Father Frank Keller. Father Keller led this church prior to me, and we all remember him for his ability to inspire others, especially our youth. It's my understanding that Father Keller also inspired one of our very own parishioners here today, world-renowned author Dr. Claudia Walden, whose latest book takes its title from one of his writings—*What You Do Matters*."

Many people applauded, and at Mark's gesture, Claudia stood for a moment and waved her thanks before Mark continued his sermon.

"Father Frank said that the examples we set and the things we do echo through time, like ripples, no matter how small, and we need to realize the impact our actions have on others and on the larger picture. Every day we have a choice to inspire others and be good or add evil to world through our actions. What we need to realize is how long our choices have an impact, how they reverberate through time. Frank was a believer in core values. He believed that if we can't find common values, then we fail. The first common value is respect for life, all life, no matter how insignificant we think it is.

"It is so easy for us these days to treasure material things even more than life. We justify taking more and more and can never get enough. We must take a step back, look at this behavior, and realize the world we create when we give value to the wrong things. Stealing and justifying it can no longer be acceptable. Doing things that hurt or potentially hurt others because we think that we may not get caught or be held accountable can no longer be excused.

"When we impose our will on others and take from them not for their well-being but to show our power over them, it is inevitable that bad consequences will result. When we tell others that good intentions only end badly because there is no trust or loyalty left in the world, then we create a world of lies and mistrust. What good can come of this?"

Mark paused and came out from behind the pulpit. He walked

down the steps and stood right in front of the first row of pews. "Father Frank asked, 'Is it not possible for us to be good to each other and treat each other with respect? Is it not possible for us to say something is wrong and participate in fixing it?' When we start taking the time to do this, the world we live in will stop being a place of pain and anger, of suffering and worry, and will be a world of healing.

"You may ask why I am sharing this message with you today at this mass. It's the same message in Dr. Walden's book. It's the same message the media are sharing." Mark paused. "One reason is that all places of worship, all faiths around the world have agreed to share this same message today. This is because you are the ones chosen to lead the way! Those of you who are here today, you come here looking for something, looking for salvation. The fact that you are already here means you have been saved. You have already turned to the truth—that there is something out there greater than we are. We cannot be the weak ones. Those who are out there"—he pointed to the door—"they are the ones who are still lost. We have to be shepherds to them. We do that by setting a good example and following the way that I have been speaking about. Now, let us bow our heads in prayer."

After the mass was over, Claudia and the others waited for Mark at the entrance to the church. Claudia invited him to the Kozy Tavern where they were all meeting for dinner, and Mark accepted.

"'When it's the smallest things you recognize, the littlest differences you notice, when all things, even the smallest, become significant, then shall you know life.' The passage I just read to you is from Dr. Claudia Walden's new book, *What You Do Matters*. A celebrated psychiatrist, she hit the best-seller list with her first book, and nobody thought she would be able to top it, but here we are with another best seller. We have Dr. Walden joining us on our morning show tomorrow. Cliff, have you read this book?"

"Yes, Audrey, and it's an amazing read. In fact, many people are attributing the fact that crime rates are down to this work. Across the country and in many countries throughout the world, there are movements centered on themes outlined in the book. I can't wait to talk to Dr. Walden and learn more about what inspired her to write it."

Chic smiled at the television hosts' remarks as he turned off the big-screen television. He had just added the fifty-five-inch television to the Kozy Tavern and mounted it above the bar. "Connor," he called across the bar, "another round for the table." He headed over to where Claudia and the others sat. "Will you need anything else?"

"No," Claudia said. "I think we are getting ready to go out."

"Cancel that last request, Connor," Chic said.

"The shadows are getting harder to find, but they're still out there, right, Samar?" Kanuik said.

Samar put his tablet down in front of everyone, displaying an electronic map of the city. "Yes, well, we haven't been to this neighborhood in a while, so I say we try there."

The group stood from their table and headed for the door.

"Don't be out too late," Chic said. "Remember your big show tomorrow."

"No problem," Claudia said. "Kanuik is flying me there."

With that, Claudia and the others went out into the night to face the shadows and continue the age-old fight of good against evil.

Printed in the United States
By Bookmasters